FROM THE ASHES

THE FORCE OF NATURE SERIES

AMBER LYNN NATUSCH

This is a work of fiction. Names, characters, organizations, businesses, places, events and incidents either are the product of the author's imagination or are used fictitiously. Any resemblance to actual persons, living or dead, or actual events is entirely coincidental.

FROM THE ASHES

Copyright © 2016 Amber Lynn Natusch

All rights reserved. This book or any portion thereof may not be reproduced or used in any manner whatsoever without the express written permission of the publisher except for the use of brief quotations in a book review.

Published by Amber Lynn Natusch
Editing by Kristen Bronner
Cover Design by Regina Wamba of Mae I Design
Layout by Incandescent Phoenix Books

www.amberlynnnatusch.com

ISBN-13: 978-0-9970765-3-0

First Edition: 2016

ALSO BY AMBER LYNN NATUSCH

The *CAGED* Series

CAGED

HAUNTED

FRAMED

SCARRED

FRACTURED

TARNISHED

STRAYED

CONCEALED

BETRAYED

The *UNBORN* Series

UNBORN

UNSEEN

UNSPOKEN

The *BLUE-EYED BOMB* Series

LIVE WIRE

KILLSWITCH

DEAD ZONE

WARHEAD

The *FORCE OF NATURE* Series

FROM THE ASHES

INTO THE STORM

BEYOND THE SHADOWS

BENEATH THE DUST

The *ZODIAC CURSE:*

***HAREM OF SHADOWS* Series**

EVE OF ETERNAL NIGHT

Contemporary Romance

UNDERTOW

More Including Release Dates

http://amberlynnnatusch.com

www.facebook.com/AmberLynnNatusch

http://www.subscribepage.com/AmberLynnNatusch

To my husband,
Thanks for tolerating all of my fictional boyfriends

PROLOGUE

There are moments in life when you see things with perfect clarity—moments when you choose to define who and what you are. And then there are those that define things for you. Lying on the floor, bleeding to death, I realized that fate had interceded on my behalf. It was all very simple, really: stay and be the weakling I had always been told I was. Stay and let my life slowly drain from me, never bothering to fight—a natural born victim. Or, in a rare act of defiance and courage, I could force myself to get up and leave. Force myself to quiet the voices in my head telling me it would all be better tomorrow. But I was no fool.

If I stayed, tomorrow would never come.

Tick tock, Piper. Tick tock.

It was then that I could hear the fighting in the distance. The voices. The others had returned home and come to my aid. I could hear the ruckus around me as they tried to restrain him. Now was my moment. This was my chance. With a surge of adrenaline, I pushed myself off the blood-soaked floor and staggered on barely functioning legs toward the doorway that led to the hall. I needed to get to my room. I needed provisions.

I would not be returning to the mansion again. Ever.

His angered roar chased me down the corridor, spurring me on. I did not know how long the others could subdue him. My failing body was sluggish and uncoordinated from blood loss and a concussion, but I managed to get to my bedroom with considerable speed—my will to live was stronger than I'd thought. I threw open the heavy wooden door and made my way inside. I took only seconds to throw what I could find into a duffel bag: clothes, shoes, a jacket. Then I grabbed my purse and fled.

I tripped just as I rounded the top of the staircase and rolled down the first few steps before I managed to stop myself and slide down the rest in a more controlled fashion. I was almost to the security door. Almost to safety.

"Piper!" he screamed after me. I shuddered instinctively. Hazarding a glance over my shoulder as I tried to punch in the code to unlock the front entrance, I found him looming at the top of the staircase. Four enforcers were trying hard to hold him back, but they were losing. Even against their combined power, he pushed forward after me.

There would be no stopping him.

My hands shook and my vision blurred from the blood dripping into my eyes, both interfering with my ability to type in the code. With his heavy footfalls echoing through the grand foyer, I tried repeatedly to press the proper buttons to no avail. My attempt to live was proving futile; he was closing in.

With only seconds to spare, I managed to unlock the main security door. I could hear his straining breaths approaching as I threw it open, turning to slam it closed behind me. Once I was through, I was free, if only for a moment. The sun would soon be rising. Once that happened, he couldn't follow, and he knew it. He'd have to wait for nightfall to come after me.

And by then I'd be long gone.

I leaned back against the solid metal door, my breath coming in ragged gasps. I needed to get outside, out of the tiny room that separated the vampires from the impending light. Outside, I could heal. Once healed, I could leave.

With ever-weakening steps, I schlepped my way to my final obstacle: the front door. Swinging it open with ease, I fell to the concrete and crawled away from the mansion. By that point, I could barely lift myself off the ground. But I needed nature—the elements—if I had any chance at repairing what had been damaged. And so I pressed on until I felt the familiar touch of newly cut grass beneath me. Face down, I collapsed to the lawn, my mind fading as I did.

"Help me," I whispered to the Earth as darkness overtook me.

And help me, it did.

PART I

BEFORE

1

It was all very unceremonious when the king of the vampires took me in. I knew he had his reasons at the time—vampires never do anything without a reason—but I happily accepted. I was homeless. I was naïve. And I was tired of watching my back.

My sob story isn't especially original; I was orphaned when I was about two and fell into the hands of the foster care system, where I stayed. The Department of Child and Family Services never could quite figure out why a perfectly healthy white toddler couldn't get adopted, but that seemed to be the case, leaving me with few options. They also had no idea where I'd spent those first two years or who had cared for me. I was no help. I was far too young to remember.

To make up for whatever shortcomings had landed me in the system, I worked my ass off in school, doing all that I could to succeed both academically and socially. Thought I excelled scholastically, I failed miserably at fitting in. I wasn't like them, and it was as if they could sense that somehow.

I was forever an outsider.

Until I wasn't.

When it came to light that I was something more than human, and that there was an entire community—an entire world—out there that was too, I cried joyous tears. But that happiness soured quickly. The more supernaturals I encountered, the more I realized that, even in their world, I still lived on the fringe. I'd find no acceptance with them, though I didn't know why. None of them showed any interest in me—unless you called being the target of their loathing interest. And they all had plenty of that. The witches all but officially shunned me. The fey wouldn't deign to have anything to do with me. The rest brought a mix of superiority and indifference to our encounters—except for the warlocks. Our relationship proved far more complicated than the others. And far more deadly.

For that reason alone, I accepted the vampire king's offer of protection.

Before that, I had been on my own for eight years after aging out of the system. I learned how to survive as a magical being in a mundane world, but not easily. I worked when odd jobs came my way, though it proved hard to find solid employment without a permanent address. Basically, I scraped by however I could. Sometimes it wasn't pretty.

What I found most frustrating was that I knew I had powers—being acknowledged by the other supernatural races at all told me as much—but I had no idea the depths of them or how to call upon them. In short, I knew little to nothing at all, and I wasn't sure anyone else did either. If they had, they might have thought twice about turning their backs on me.

That fact made me question early on the motives of the king.

From the Ashes

"HEY PIPER," Jase called from the kitchen. I walked in to find him pilfering another twelve-pack from the fridge.

"You know it's only ten in the morning, right?"

"Ah, but you forget, my young Jedi. Your morning is my night. This is merely a nightcap before I pass out for the evening."

I rolled my dark-blue eyes, irritated that he once again had a point. Jase loved to be right, a fact that was blatantly displayed in the grin he wore.

Living in the mansion was a strange life to adapt to in the beginning. Located in lower Manhattan, the property spanned multiple city blocks, cleverly shrouded by magic. While humans saw the standard multi-story buildings that predominated in New York City, what really existed was a lush, expansive estate surrounded by woods. Every time I crossed through the perimeter, the pull of that magic was impossible to deny. Then there was my perception of time, which was turned on its ass; day was night and night was day. My sense of self was somewhat lost as well, surrounded only by the strongest of the strong, the toughest of the tough —the most gifted. The enforcers were all total badasses in their own right, and that was a lot to live up to. At some point early on, I stopped trying.

Most of them had been welcoming to some degree, but they all seemed somewhat suspicious of me. All but two. The brothers of the crew—Jase and Dean—were massive and intimidating. Both were known for their incredible speed and ability to "ghost" from one place to another, which made them special and therefore highly prized by the king. The rest couldn't do what they could. From what I'd heard, it was a pretty impressive party trick.

Jase and Dean took me under their collective wing and showed me the way of things in the vampire world. Under their tutelage, it didn't take too long for me to get the hang of things. As much as a non-vampire ever could.

Their lives weren't all that complicated, really. They drank (booze, not just blood), they partied (hard), they scammed on women (supernaturals and humans alike), and, when necessary, they brought a little punishment down on deserving parties (euphemism of the century). They, and the other enforcers, were a policing body for the vampires and, for a price, the other breeds of otherworldlies that inhabited the Earth. In plain English, they were a force to be reckoned with.

They, these party-loving bringers of pain, were my family.

"You'll catch on eventually, kid. Promise."

"It's been months...almost a year. I don't think it's looking too good for me."

His smile widened.

"Well, look on the bright side. If you're not a quick study, at least you're really hot."

My eyes did another loop of their sockets.

"And out of your league," I retorted, pushing past him to grab some food—the only food—out of the refrigerator. Vampires didn't need to eat solids, so I had become the queen of takeout, a crown that I wore with pride.

The truth was, I wasn't out of Jase's league at all. Dean's either. They were out of mine.

I was petite, thin—weak. My pale skin was harshly contrasted by my straight black hair, making me look more dead than the vampires I lived with, an accomplishment in and of itself. The boys, however, were practically carbon copies of one another. Tall. Thick. Strong. And painfully good-looking. Their short, dark hair framed their angular features perfectly, and their brown, almost black eyes looked at you like they were staring into your soul. Women, human and otherwise, were putty in their hands. I seemed to be one of the only beings that could withstand the power of their good looks. I think they found me amusing solely because of that fact. Amused or not, I wasn't messing up our relationship by sleeping with either of them. I'd seen others in the house do that.

It always ended badly.

"We're going out tonight," he continued, not acknowledging my dig.

"Wait...isn't it night now?"

"Yes, technically. I meant YOUR night. So you'd better go nap or whatever it is you need to do to stay out with the big dogs. We're going out hard..."

"Don't you always?"

"Yes, but tonight we're going out harder than usual."

"What's the occasion?" I asked, popping out of the fridge with a leftover Chinese food container in hand. An arm snaked around my shoulder from behind me, startling me for a second until I turned to find Dean smiling down at me, just as his brother was.

"Merc is back in town."

"Merc?"

"Mercer, a.k.a. Mercenary, a.k.a Merc. It's our pet name for him."

"Sounds charming."

"You have no idea."

"So where's he back from?" I asked. It seemed an innocent enough question. But judging by the quick devolution of their expressions, I guessed I'd hit a nerve.

"That's a bit of a touchy subject," Jase started, always the more diplomatic of the two boys.

"And don't you dare fucking ask him about it," Dean chimed in. "He'll go postal. You do NOT want Merc to go postal, understand?"

"Yeah. I got it. Don't poke around at the new guy's past. No problem."

"It shouldn't really be an issue anyway," Jase added. "He's not much of a talker."

"More of the strong silent type?" I deadpanned.

"Something like that."

The two males exchanged looks before heading toward the swinging door leading out of the kitchen.

"So where are we going exactly? I need to know what I'm wearing."

"You know where we're going..."

"Didn't we practically get kicked out of there last time?" I groused.

"Yep. But that's all been smoothed over now," Jase said with a grin.

"We'll find you later," Dean added, following his brother out of the room.

They disappeared, leaving me to my takeout and contemplations. Did I want to partake in their night of debauchery, which would end as it always did: with them finding a light snack (should read "human to feast on") and me waiting for them to finish up? And then there was the mysterious return of Merc. Was I going to be stuck entertaining him while the boys did their thing? From what they'd told me, he sounded like the perfect companion to ensure a horrible night. I didn't need another moody vampire in my life, or one with a short fuse for that matter. I was all set with hair-trigger vamps. I lived in a house full of them.

One way or another, I needed to duck out of Jase's planned festivities.

※

ANOTHER DIFFICULT PART of living with vampires was trying to evade them. It was virtually impossible once the sun went down. And unfortunately for me, that was when they (and fun-loving humans) went out. My plan to avoid going clubbing with them was dead in the water. Jase and Dean tracked me down without even trying.

"Did you really think hiding in the pantry was going to get you out of this?" Jase asked, clearly entertained by my antics.

"Hoped would have been the word I'd have chosen, but yes. I did."

"Aw, don't you love us anymore, P?" Dean asked, draping his arm over my shoulders as we walked out to the parking lot.

"I do. I just don't love your harebrained antics when you're drunk off your ass," I retorted. "And so help me, if you two leave me alone with this Merc character, I will never forgive you. Understand?"

"Yeah, that will *never* happen," Jase replied, all joviality gone from his tone. "Merc is fine if we're around, but you are not to go anywhere near him if we aren't. Got it?"

"Seriously?"

"Very serious...ly."

"Does he live at the mansion?" I asked.

"He does now."

"Then what the hell am I supposed to do if I'm walking

down the hall and he just happens to be there? Clearly I can't just avoid him indefinitely..."

"You can and you will," Jase countered. "Turn around slowly and go the other way. That's what you do."

"Holy shit!" I exclaimed. "You guys aren't kidding? You really want me to avoid him!"

"That is what Jase said," Dean pointed out unhelpfully.

"Who is this guy exactly? Some fucking vampire serial killer?" Silence. "You two are so comforting."

"Realistic would have been the word I'd have chosen," Jase corrected, throwing my words back at me. "But I mean it, Piper. Merc is volatile at best, and it doesn't take much to set him off."

"Is that why he's been gone?"

Again, Jase and Dean exchanged looks before answering.

"Sort of."

"Fine. I won't poke the bear with a short stick and I'll retreat if I see him coming. Happy?"

"Yep."

"So where is he, anyway? If he's coming to the club with us, why isn't he out here?"

"He is."

"What? Where?" I blurted out, looking around the various vehicles for this loose cannon brother-in-arms of theirs.

"Right on cue," Dean said under his breath, looking back at the mansion. I turned to follow his gaze. What I found approaching was a veritable wall of brooding darkness. Clad in all black, he stalked toward us like a midnight assassin. Merc was easily as tall as the boys and equally built, but he had an edge that they lacked. An arrogance that permeated the air around him. His black, shaggy hair was partially pulled back, letting the moonlight highlight the sharp angles of his face. I expected his eyes to be almost as dark as his hair, but as he grew nearer, I saw that they had a surprising hue. Pale gray-blue eyes fell on me, staring me down as though I were an alien—a being like nothing he'd ever seen before.

"Merc," Jase said, edging himself strategically between the new guy and me. "This is Piper, the one we mentioned earlier. She's coming with us tonight."

Merc continued to stare silently at me before walking past us toward the SUV. He opened the passenger door and got in, leaving the boys and me standing in his wake. I looked up at the brothers incredulously, trying to give them my very best "what the fuck?" face.

"You didn't tell her?" Dean asked his brother, mimicking the expression I wore.

"I thought you did!"

"Well, I didn't."

"Tell me what?" I asked, not wanting to bear witness to one of their epic verbal battles. Those things had been known to drag on for hours.

"So, there's one other little catch with Merc," Jase started, ushering me toward the vehicle. "Like I alluded to before, he's not really a talker."

Dean scoffed.

"Like he's quiet?" I asked.

"No. Like he never talks. *Ever*," Dean clarified.

"You've got to be kidding me..."

"Sorry, P. Wish I was."

"Well, I guess it's a good thing you hadn't planned on leaving us alone then," I mumbled to myself.

The boys grinned simultaneously before replying in unison.

"This should be a fun night for sure."

※

I'D NEVER BEEN SO happy to escape a confined space in all my life. Jase and Dean did their best to make the ride to the club tolerable, but their efforts were in vain. The second we were parked, I bolted from the SUV toward the line stretched around the outside of the three-story red brick building. We had an easy time getting in, which meant that Jase really had smoothed things over with the owners. The vamps were a bit like the mob. They practically ran parts of NYC (the non-supernatural parts). And because of that, we had ins at nearly every place worth going to in the city.

Bruno, the bouncer working the door, patted me down, being extremely careful not to linger too long near any of my valued areas. He had done that once. After that night, his fingers had never quite looked right, remnants of the anatomically impossible angles they'd been bent into still present.

Dean was a little sensitive when it came to me and my virtue.

Once we entered the main room of the club, the boys made their way back to their usual spot in the VIP section above while I hit the ladies room. I needed a break from Merc's intense glare. Since the place was run by the vamps, I didn't have to worry about any unfriendly supernaturals showing up there. It was a safe haven of sorts for me. Even though I bitched about the boys and their all-night partying, I secretly did love going there.

The line to the ladies room ran the length of the hall, but I eventually got to use it before I peed my pants. I then made a pit stop at the bar to talk to Kat, the werewolf who bartended there a couple nights a week. Even after "marrying" one of the enforcers, she insisted on maintaining an air of normalcy, as well as income of her own. The sad reality of which she was all too aware was, in the event that her mate, Jensen, was killed, the vampires would kick her out of the mansion to find a pack to take up with. Most supernaturals tolerated mixing, but it wasn't their favorite practice, especially in the vampire community. Kat was by far and away an exception to the rule, but it wasn't hard to see why. She was five-foot-eleven and built like a swimsuit model with the looks to match. Her clear blue eyes were almost too large for her face, but the almond shape of them gave her a mysterious beauty that boys of any species had a hard time ignoring. Hell, I'd checked her out when I'd first met her. Nobody should be that good-looking.

Nobody.

"The usual?" she asked, leaning over the bar so that her breasts rested on top of it. The guy next to me was mesmerized.

"Please," I replied and watched as she fixed me a vodka cran the size of Texas. I saw no point in ordering drinks all night long. I preferred to get mine Big Gulp size so I wouldn't have to make a return trip.

She plopped it down on the bar in front of me and waved me off when I reached for my wallet.

"You know your money is no good here," she said with a smile before her eyes lifted toward the VIP section. "You keeping the boys company tonight?"

"Ugh...you know it isn't like that, Kat," I sighed. She'd always hoped I would hook up with one or the other. She adored Jase and Dean, though she would never directly admit it when asked. "Besides, I think they have their hands full enough."

Before she could interrogate me about my remark, some rowdy guys at the other end of the bar started to razz her about slow service. She rolled her eyes at me, then turned to give them a wink. As soon as they laid eyes on her, their expressions lightened. Werewolves really did have an animal appeal that couldn't be ignored. Or maybe it was Kat's amazing boobs. It was hard to tell.

"I'll catch you later, Piper," she called over her shoulder, running her hand through her short auburn hair as she made her way over to take their order.

With drink in hand, I wove my way up to the VIP section, a growing sense of dread accompanying me. By the time I made it to the table, I was ready to place it down and retreat to the dance floor immediately. The boys, however, had other plans for me.

"No you don't," Jase said, grabbing my arm when he figured out my plan to escape. "You're hanging out tonight. No more of this drink and ditch bullshit. You've been playing that game for the last two weeks."

"Yeah," Dean chimed in. "I'm starting to think you don't like us."

"Fine," I declared in surrender before flopping down into the empty seat at the table. "I've had a lot on my mind for the past couple weeks. You know music is how I escape. How I deal. Dancing is my vice."

"What's been going on?" Jase asked, leaning forward onto his elbows. "You haven't mentioned anything. Is it the warlocks? Do we need to crack some skulls?"

I considered his offer for a moment, then thought better of it. Though the boys knew I had an extensive and occasionally violent past with the warlocks—more specifically a small faction of them—I never did tell them, or anyone else for that matter, how things came to be so bad between those warlocks and me. I usually did all I could to block those memories from my mind.

I had been young and impressionable and desperate for supernatural guidance, a link to the world I belonged to, yet wasn't a part of. I found that link, if only for a while, in a warlock named Kingston. He took an interest in me when nobody else bothered. He cared about me and tried to be my mentor. But when I proved unable to deliver magically, he turned on me. And his buddies followed suit.

For those eight years on my own, I'd done all I could to evade them, succeeding for the most part—narrowly escaping them for the rest. With every encounter, Kingston's rage grew, his hatred of me poisoning his mind. Kingston abhorred the weak.

And weak I was.

Knowing that the brothers would do anything to keep me safe—especially bend the rules until they broke—I did what I could to keep them from knowing all that went on with me when they weren't around. They didn't need to know that my warlock situation had recently escalated. At least not yet. If the boys intentionally went after them, it would only cause trouble for all of us.

It wasn't yet time to raise that alarm.

"Nothing like that," I sighed, looking annoyed by his over-protectiveness, even though I thought it was endearing. "It's just more of the same old. It wears on me after a while."

"Define 'same old'."

"It's nothing crazy, Jase. It just seems like New York isn't big enough to avoid those that I want to avoid, that's all," I explained with a sigh. "Things have been so much easier for me since I moved in with you guys, but that doesn't mean that the past has changed. I may be much more tolerated than I was before, but I'm far from accepted."

"Then why go out during the day by yourself?" Dean asked, mimicking his brother's posture.

"My options are kinda limited. Kat's about the only one who can venture out into the sun with me, and she's usually spent after her nights working here. What am I supposed to do? Stay inside all the time? Hole up like a daytime recluse? No," I said shaking my head. "I'm not going to do that. I need the sunshine, the blue sky...normal things like that."

"Piper," Jase started, his tone taking on its big brother affectation. "Things between the different supernaturals are not so stellar right now. There are...*tensions* brewing."

"What he means to say is that shit's about to hit the fan because everyone is so twitchy. It won't take much, and knowing how some of them get around you—"

"You mean the warlocks," I specified.

"Yeah. Them," he replied with a sour expression. "We just don't need to give anyone a reason to drop the first bomb, you feel me?"

"Um, not really, but..."

"The different races are just looking for a reason to go at it. I don't want you to be the reason."

"Oh."

Merc, who I'd nearly forgotten was there, leaned forward out of the shadows and looked at Jase.

"Long story," the older of the two brothers replied to a question that hadn't been asked. I looked on while Merc and Jase stared at each other, trying to flesh out what the change in Jase's expression meant. If I hadn't known better, I would have thought they were having a telepathic conversation. "Ha!" Jase laughed, finally breaking his silence, "that's an even longer story."

"Don't go down that road, bro. Trust me. It won't get you anywhere," Dean chimed in, confusing me even further.

"What are you two talking about?" I asked, trying to make sense of what was going on.

Jase and Dean both smiled.

"Just having a little informative chat with Merc."

"But he doesn't talk," I whisper-shouted, leaning in toward Jase. My eyes darted to my left to find Merc staring at me, his dark, veiled expression unchanged. I wondered if it ever did.

The boys' smiles widened.

"Not in the way you do," Jase said unhelpfully.

"With us, he's never needed to," Dean added.

"What the hell does that mean?"

"It means that he speaks directly to our minds."

Holy shit. Suddenly my telepathy theory was back on the table.

"So he was talking to you? Just now?"

"Yes," they replied in unison. It always freaked me out when they did that.

"*Can* he talk?" I asked, wondering if he was truly mute or just chose to be because it suited his creepy, mysterious vibe.

"He could once, but I haven't heard him utter a word aloud in...shit. I don't even know how long."

"It's got to have been, what? Eighty years or more now?" Dean said, looking to Merc for confirmation.

In a rare act of acknowledgment, Merc nodded.

I stared in disbelief, not because they were at least 80 years old and looked 30. I stared because I couldn't imagine going eight decades without communicating verbally. No wonder he was crazy. I'd have been nuts too, if that was the case.

"Why you two?" I finally asked, wondering what made them so special. Why he could talk to them, hang out with them, and seemed to tolerate them when he allegedly tolerated no one.

"Because he's our brother," Dean said, looking utterly confused. "We didn't tell you that either?"

"What did you two actually tell me, since everything worth mentioning seems to just now be coming out?"

Dean's eyes shot to Merc suddenly.

"Yeah. Pretty much."

"What did he just say?" I asked, wondering if that was how the night would play out; they would have their little conversations and I would be left demanding explanations for the bizarre and random responses they gave.

"He asked if you were always like this."

"Like what?"

Dean hesitated.

"So uptight."

"I'm uptight? The guy that doesn't fucking talk for almost a century thinks I'm uptight?" I exclaimed before slamming the better part of my drink. "I've officially entered the twilight zone. If you need me, I'll be on the dance floor trying to sort all of this out." I got up abruptly and walked away to the sound of Jase and Dean calling after me. Merc didn't say a thing, not that that was surprising. I probably would have fallen over if he had. How did those two manage to not once mention this strange brother of theirs to me? Dean couldn't keep a secret to save his life. Jase, though better than his younger brother, must have had a hard time sitting on that little detail—or not so little detail, as the case seemed to be.

Either way, the cat was out of the bag, and it left my mind reeling. Why had he been gone? Why was he so dangerous? And why was he selectively mute? The last thing

I needed were more questions in my life. I had plenty of my own, thank you very much.

Thankfully, the pounding bass line reverberating all around me offered reprieve from the barrage of questions that ran through my mind. Instead, I let the rhythm take over, carrying me deep into the crowd of humans. It was easy to lose myself in there, to go unnoticed. It was a welcome feeling. While I danced until beads of sweat started to gather at my hairline, the boys hung out in their lush VIP section, drinking, canoodling with the high-priced ladies of the night that frequented the place, and, from what I could tell, trying to coax Merc into joining in their fun. Not surprisingly, he wasn't having any of it.

After an hour of dancing, my body demanded liquids of some kind, so I made my way through the crowd (with a lot of difficulty) to find Kat at the bar.

"Having fun, I see," she said with a wink, handing me a bottle of water.

"It's better than the alternative," I replied after taking a huge drink.

"Which would be not having fun?"

"Ha! No. Well, actually yes, but maybe only kind of. Jase and Dean brought someone with them tonight. He's not very entertaining, so I've decided to do my own thing."

"He?" she asked with mischievous look in her eyes.

"Oh my God, no! Not like that. Holy crap, Kat. You know the boys don't swing that way. And besides that, ew! He's their *brother*."

Her expression fell just as quickly as the color drained from her face.

"Merc is back?"

"So it seems."

Her hand darted out, catching my arm as it brought the

bottle to my mouth. I got doused with water in the process, my white tank now translucent.

"Stay away from him, Piper. I mean it."

"Well, that's a bit challenging since I came here with him and the—"

"I am not bullshitting about this, Piper. I really mean it." Her eyes pierced mine with a desperate intensity that I couldn't overlook. She looked more than concerned. She looked scared. "If even a fraction of what I've heard about him is true, he's no joke, girl. There's a reason he's been gone."

"Which is?" I probed, hoping for some answers about the newcomer.

"No clue. All I know is it can't be good, and I don't want you around that."

"The boys already warned me about him; that I'm not to be alone with him."

"Ever!"

"No objections here. He's super creepy," I added. I conveniently left out the 'hot' part of my analysis, thinking it wouldn't do much for Kat's blood pressure. "I think this avoidance plan might prove problematic given that he and I both will be living in the mansion."

"I don't care. Find a way to do it. Live in my room if you need to. Whatever, just promise me you'll stay away from him after tonight."

"Okay. I promise. But you're going to have to explain to Jensen why I'm sleeping on the floor of your room. And you're also going to have to explain to the boys why I can't hang out with them anymore."

"Deal," she said with a hesitant smile. "Need anything else?" She jerked her head back toward the wall of alcohol behind her.

"Good thinking," I replied, eyeing the backlit bottles. "Make me something strong. Really, really strong."

"You're going to need it." I watched her walk over and start pulling various liquors down from the shelves. I stopped counting after the fifth one. It seemed Kat was about to make good on her word.

2

Thirty minutes later, things were looking up.

I had rejoined the boys in VIP with my new favorite beverage, and I proceeded to drink it as quickly as possible. Given that I'd all but chugged the previous one, I was well on my way to drunk as it was. I wasn't much of a partier, so I had lightweight drinking status at best. My size didn't exactly work in my favor either. After Kat's concoction was done, I was lit up like a Christmas tree.

The women that had amassed in my absence cleared out not long after my return, putting an end to any potential shenanigans for the boys. Dean pouted. Jase looked concerned. And Merc just brooded in the corner like nothing had changed.

"So now what are we going to do?" I asked, leaning back in my chair to prop my feet up on the table. "Looks like none of ya will be getting laid, I know that much." I laughed heartily at what I'd thought was a joke. When nobody joined in, I sat up a bit straighter. "What? Why are you staring at me like that?"

"You're wasted," Jase observed.

"And you're grumpy. Waitress!" I yelled, hoping one of the scantily clad girls that served the VIP section would come running.

"Piper, what has gotten into you tonight?" Dean asked, a faint look of disgust in his expression.

"A whole lot of tequila?" I replied before erupting into another drunken outburst of laughter.

"I think it's time we get you home," Jase said, rising from his seat. Suddenly, he paused and looked over at Merc, who hadn't moved an inch. "Yeah, I don't think so, bro. She's coming home with us. All of us. Now." Merc still maintained his position, lounging back against his chair, his arms folded across his chest. When his hooded eyes fell upon mine, I sobered up, if only for a second. There was a palpable tension between us in that moment. He was concentrating on something, staring at me in a way that no one ever had before.

After what seemed like an eternity, his pale eyes darted back to Jase, whose eyebrow cocked strangely.

"You can't? That *is* rather interesting," he muttered, looking to me. "But don't pull that shit, especially not on her. I mean it. No more fucking around. That's what landed you in trouble last time. Now, let's go." Without awaiting a response from anyone, Jase walked over to me, scooped me up under my arms, and pulled me out of my chair to my feet.

"But I wanted to hang out!" I objected with a pout.

"The only thing you're going to do is *pass out* in the car on the way home, party girl. You won't be missing anything. I promise."

"What did Kat put in your drink anyway? Rubbing alcohol?" Dean asked, following Jase and me as his brother ushered me toward the exit.

"Nope. It was way too yummy for that."

"Might as well have been for as much as you tasted it. You downed that thing."

I shrugged in response, tripping over my foot as I tried to look back at Dean. Jase caught me, mumbling something to himself about the lightweight queen. I decided (in all my drunken wisdom) that I would give him a quick jab in the arm as payback. Unfortunately, all that earned me was a near-faceplant in the crowd of clubbers.

"Can you try to stay upright?" Jase admonished. When I bounced off the nearest wall in reply, he sighed heavily, then picked me up over his shoulder in a fireman carry. The position did little for the pressure in my head or the rolling sensation in my stomach.

"Put me down!" I yelled, my words coming out a bit more slurred than I remembered sounding earlier. I tried to push against his back to lift myself up, but all that earned me was a close-up of Merc, who trailed directly behind us. Our faces were only inches apart. I stifled the squeal that threatened to escape and flopped back down, my head resting against Jase's back.

The cool night air felt good against my overheated skin. I was starting to remember why I didn't drink much. The stuff never did jell well with my system.

"Shall we try this again?" Jase asked, placing me down gently on my feet. I wavered for a second, but waved him off with floppy hands when he came to aid me.

"I'm good. Nothing to see here," I quipped, spreading my arms wide to catch my balance. I heard Dean snicker from my left and shot him the nastiest glare I could. "What's so funny?"

"You," he said, stating the rather obvious, "and him." He jerked his thumb over to Merc, who stood between his brothers, staring at me intently.

"What about him?" I demanded, pulling myself up as straight as I could.

"Like there's any point in me telling you. You won't remember tomorrow anyway."

Before I could launch my rebuttal, Jase grabbed my hand and led me down the street. He was walking briskly, which meant he was mad. For a second I felt like shit, knowing that I was the reason behind that anger. Me and my drunk ass.

I opened my mouth to tell him that I was sorry, but snapped it shut the second we rounded the corner leading into the alley. Shortcuts; I'd learned long ago that they just weren't worth it.

"Fancy running into you here, Piper," an unwelcome voice called out from the depths of the narrow way. I stopped dead in my tracks. "And look, you even have your goon squad babysitters with you, not that that's surprising. Maybe you're smarter than we thought."

"Kingston," Jase drawled, covering his irritation with an ambivalent tone. "Always such a pleasure."

"Fuck you, Jase," the warlock snapped, stepping out from the shadows. The very sight of him made my whole body shake with fear. To one who didn't know better, he looked like a model with a hint of goth flair: tall, wiry, with black hair and piercing dark eyes. But to me, he looked like the grim reaper.

My eyes immediately went to his hands. They always had the subtlest hint of blue under that pale white skin. I doubted humans ever noticed. But I did. I knew what that thin veil of flesh withheld.

"It seems we won't be doing any fucking tonight, thanks to Piper," Dean said coolly. "But you're hardly our type anyway. Thanks, but no thanks."

"Is *she* your type?" Kingston fired back. "Because I have to warn you, she's hardly worth it. Pretty disappointing, if I'm being honest."

I cringed at the reference, my skin crawling at the memory of his hands on my body. My traitorous mind recalled the event Kingston was none-too-subtly referring to in vivid detail. A night I deeply regretted. I had fallen victim to temptation and given myself to him, all under the promise that it would help unlock my powers. Help free my gifts.

The only thing it freed me of was my dignity.

Not long after he cast me aside, disgusted by my inability to live up to the magical expectations he held. It was then that I knew I'd been played all along—that he'd used me to gain access to whatever power he thought I possessed. It was then that everything started to go wrong.

Every nerve in my body was begging me to run as I stood in the alley, my focus now returned to his hands. The second they started glowing, all hell would break loose.

"Watch your fucking mouth," Jase ground out through gritted teeth, pulling me from my downward spiral. "Unless you want a war on your hands, *warlock*, I suggest you get the fuck out of our way."

"War, you say?" Kingston queried. "Well now, we wouldn't want that, would we?" His sarcasm was hard to miss. Right on cue, his warlock brethren poured from the darkness at the end of the alley as though it were a direct portal to all things corrupt and evil.

I felt Dean brush past me, putting himself in the line of fire. Jase stood right beside him. Then I felt a body directly behind me. Merc and his brothers had me encased in a ring of vampire enforcers. I was as safe as I was ever going to be around Kingston.

"You know better than that, Kingston," Jase cautioned, reaching behind his back for the blade he kept holstered there. He never took it off. "You come after her, then you come after me. After us all."

"Why do you protect her? She's not one of you," the warlock snarled.

"And she sure as fuck ain't one of you either," Dean countered.

"She shouldn't be at all," Kingston growled under his breath.

"That's not your call," Jase said, stepping forward. "So make your play for her or back the fuck down for good. Either way, this ends tonight. Now."

The two stood only paces away from one another, Kingston's hands a faint icy-blue glow. He was going to fight the boys, and they were terribly outnumbered. The enforcers were some of the most powerful warriors the supernatural world boasted. But they were not invincible. Not by a long shot.

"Make your move, Kingston. It's now or never."

I peeked around the side of Dean to see the warlock staring me down. A smile tugged at his lips when he saw the fear in my eyes. I was in trouble. We all were.

In a blur of motion, he blasted a blue flaming orb at Jase. From where I stood, it looked like it hit him, sending him flying backward. But before he crashed to the ground, he just disappeared altogether. While I screamed in horror, Dean and Merc charged the warlocks, weapons drawn.

"Run, Piper!" Dean yelled. But I couldn't. My feet were glued to the ground with a thick film of fear. I was paralyzed by it. I watched as the two of them took out warlocks left and right, but there were still so many coming. They crashed upon the boys like waves on a pier.

"When somebody tells you to run, you fucking do it!" Jase whispered in my ear, causing me to scream again.

"Jase—"

"GO!" he shouted, shoving me toward the alley's exit. Toward safety.

I listened to him and took off in an uncoordinated sprint. Within seconds I rounded the corner in a stumbling run, trying hard not to fumble the keys Jase had put in my hand before he'd pushed me away and rejoined the fight. I managed to keep hold of them as I wove my way down the sidewalk to the SUV. When I finally reached it, I hit the alarm key instead of the unlock button. The screeching sound that echoed off the tall brick buildings surrounding me did little to settle my nerves.

While I tried to shut it off and get in the car, I heard a tremendous roar that demanded my attention. I looked over my shoulder to see a blue inferno dancing in the sky above the alleyway where the boys were fighting.

"Oh no..." I whispered to myself. Without thinking, I started running back toward them, fearing that somehow Kingston and his boys had found a way to take the enforcers out. Along the way, I felt the wind picking up, a magical storm brewing. There was nothing natural about the way it swirled in the road in front of me or the way it appeared sentient, pausing the moment I came into view.

I instinctively stopped running toward it.

I looked on as it grew in height and breadth, the debris it collected along the way making it gray in appearance. It was nearly as wide as the street I stood in by the time I realized what was happening. Kingston was too occupied with the enforcers to come for me himself, so he sent a minion of sorts. Death by tornado wasn't really his style, but he was a master of adaptation, a trait I could have benefited from a time or two.

Turning back toward the car, I ran as fast as I could, but I could feel the pull of the vortex trailing me. I didn't have long before it would claim me; that much I knew. I needed to figure something out quickly.

Not too far ahead of me, I saw a sewer drain. If I could get there with enough time to wiggle my way into it, I would be safe. But that was a big if. I looked over my shoulder to see the wall of doom only yards away, barreling down on me. There was no way I was going to make it.

I choked back the tears that were threatening to escape.

Don't give up, Piper. Never give up...

With every ounce of strength and adrenaline I could muster, I poured on my speed, darting toward that drain. I was closing in on it: five yards. Four yards. Three yards...

A massive body crashed into me from my left, driving me deep into the entrance of an old storefront. Heavily muscled arms encased my body, locking me tight against the door at my back. Then I felt the pull of the supernatural tornado, my hair and arms unwillingly sucked past the body holding me in place. I looked like a rag doll. His whole body tensed as the magical vacuum effect grew, his mass pressing against me so hard that I could barely breathe. The metal security bars behind me rattled with the force of the storm, shaking me while they bit into my back, but still I went nowhere.

Then suddenly it stopped. Abruptly, inexplicably, the vortex disappeared. I tried to move but couldn't, the wall of male in front of me still very much in place. When he did finally pull away, I looked up to see Merc, his shadowed face hovering close to mine.

I swallowed hard.

"Thank you..." The words barely made it past my lips. Fear had its grip on my throat, closing it. The fearsome Merc had me cornered—exactly what the boys had warned me against. But as I looked up at him, that fear slowly abated, even if it shouldn't have. Something in his stare eased my anxieties.

"Piper!" Jase cried from somewhere down the street. There was definite fear in his voice.

"In here," I called, unable to pull my eyes away from the vampire staring at me. There was no malice in his gaze, but the warnings of his brothers and Kat still ran rampant in my mind. He was capable of terrible things, of that I was sure, and yet there he stood, still sheltering me from a threat that no longer existed. My mind couldn't reconcile the incongruities.

"Holy shit," Jase exhaled as he approached us. "Are you okay?" I watched him turn into the store entryway, his expression bleeding from concerned to frightened in a second. "Merc," he said calmly, like a cop in hostage negotiation. "Back away from her. Everything is fine now. They're gone." When his brother didn't move, I assumed he was relaying some telepathic message to Jase. Then I realized Jase's hand was slowly sliding up his back for his blade. Perhaps they weren't talking at all. "Let her go." There was no mistaking that his words were an order, not a request. Even still, Merc paused. He looked down at my wild eyes and disheveled appearance as if he were taking stock of my well-being, not contemplating how he could harm me. My hair was stuck to my face in places with sweat and dirt, obscuring my vision slightly. As if he'd known it was making me crazy, he reached up and gently slid the unruly locks behind my ear, then turned and walked away from me and Jase like nothing interesting had happened that night.

As soon as Merc was out of sight, Jase grabbed me and pulled me to him, hugging me fiercely.

"Are you sure you're okay?"

"Yes. I'm fine," I replied absentmindedly, my thoughts occupied by the feel of Merc's body against mine and his finger grazing my cheek.

"Piper," Jase said, his tone warning. "This isn't one of those times where you should hold out on me."

"Honestly. I'm fine. Merc saved me from death by tornado. That's all."

Jase looked at me with doubt in his eyes. He thought I was lying. He didn't seem to believe that Merc would have done what he had.

"That's all? You swear it?"

"Yes. I swear it, Jase! He saved me. You showed up. He left. End of story."

He muttered something under his breath about cracking someone's skull, then returned his focus to the matter at hand.

"We need to get out of here, Piper. Now. I have to go report to the king..."

"Oh my God! You guys are going to get in trouble, aren't you? And wait...where's Dean?"

"I'm fine, Piper," a disembodied voice called from the street. "I was cleaning up Jase's mess. As always."

I pulled myself from Jase to find Dean, hugging him the second I did. He was covered in blood and other questionable bits, but I didn't care. I was just happy he was alive. The boys had gotten off easily that night. Luck had been on their side for sure.

Mine too, for that matter.

"What happened to Kingston and the others?" I asked, my face still pressed tightly to Dean's chest.

"Some met untimely ends. Others ducked through portals like the chicken shits they are."

"So I wasn't imagining that then? They really did come out of nowhere?"

"Yep. Motherfuckers are sneaky like snakes. Never, ever trust a warlock."

"It was an ambush," Jase called from behind me. "It had to be. What other reason did he have to be lurking where he was?"

"Unless we stumbled upon something else," I suggested, knowing full well that the warlocks were into some shady dealings with humans, though those particular humans had no knowledge of who and what they were actually dealing with.

"Like what?" Jase probed, taking me by the shoulder to turn me around.

"I don't know...you name it. Drugs. Guns. Prostitution. All of the above."

"With humans?" Dean asked incredulously.

"Yep."

"That can't be right," Jase said thoughtfully. "Reinhardt would never stand for that. He's no saint, but he's above that. And he sure as hell isn't careless. Interactions with humans that go beyond the occasional lay or casual work relationship are strictly forbidden by all factions of the supernatural. It's written in the treaty itself. The exposure risk is too great. There's no way Kingston could be doing that shit without repercussions from his own kind, let alone all the others."

I shrugged, not knowing what to say. I'd seen it with my

own eyes long before I'd ever come to live under the protection of the king and his enforcers. There was no doubt in my mind that what I'd told him was a viable reason for Kingston's appearance in the alley that night. And I wasn't nearly as convinced that Reinhardt, their leader, would have disapproved.

"Something else to report, I guess," Jase said with a sigh.

"What will happen now?" I asked, concerned for what would happen to us all, knowing that carrying out supernatural business that publicly was also forbidden. Dean may have cleaned it up, but there was just no way to be sure that nobody had seen the battle, the raging blue inferno, or the bizarre tornado that had ripped through the business district before disappearing. The odds were not in our favor.

"It'll be fine, Piper. Don't stress out about it," Dean said casually. But when I looked up at him, there was nothing casual about his expression as he stared over the top of my head at Jase.

"Do you think they got the message?" I asked, wondering if the warlocks might finally leave me alone now.

A dangerous pair of smiles overtook the brothers' faces.

"I think you'll find that Kingston isn't a problem anymore," Jase finally offered.

"Is he dead?"

"Worse," Dean said with a laugh.

"What's worse than dead?" I pressed.

"Useless," Jase said callously. I knew he didn't mean anything by it, but his reply cut through me like a knife. He clearly saw my flinch at his words and came to stand directly before me, placing both hands on my shoulders. "Piper, you are far from useless. You are untrained. That isn't the same thing." I tried to force a smile, but it was a weak attempt. One that he saw right through. "C'mon. Merc hates waiting. He's not especially patient. I'll let Dean detail the whole fight on the way home." Jase looped his arm around my shoulder, ushering me toward the SUV down the road. "But I get to tell you the best part."

I looked up at him to find a genuinely amused expression on his face.

"And which part is that? The part where none of you died?"

He leaned in close to whisper in my ear.

"No. The part where I cut off Kingston's hands."

AFTER WE RETURNED HOME, I collapsed into my bed the second I entered my room. I was emotionally, mentally, and physically exhausted. I wanted to sleep off what had almost happened that night and ignore the impending consequences that we were certain to face the next day, even if Jase maintained that there wouldn't be any. I knew better than that. I'd been at the mansion long enough to see what happened to those who bent the rules.

Sleep would provide the perfect safe haven for several hours.

It didn't take long to feel the depths of slumber pulling me in. Once there, I found myself lying naked in an unknown bed in an unfamiliar room. It was clean, modern, and masculine, and I seemed strangely at peace there, luxuriating in the feel of the soft sheets against my skin.

Then my leg brushed up against someone.

Startled, but not frightened, I rolled over to find Merc lying next to me, his hands tucked behind his head, his eyes closed. My heart raced at the sight. I inched closer to him, wanting to assess him the way he had me. There was a serene quality about his face that almost looked wrong on him. How could one so deadly appear so placid?

Suddenly feeling bold, I wove my arm over his stomach, teasing him with trailing fingertips. His eyes opened slowly, falling immediately upon me. Then his body followed. Pinning me to the bed with his formidable weight, he hung his head down, his lips a hair's breadth from mine.

My heart skipped a beat.

"Time to wake up," he said, though his mouth never moved. The sound of it was distorted and fuzzy, like listening to the radio while submerged in water.

With my heart now hammering in my chest and my breath caught in my throat, I awaited his touch. Silently, I begged for him to lay his hands on me—pleaded for his lips to meet mine. Arching my back and extending my neck, I tried to close the distance between us. The anticipation of what could happen next was almost more than I could bear.

"Piper, seriously! Wake the fuck up!" the voice called again, though this time it sounded strange—far away. And female.

A pillow to the side of my head jarred me from my sleep, leaving me frustrated and confused. The dream had seemed so short, so real. Waking to find myself alone in my bed, an irritated-looking Kat hovering over me, was not what I'd envisioned.

"You need to get downstairs," she said, staring at me like she had a bone to pick with me for some unknown reason.

"I'm getting up," I grumbled, wiping my eyes.

"You guys," she grumbled under her breath. "You guys are in some real shit."

Before I could get her to elaborate on why, she stormed out of the room, slamming the door behind her.

I sat up in bed, trying to remember the details of the

dream I'd had, but they seemed beyond recollection. It was as if it had never happened. I started to question if that wasn't the case. But there was a lingering sensation deep in my core, a feeling of need that hadn't abated when I awoke. Something had caused it.

And his name was Mercenary.

3

I stumbled out of my room, still sleep-drunk and hungover, and made my way down the butler's stairs to the kitchen. I needed coffee and lots of it. A croissant wouldn't have hurt either, but I doubted we had anything like that lying around unless the pastry gods were watching out for me.

They, like all the other gods, usually weren't.

I peeked around the corner to find that the coast was clear, then made my way over to the coffeemaker and got down to business. It was pretty clear when Kat woke me up that she was pissed. I needed to talk to her to find out what had her so riled up. But there was no way I was even going to attempt that until I had at least two cups of the black liquid-of-life coursing through my veins.

Maybe three.

On the counter next to the coffee machine was an iPod dock, equipped with the iPod I had left in it a couple of nights ago. I scrolled through until I found something cheery that would pick me up and prepare me for a potential battle with Kat. The speakers sprang to life with a peppy

80s song that always put a smile on my face. I bopped around the kitchen, acquiring the things I needed to brew a monster-sized pot of coffee. Wearing only my boyshort undies and a white tank, I danced like an 80s queen.

Tom Cruise a la *Risky Business* would have been jealous.

It was a gift to be able to bounce around and not spill the water as I filled the reservoir at the back of the coffeemaker, and I had it in spades. I turned around to refill the pot and found myself prancing toward a formidable figure leaning against the far wall of the room. I yelped, managing not to let out the full-blown scream that wanted to escape.

"Holy shit!" I exclaimed, clutching my chest. "You scared me." While I battled to control my breathing, I realized that I was standing virtually naked in front of Merc. And judging by the level of his gaze, that little detail had not been lost on him.

I quickly put the pot down and crossed my arms over my chest, hiding the rest of me behind the cover of the island. There was an intensity in his stare—a familiarity to it—that made me squirm. Apparently the dream I'd had that night had been more real to me than I'd thought.

If I hadn't known better, I'd have thought it was real to him too.

"Do you want some coffee?" I asked nervously, cursing my lack of clothing and need for a caffeine fix. I should have gone after Kat as soon as I'd gotten up, but instead I'd sought refuge in the kitchen and that plan had backfired miserably. Evasion, distraction, and diplomacy had long been my tactics. They were how I'd survived on my own. And it was time to employ them with Merc.

He looked at me strangely, silently refusing my offer.

"Right," I admonished, shaking my head slightly. "Probably not a big fan of the stuff."

He took a step deeper into the room, right toward me. All that separated us was the huge square island that I was hiding behind. Not much of a barricade to a two-hundred-plus-pound vampire.

"It's great for hangovers," I continued, pretending not to notice his approach. "I usually don't party that hard, though. Never could handle my booze very well. But coffee is my best friend the next day. Don't know how I'd survive without it on mornings like these." I turned to grab a mug from the cabinet. Giving him my back (or my butt, as the case might have been) wasn't something I wanted to do at all, but I needed to appear calm, collected, and unfazed by his presence, even if I was anything but. I also needed to keep talking. "I swear Dean hides my favorite cup at the top just to piss me off," I said, straining to reach the top shelf. I held my tank top's edge down with my other hand, not wanting to expose any more skin than I already was. "Your brother can be a real pain in the ass sometimes."

I was as far up on my tiptoes as I could possibly be, and still I could barely touch the handle of the mug, my fingers grazing it before I'd waver slightly and lose contact with it. Anxious and frustrated, I reached up one last time only to miss again. This time, however, my height wasn't the issue. The large hand holding the cup above me was.

I could feel Merc behind me. He had to be only an inch or two away, his massive frame looming as he reached over me into the cabinet for the object I desired. I froze, but my heart raced uncontrollably. As I stood there, paralyzed with growing panic, his arm wrapped around in front of me and placed the *Morning Princess* mug down on the counter.

"Thanks," I whispered, my voice catching in my throat. My nerves had closed it down too tight to speak normally. When he didn't reply (not that I expected him to), I hazarded a glance up over my shoulder at him while he remained behind me, unmoving. His gray-blue eyes nearly bore through mine just like they had when he'd saved me. Just like they had in my dream. And just like on those occasions, despite my growing anxiety, I could not look away from him.

I was utterly entranced.

His eyes narrowed slightly as he cocked his head to the side, moving it toward me. I gasped, memories of the dream I'd had flooding my mind—accompanied by the sensations it had sent through my body. Knowing the warnings I'd been given by the boys and Kat, I should have run from that room, screaming for help from anyone around like I'd been told to. But instead, I stood there awaiting whatever he had planned. The potential consequences of not fleeing seemed swallowed up by anticipation. It made me question if the warlocks hadn't been right about me after all.

Maybe I was too stupid to live.

With his head hung low to reach mine, his lips dangerously near my ear, a voice cut through the kitchen, startling me. I jumped, flinging my hands out wildly around me. My *Morning Princess* mug flew through the air and crashed to the floor, shattering into pieces.

The first casualty of the day.

"Piper!" Kat shouted, her tone chastising. "We've been looking all over for you!"

"Sorry," I replied, slinking away from Merc. "I just wanted to wake up fully before the shitstorm settled in."

"Yeah well, it already has. Jase and Dean are expecting a call from the king any minute. They're trying to get their story together, and you need to be there to vouch for them." Her angry eyes fell on Merc, then widened slightly. "I'll take you to them now, Piper. Let's go."

"Yeah, okay," I replied, stepping over the shards of my favorite mug.

"Maybe you should put some damn clothes on first," she scolded as I walked past her. "If things go wrong, you'll be heading over to see the king instead of settling this over the phone."

"I got it, Kat. I got it." I looked back at her, giving her my most irritated expression, which did nothing to improve her mood. Then my gaze reached past her to Merc, who stood exactly where I'd left him, his eyes fully trained on me.

Something in them begged me to see what I had not yet seen. And I as I walked away, I tried to make sense of his expression. But with every step I took, all I could think of was how close he'd just been to me—and how much I'd liked it.

Just like when he'd saved me.

Just like in my dream.

With a shake of my head to clear it, I ran back up to my room to throw on some pants and a top, then hightailed it down to Jase's room, where the call had already begun. The king's voice was calm as he spoke, but I had no doubt in my mind that he was forcing himself to sound that way. He had to have been pissed about what had happened.

I slipped through the door and closed it behind me, doing my best not to make a noise.

"Am I to assume that Piper has just joined us?" the king asked.

"Yes, it's me, your highness. Sorry I'm late."

"I was just about to inform the brothers about the conversation I just had with Reinhardt." I looked over at Jase and Dean, their expressions tight. Then I noticed Merc, leaning against the far wall looking totally unfazed by the situation. "I'm not sure that you all are aware of just how precarious this matter is. I have done all I can as of late to keep this information to myself, but now it seems I must relay it to you: the treaty is in jeopardy. More so than it has ever been before. The unrest in the supernatural community is at a fever pitch, and your antics last night have done nothing to help that, let alone the risk of exposure to humans you so carelessly ignored while embroiled in your petty battle."

"Sire, I can assure you that it wasn't—"

"Enough," the king said, cutting Jase off at the knees. "I do not wish to hear your excuses. You are here to listen and listen only. Is that understood?" We all quietly agreed. "Excellent. Now Reinhardt, clever as he is, was willing to see the reason in keeping this matter between us. After some convincing, he saw that it was his warlocks that were the aggressors and has taken measures to ensure that it will not happen again."

Both Jase and Dean's gazes fell upon their silent brother, looks of disbelief on both of their faces.

"Piper," the king continued. "You should not fear the wrath of Kingston and his crew anymore. They will no longer be a threat to you."

I didn't know what to say or if I should say anything at all. Instead, I just stared at the phone in Jase's hand, utterly dumbfounded.

"Thank you, sire," I said softly, wondering what he must have had to give up in order to ensure such a concession on Reinhardt's part.

"I would not thank me yet, if I were you," he said. "You are all on thin ice with me. I want to make that point very clear. Though I understand your options were limited last night, you need to know that I cannot have a repeat of this behavior, no matter what. If I catch wind of any, and I mean any, vigilante activity or unsanctioned attacks on any of the supernatural breeds, you will be staked. No questions asked. Have I made my position clear?"

"Yes," Jase and Dean quickly agreed.

"And what of Mercenary? Does he too agree to my terms?"

"He does," Jase replied, looking over at Merc with a rather strained expression.

"Excellent. Then I will deem this matter closed."

With that the king hung up, leaving us all standing there, our collective minds reeling. Except for Merc. He looked no different than he had when I'd noticed he was in the room.

"Well that could have been worse," Dean said, letting out a breath.

"I'm so sorry," I said softly. "I didn't want any of this to happen."

"It's not your fault, Piper," Jase argued. "We had no choice, though I'm sure Kingston did all he could to paint that picture differently."

"The good news is that Reinhardt finally promised to keep that douchebag and all his little friends in line. For that alone, it was worth it."

Jase and Dean both suddenly turned their attention over to Merc.

"What do you mean 'can he be trusted'?" Jase replied to the question Merc had apparently posed. The silent brother cocked his head curiously at Jase. "What reason would he have to lie, Merc? The only ones we need to worry about lying are Reinhardt and Kingston."

"And Reinhardt isn't dumb enough to lie outright to the king. Treaty or not, he knows what that would mean," Dean added.

Merc nodded once, then pushed off the wall to walk toward me. My heart raced with every step he took. I couldn't decide if it was out of fear or anticipation.

Maybe it was a little of both.

He stopped in front of me and lingered for a moment, staring at me with a curious expression. He looked as though he were trying to tell me something. Hovering for only that brief moment, he continued on and out the door.

I watched him disappear into the hallway. The pang of disappointment I felt was undeniable, though difficult to understand. Though I wanted to dissect what I was feeling, there was no time for that. With a sigh, I turned to see Jase eyeing me, his jaw clenched so tight that I could see the muscles in his neck straining.

"Anything you want to tell us, Piper?"

"Me? About what?" I replied, volleying a question back at him.

"About whatever that just was." He looked at me, irritation in his stare. "You two sure do seem to enjoy sharing dramatic pauses and quiet little moments together," he explained. The accusation in his tone was plain.

"What in God's name are you getting at, Jase?"

I balled up my fists and planted them firmly on my hips, trying to make myself look as intimidating as possible. It was a laughable attempt, but I was getting mad (or defensive). I didn't feel like being interrogated or berated for a third time that night. The king and Kat were enough.

"I'm wondering if you have forgotten my previous warning about Merc."

"You mean the 'he's dangerous...stay away' one?" Jase nodded. "No, I think I have that one filed away."

"It doesn't appear that way."

"Listen, I get it. You know things about him that I don't.

But all I've seen so far is his ability to save my ass...and reach my coffee cup." I shot Dean a scathing look to punctuate my last remark. "I know you think he'll hurt me, but I've spent a long time running from people wanting to do just that. So far, I get no hint of ill intent from him."

...Not that Kingston had displayed any warning signs of his impending betrayal.

But still, in hindsight, it was easy to see how he'd manipulated me, magically or otherwise. He'd wanted something from me and had exploited my desires to fit in, to know how to call upon my magic, and to be loved. Merc, on the other hand, just seemed interested in me—or keeping me alive, to be more precise.

At least for now.

"Merc can be misleading."

"So can a lot of people, Jase. But either way, I haven't forgotten what you've told me about him. He just shows up wherever I am."

"I'll take care of that. You work on avoiding him. Got it?"

I let out an exasperated sigh.

"Got it."

"Good," he replied, looking relieved. He ran his hand through his dark hair a few times, messing it up in the most perfect way. "I'm not trying to be a dick, Piper. It's just with everything going on, I wanted to make sure you didn't forget what we told you. That's all." He let out a heavy sigh of his own. "I get that you've kind of been thrust into the crosshairs recently and Merc did right by you. I just don't want that to lull you into a state of complacency, okay? He's my brother and I love him, but he can be dangerously unpredictable. I don't want to see you get hurt. That's all."

I wanted to be mad at Jase, but I couldn't. He was like a

brother to me, and I loved him. He was watching my back as he always had. That's what family does.

"I understand," I said, walking over to hug him, then Dean, who had remained uncharacteristically quiet throughout Jase's and my exchange.

"I'm going to have a chat with Merc later tonight," Jase said as I pulled away from Dean. "But for now, Dean and I have some planning to do."

"Planning for what?"

"Before you came in the king suggested that we start training some of the younger vamps to see who is cut out to be an enforcer. He wants a list of potentials drafted before the day is done so that we can round them up to begin by next nightfall. Dean and I need to get on it if we have any chance of organizing this in time."

"That's fine. I'll find something to do," I told him, turning to leave.

"And try to stay out of trouble while you're at it," Dean called after me. I looked over my shoulder to find him grinning from ear to ear.

"I'll do what I can. I can't seem to help that trouble always finds me."

"Please steer clear of Merc until I talk to him," Jase added. "This interest he seems to have taken in you—it makes me uneasy. I'll feel better once I know more."

I felt a spike of fear and excitement shoot through me.

"Okay," I replied, trying to keep my tone even and calm while my body felt anything but. With his closing remarks running wild through my mind, I exited the room, closing the door behind me. Leaning against the heavy wood, I sighed heavily, trying to slow my racing heart. Then I remembered what the Merc debacle had eclipsed. A smile grew wide across my face. For the first time in as long as I could recall, the threat of the warlocks had been lifted. It was as though a weight had been lifted off of me. The freedom from that burden felt better than I ever could have imagined.

Unfortunately for me, that freedom was just an illusion.

4

I'd gone for a run that evening.

It seemed like the perfect time to do it, given the conversation we'd had with the king. His message that the warlocks were no longer a threat to me was greatly reassuring. Reinhardt was many things by reputation, but stupid was not one of them. He wouldn't dare cross the king. The consequences would be far too dire, and for what? To eliminate someone like me? Even Kingston wouldn't put himself in the king's crosshairs. He was too committed to living to sign his own death warrant so easily.

Since it was not quite dark yet, I threw on my running gear and made my way outside. I knew the vamps wouldn't be up for a while, and Jase and Dean were still busy rounding up potential candidates to pick up for enforcer training, so I decided to capitalize and take some time for myself to recharge a bit. The perfect way to clear my head.

I stretched for a minute, taking in the smell of the freshly cut grass, then I started off on my normal path, my pace easy but quick. But the farther I ran, the more my mind wandered, turning over and over the events of the prior night. I wanted to believe they hadn't affected me, but it seemed I was wrong. That dream—it had seemed so real. And the way Merc had looked at me in the kitchen afterward? Something seemed so different. Or maybe I just wanted it to be. Maybe I was reading into things.

But then there was the moment in the store breezeway...

With every stride I took, I dove deeper and deeper into the mystery that was Merc. I wound my way through unfamiliar streets, my mind determined to sort out what I was feeling and why I was feeling it. By the time I realized I was lost, I wasn't any closer to the answers.

"Shit," I muttered to myself, bent over at the waist to catch my breath while I surveyed my surroundings. I'd gone way farther than I'd meant to, and now I was too exhausted to run home before dark. "Just what I need."

With few options, I turned around and attempted to jog back toward the mansion. After three blocks of that, I slowed to a walk. Running home just wasn't an option. Luckily, I knew that the boys were meeting the new recruits at a vampire-owned bar just across the street from Central Park. I decided to head there and wait for them.

It didn't take long to walk over to the park's edge, the dying light of day casting a soft orange glow around me. The park was huge, spanning well over a square mile, so it was no surprise that I had arrived at a section I was unfamiliar with. I decided to head into the center, where there was a map posted in a large concrete fanfare. Once there, I could figure out which way I needed to go to cross paths with the boys. It all seemed so simple really.

It should have gone off without a hitch.

Darkness had nearly settled around me by the time I reached the map, but the surrounding lampposts illuminated it, making it easy for me to read. According to what it said, I needed to get to the opposite side from where I'd arrived if I was going to have any chance of catching Jase and Dean.

Missing them was not a very appealing thought.

Trying to avoid that outcome, I decided to veer away from the delineated paths, hoping to take a more direct route and shave some time off the trip. I knew that Jase and Dean had wanted to leave the house the second the sun was down, and judging by how dark it was, that had already occurred. With my anxiety rising, I cut through a copse of trees, jogging toward the intersection where the bar was located, and came upon an unwelcome sight.

Warlocks.

I stopped dead in my tracks, hoping they hadn't yet seen me. I knew that the king had said all was well—that Reinhardt would be taking care of those that had ambushed us near the club—but my survival instincts were on high alert. I was desperate for a way out.

But it was far too late for that. They had already spotted me.

"Well, well, well, what have we here, boys?" a voice called from behind the others. A voice that made my blood run cold. Ice cold. "Looks like the little lamb has happened upon us." With a degree of fanfare that only he could create, Kingston stepped forward from the group. A long leather coat draped over his shoulders, covering his arms. With an ambivalent shrug, it fell to the ground, exposing the gruesome aftereffects of Jase's handiwork. Where there had once been hands, only raw stumps remained. Kingston seemed almost amused by my inability to not stare with mouth agape.

"Jase is not without a cruel sense of justice," he said, lifting one of the blackened wrists up to his face, twisting it at various angles while he inspected it. "Speaking of Jase, where are he and the rest of your vampire buddies? You didn't venture out alone without them, did you? Because that would be a really stupid thing to do, you know? The world can be such a dangerous place..."

"They'll be here any minute. They're picking me up."

Kingston looked around at the trees surrounding us.

"In the middle of Central Park? That seems a tad unlikely, doesn't it, Piper?" He took a step toward me and I retreated a pace to match his advance.

"I wouldn't think of touching me if I were you. I spoke to the king myself only hours ago. He said that he and Reinhardt had come to an understanding regarding your attack in the alley. I don't think your leader was overly happy about your antics, from what I understood."

"No," he replied with a smirk. "He wasn't."

"I know you, Kingston. You're smart. Too smart to invite the wrath of your leader and the vampire king down upon you. We both know that," I babbled, hoping to defuse the situation enough to get away intact.

"Is that the tactic you're going to employ tonight? Leverage me to let you go based on fear of retribution?" he asked, advancing toward me again. His collection of fellow warlocks followed his lead and moved toward me as well. "You see, the thing is, Piper, I don't give a fuck about any of that. I stopped caring about politics the second your little babysitter lopped my hands off." The fury in his dark eyes somehow cut through the night and pierced my heart, stopping it entirely.

Or perhaps that was the fear that surged through me the second I saw the faint blue glow emanating from the marred stumps Jase had left him with.

Either way, I didn't bother waiting to hear what he was

going to say next. Instead, I turned to make a break for it. Unfortunately for me, I didn't stand a chance at escaping. I barely made it two steps before I crashed to the ground, a searing pain shooting through my body.

As I writhed on the ground, the pungent smell of burnt flesh assailing me, Kingston came to tower over my wounded body. He and all the rest of his minions. The situation was grim. The last time I'd run across the warlocks, I'd narrowly escaped with my life. And when my eyes fell upon the growing fireball occupying the space where his hand should have been, I wasn't so certain I was going to avoid death this time around.

"You really don't deserve to live," he laughed. The tone of it held a note of instability. Kingston was coming unhinged. "I'm really doing us all a favor here, Piper, yourself included. Being the enforcers' pet is no way to live. Consider this a mercy kill."

"The second Jase and Dean realize I'm missing, they'll come after you!" I shouted at him through gritted teeth. The scorch mark on my back was throbbing like crazy. "You'll be dead before sunrise."

"Come after me for what?" he asked, feigning ignorance. Then he bent down close to me, wiping the hair from my eyes so that I could see his face clearly. He wanted his visage to be burned into my memory. "They'll never find a body, Piper. And you said it yourself; the king and Reinhardt expressly prohibited any such behavior as was exhibited last night near the club." My eyes widened with fear. "And you know that I wouldn't dare act out against such forces, don't you?"

I couldn't believe what I was hearing, let alone the wild conclusions his words forced me to draw. The previous night had been an ambush. There was no doubt about that.

Kingston had orchestrated the entire thing just to give himself the perfect alibi for my murder. And it was undoubtedly going to work. The king had forgiven Dean and Jase for their unsupported actions against the warlocks. He would not do so again.

My murder would go both unsolved and unavenged.

"Don't worry, Piper. This will only burn for the first few minutes or so. You'll eventually pass out from the pain," he informed me as his signature smug expression overtook his face. "And you can scream all you want. Monroe has already cast an illusion around us. Nobody will hear or see you."

He stepped back away from me, his lackeys flanking him as his hand-less arms somehow called forth an electric blue flash of fire so bright that I squinted hard against the visual assault. Then I realized he had set me ablaze. Initially I did what any sane individual would have done; I screamed, panicked, then started to roll frantically across the ground in an effort to put out the flames. But in my heart I knew there was no hope. Magical fire doesn't fuel itself with oxygen.

Stop, drop, and roll doesn't really apply.

I heard their laughter cut through the roar of the inferno and my own screams. Then they left me to burn slowly. Painfully. I cried out, but no one heard my pleas for help, just as Kingston had promised. I had no doubt that his warning that no one could hear me was true. The scorching heat melted what little clothing I was wearing into a patchwork of pieces dangling precariously from my fiery body, but the epicenter of the fire remained right over my stomach. My core. The alleged source of all the Magicals' power —including my own.

I prayed hard to anyone and anything I could think of that maybe someone would smell the stench of my burning flesh. Kingston hadn't said anything about making his illusion smell-proof. I was desperate for someone to come put me out of my misery.

But nobody did.

I wanted to continue to cry for help, but I knew my efforts would be in vain, and my energy was fading. I felt the well of tears in my stinging eyes intensify as my resignation grew. I was going to die alone there that night.

"Make it stop," I whimpered, my consciousness fading.

And then, as if my prayers had been answered, the clear night sky clouded over in what seemed like an instant, and those clouds ripped open, releasing a punishing downpour that extinguished the flames that had nearly engulfed me. Unfortunately for me, the rain did not extinguish my agony.

The pain was indescribable. In some places, like my abdomen, I felt little if anything at all. Though it felt like a blessing, I knew that it was anything but. My nerves had clearly been damaged. Third-degree burns for sure. The parts that were less charred felt as though they were still on fire, the heat searing through my flesh. It hurt to breathe. Moving seemed out of the question, but I had to get out of there. I had to get help.

Curled up in pain, I managed to push myself up to crawl through the park toward my initial destination. I held out little hope that I'd get there before the boys drove by, but I had to do something, so I painfully made my way there. Every inch of ground I covered was anguish, and I cried the entire way, nearly passing out from the pain on several occasions. When I arrived at a small downhill slope that led to the road, I collapsed, rolling toward the street, though still hidden by the trees. My vision blurred as I tried to push myself off the ground to no avail. I was mere yards away from humans that could rescue me, take me to the hospital. But I was too far gone to reach them.

As the darkness overtook me, I whispered into the night. "Please let them find me..."

🙢

"OVER HERE," I heard a familiar voice shout. I thought I was dreaming. Actually, I thought I was dead until Jase's words roused me. "Oh my God, Piper. What happened?" There was true terror in his voice as he spoke to me. I'd never heard him quite that rattled before.

"Sweet Jesus," Dean said from somewhere near me. "Piper?" In his haste to see if I was okay, he reached to turn me over. I cried out in pain.

"Don't touch her!" another male yelled. His voice was utterly foreign to me.

My body was in shock by this point, shaking erratically, my pulse thin and thready. I was barely coherent enough to know what was going on, but I was aware that someone was picking me up delicately. Reverently. As if I would break at any moment.

I thought I already had.

From that moment on, the trip home was a series of me losing consciousness only to be awakened by the pain. I remembered a calming voice in my ear and the soothing sound of his murmured words as we drove back to the mansion. The vampires had everything there that I could possibly need, medically speaking. I would be in good hands.

I would possibly live.

My eyes still refused to open when we arrived at the compound, my body still shaking but exhausted. The pain, when it broke through my hazy, almost unconscious state, was unbearable, but I was too weak to scream anymore. Too weak to cry.

There was a frenzy of voices and shouting when we burst through the front door, the boys rushing me through the maze of hallways and down several flights of stairs to the infirmary deep below the ground. Vampires rarely if ever needed medical care, but the enforcers offered it to supernaturals outside their own race there—for a price, of course. Supernaturals that lacked their immortality and near-invincibility.

Whoever was carrying me crashed through the double doors and placed me down gently on a bed of some sort. I heard him yelling orders at the others who had come down to help. Then I heard Doc come in and silence them all, sending everyone out to wait in the hall while she worked on me. Her voice, too, held a measure of concern that I'd never heard in it before. I hoped it was due to my fading in and out of consciousness, but I doubted it. I was in bad shape and I knew it. Perhaps things were even worse than I had bargained for.

Perhaps the warlocks really would succeed this time.

"I'm going to give you something for the pain," Doc whispered in my ear before I felt her lift my arm and slide the needle in. She waited a moment, presumably to allow whatever medication she'd injected to work. She then attempted to remove the last remnants of my clothes from my body before they became encrusted in my burns. I heard the shrill sound of my screams echo off the tile walls.

Then I heard a roar from the hallway outside eclipse my cry.

In what seemed like the blink of an eye, the now-familiar voice was in my ear, lulling me into a peaceful state.

Then I felt a hand on my forehead, stroking my hair back gently from my face and tucking it behind my ear.

"Sleep now, Piper," he said, his voice so low that I barely heard him. "The pain will be gone soon."

A moment later, I felt the comforting arms of slumber wrap around me, pulling me into her depths. There, I felt nothing. There, I would be safe.

I HAD no idea how long I was out, but I woke up to a sharp and sudden pain that tore through my body. I tried to shoot up in bed but was quickly accosted, large hands on my shoulders, holding me down, restraining me gently. With every movement I made, the pain worsened. My screaming returned.

"Sleep, Piper. *Sleeeeeep*."

His words pressed against my brain until his command sunk in.

Then the world went dark again.

THAT CYCLE REPEATED itself several times until finally I awoke to no pain, or at least a bearable amount of it. Now able to open my eyes for the first time since the incident, I looked around to find myself alone. No Doc. No Jase. No Dean. No mysteriously-soothing-voice man either.

I glanced to my right to find a battery of equipment and machines there with myriad wires and tubes extending from them to me. Monitors beeped rhythmically: the soundtrack to my reawakening. Trying gingerly to shift in the bed, I immediately regretted the decision. A sharp tugging sensation in my abdomen radiated out in nearly every direction possible. I stifled my outcry by biting my lip, only a squeak escaping, but in a household of super-hearing vampires, I might as well have sounded an alarm. It wasn't long before one of them arrived.

The last one I would have expected to see.

I stared at Merc as he hovered just inside the infirmary doors, my expression undoubtedly incredulous. Neither of us said anything at first (but why would he?). I was too busy trying to wrap my head around his presence there to form a sentence.

"I heard you," he finally said, and my heart raced instantly. That voice. I knew that voice.

Of course, I thought to myself. Of course it had been Merc that night in the park. Any other vampire that could have been there that night I would have recognized. It made perfect sense that it was Merc that had whispered in my ear; but then again, it didn't. Until that night, he'd never uttered a word to me, or anyone else for that matter. Not for decades. So why to me and why at that moment?

"I tried to move," I said softly, not certain why I felt the need to explain myself.

He nodded once before taking a step toward me. I tensed instinctively, making me wince. Merc stopped dead in his tracks, his mask of darkness taking over his countenance.

"I'll go get Doc."

Without another word, he disappeared from the room. Doc arrived moments later to check on me.

"I need to look at your wounds, Piper," she said with a grim expression. "I don't want you to be alarmed when you see them. I can't figure out why they're not healing…" Her voice trailed off, as though she were going over the possibilities while she spoke. "At any rate, you might not want to look at them until they're in better shape. I don't want you to be traumatized any more than you already have been."

It was my turn to nod silently, turning to focus on the mint green tiled walls off to my left. I felt the blanket lift off of me, Doc being meticulously careful as she pushed both it and my gown to the side, exposing all of me from the breasts down. The air in the room felt exceedingly cold on my damaged tissue, but I tried to ignore it, counting the porcelain squares on the wall to occupy my mind instead.

A sound escaped Doc's mouth that I didn't think she'd meant to let out. It was ominous to say the least. Without thinking, I let my eyes dart to the sight that had drawn that noise from her. When I took in the charred and oozing, festering mess that was my torso, I choked back a sob. Doc had been right. I wasn't healing. In fact, my guess was that they were getting worse—infected.

"I just don't understand," she whispered in disbelief.

"Am I going to die?" I managed to squeak out, tears streaming down my face.

"You shouldn't," she replied in a faraway tone as she stared at my abdomen. Her answer was evasive and far from comforting. "Something is wrong, though. I've worked on every kind of magical being this world has to offer, and never once have I come upon one who could not heal wounds like this. Some may have required more intervention than others, but..."

"But what?"

"But I've done positively everything I could think of for the past two weeks, and you're still no better off."

"Two weeks?" I blurted out.

She frowned slightly, pulling her gaze up to meet my eyes.

"Yes. I needed to buy time to try out different forms of treatment. It's taken more time than I expected it to."

"How could I be out for that long and not know it?"

"Nothing I gave you for the pain worked, Piper. I had to explore other options and quickly."

"Meaning?"

"Merc," she replied with a sigh. "He's been with you this whole time, waiting for you to wake up in pain only to work your mind back to rest again."

"What do you mean 'work my mind'?" I asked, knowing that some vamps could mess with the minds of humans to maintain their unknown status, but they couldn't do it to other supernaturals. Not that I knew of.

What a powerful vampire that would be.

She exhaled heavily before she pulled up a chair to sit next to me. She looked stressed. Tired. It appeared that she truly had been working night and day to find a way to help me.

Apparently Merc had as well.

"Merc is special, Piper. He has...*gifts*. Gifts that are rather extraordinary, but they come at a price."

"How so?"

"They've left him a bit remote. Antisocial. And, at times, unstable," she explained. "One of those gifts is the ability to work the minds of other supernaturals as though they were human."

Holy shit. A memory flashed through my mind, one of Jase and Dean exchanging a dubious look when the king spoke of Reinhardt's willingness to not seek retribution for his warlocks after the attack in the alley. Had Merc been responsible for that pardon?

"The night he brought you in," Doc continued, pulling me from my thoughts, "he'd already been trying hard to keep you calm, your pain suppressed. He's been doing that ever since, but he's nearly pushed himself over the edge in the process. I had to sedate him after his last session on you. By then he had finally found a way to permanently dull your pain to a manageable level, but—"

"But what?" I implored, my chest tightening at her words. "What happened?"

"It's your mind, Piper. I don't think he's ever encountered anything like it before. It's like a code he couldn't break, and he nearly broke his own mind trying to." She took my hand in hers gently, trying not to disturb my body in the process. "There's a reason he's been gone for a long time. He's special beyond compare, but it comes at a cost to him and those around him. From now on, you need to stay away from him for his own good as well as yours. He's only just returned to us and it seems he's teetering on the edge of sanity."

"And you think I will be the one to push him over?"

She nodded silently.

My mind—my enigma of a mind—was working overtime, trying to make sense of everything that had occurred from the time the attack had happened until the present. It was a lot to try and process. Especially the parts regarding Merc.

The infirmary phone rang, distracting both Doc and me from our conversation. She rushed over to answer it right away. Her skin grew pale when she saw who was calling.

"Yes, your highness," she said, curtsying as though she were standing before him. "Yes. She is. I will put you on with her immediately." She rushed to my side, hesitating for a moment while the king spoke to her. "Yes, of course, sire."

She handed me the receiver.

"I'll be outside. Please let me know when you're finished."

I nodded once and she took her leave.

"Piper," the king began before I could even address him. "I am so pleased to hear that you are awake now. I know my timing is unfortunate, but I need to speak with you. It's rather urgent."

"Of course," I replied, wondering what urgent matter the king could possibly have to discuss with me.

"What happened to you...do you remember anything about it?"

"Yes. I remember it all."

"Who did this to you, Piper?" he asked, concern in his tone.

"Kingston and his crew."

My reply was met with silence that lasted longer than was comfortable. Just as I was about to explain further, the king spoke.

"This presents a problem, Piper. As I said before, the treaty hangs in a very precarious balance at the moment."

"I know..."

"If certain parties were to be made aware of who did this to you, I fear that a deep-seated need for retribution would overshadow the bigger picture," he said tightly. "Do you understand what I'm saying, Piper?"

"I think so," I said quietly.

"Jase and Dean adore you. I do not think you need me to tell you that. Their actions the other night along with Merc's are evidence enough."

"You think they'll go after Kingston despite your direct order not to..."

"Though it pains me to admit it, yes. I do." He fell silent again, and my anxiety with the situation grew. Just when I felt like I was going to jump out of my skin, he began to speak. "Piper, do you know why I took you in?"

"You felt sorry for me?"

"Hardly. I see something in you, Piper. I always have, but the trouble is and always has been that you yourself do not see what I do. I fear that your insecurities will be your undoing one day. Maybe the undoing of those that are closest to you as well," he explained gently. "Our world is one without forgiveness, as you well know. One where the weaknesses of some are exploited for the benefit of another. Imagine what will happen if the treaty fails? If I am unable to hold together the very agreement that keeps such behavior within our community to a minimum—crimes punishable under the stipulations set forth?" I swallowed back my fear. "We cannot afford for things to go back to the way they once were, Piper, and so I am going to ask something of you that brings me no pleasure."

"Okay," I whispered, sensing what he was about to suggest.

"I need you to keep quiet about who was behind your attack." My blood ran cold. "Rest assured that Reinhardt and I will be revisiting our previous agreement that resulted from the incident two weeks ago." I still sat silent, my heart racing. "Please do not mistake this as my ignoring the despicable events that you suffered, Piper. Someone will pay dearly for that, but it needs to be handled carefully. Quietly. Say yes if you understand."

"Yes..."

"Thank you for your compliance in this matter, Piper. You are a good girl in a harsh world. A world that you must one day learn to navigate."

The line went dead in my hand.

I sat there speechless for a minute or two, trying to sort through the reeling emotions that replaced my fear and concern over my unhealed wounds. But before I could wrap my head around what had just happened, I heard the clacking of Doc's heels from across the room as she approached me.

"All done?" she asked, knowing full well that I was. She could hear the buzzing sound of the phone. "Is everything all right?"

I nodded.

"Is it about your attack?"

I nodded again.

"Piper, do you remember something?"

I looked up at her with tears in my eyes, then shook my head no.

"Let's not worry about that for now, okay?" she said, patting my hand sympathetically. "For now, we need to focus on helping you heal. I have to say, Piper, I'm at a loss. I'm seriously considering bringing in some others on this case to help me. Maybe the witches know of something—"

"NO!" I shouted, grimacing as the pain my outburst caused shot throughout my body. They couldn't know. Nobody could, for more reasons than I could count, not the least of which was the treaty. Nobody could know what had happened to me. "No. Please. They all hate me. They'll do nothing to help. If anything, they'll find a way to capitalize on the situation and make me more miserable."

Doc's eyes grew dark at my words.

"They wouldn't dare." Her tone was ice.

"Maybe not, but they certainly wouldn't help you even if they knew how. And the—" I cut myself off before letting loose the truth, lest I should start a war.

"Do you have something you want to tell me?" she asked, her eyebrows furrowing slightly.

"No. It's just that we need to find a way to fix this on our own. Without any outside help. Okay?"

She continued to eye me strangely. There was suspicion in her gaze.

"What aren't you telling me, Piper?"

"Nothing. I promise. I just don't want any of the Magicals brought in on this."

Her expression softened slightly.

"Then we need to start thinking outside of the box, or I'm afraid your status may never change for the better."

I quickly read between the lines.

"Will it change for the worse?"

She hesitated for a moment.

"I don't know. But I won't let that happen without a fight."

Neither will I, I thought to myself. *Neither will I.* Suddenly I felt a strong sense of conviction. A fortified will to live. I was going to find a way to heal my injuries.

And then I would find a way to pay back those who had inflicted them upon me.

"Excellent," I replied, a smile overtaking my countenance. "Let the cage match begin."

※

IN A HAREBRAINED ATTEMPT TO help me, Kat offered to take me outside in a wheelchair that Jase had found for me. She thought the fresh air might do me some good—let my wounds breathe a bit. Understatement of the century.

I learned a thing or two about myself and my magic that day. Something that I'd never fully put together until the moment she pushed me gently through the front door of the mansion and into the sun that awaited me, greeting me with its warmth on my face. All beings were creatures of the Universe, supernatural and human alike, but not all of us were connected to her equally. To me, the Earth, more specifically nature itself, was like a touchstone, a place to recharge—to heal. I felt the pull to her almost instantaneously. With some help from Kat, I was able to stand and inelegantly shuffle my way over to the lawn. I refused to let her carry me there. I needed to do this for myself as much as possible. I needed to know that I wasn't as weak as I'd long thought I was.

The reason why the others shunned me.

The second my foot touched the lush green grass, I collapsed to it.

"Help!" I cried, reaching out for Kat before I landed face first on the lawn.

What should have been a painful slam was more like a gentle caress—like the ground itself enveloped me. I could feel its energy coursing through my body, centering primarily on my wounds. Kat grabbed me to help me up, but I waved her off.

"It's okay," I mumbled, my face still smooshed into the front lawn. "It feels good. Just leave me here."

"Piper, I'm not—"

"Can you take this stupid gown off first?"

I watched her feet as she hesitated for a moment, ultimately stepping closer to do as I'd asked.

"This can't be good for your burns, Piper. They're already infected. They're going to get dirt and God knows what else in them..."

I could hear the irritated concern in her voice, but when she rolled me over to help me out of my clothes, she gasped in disbelief.

"You're healing!"

"Just get it off. Please." She ripped it off in two pieces,

exposing my wounds to the blazing sun above. "I'm going to be fine, Kat. Just leave me here."

"I'm going to go tell Doc."

"Great. Tell her I'll see her once the sun goes down."

Although I was still weak and my delivery wasn't up to par, Kat caught the humor in my words and laughed.

"I think you can probably bet on that. You'll have a whole gaggle of vamps out here to join you in your naked lawn party."

"Sounds great. Tell Dean to bring me a margarita. With salt."

"Will do," she said, walking away slowly to alert the good doctor, leaving me to lie naked in the yard of the mansion. Werewolves never seemed too concerned about nudity, so I didn't let it bother me. Instead, I placed my hands behind my head and shamelessly basked in the glorious, healing sun, letting whatever magic was to be found in it heal my burns.

When I awoke hours later, the sun nearly gone from the sky, I pushed myself up onto my elbows to inspect the state of my wounds. My eyes went wide when they took in the sight.

Then I screamed.

5

"You have to get out of this house, Piper," Kat argued, throwing her purse over her shoulder. "You've practically been a recluse ever since you healed. More than you were before. It's not healthy. And you smell. I swear to God, if you don't start showering soon, I will hose you off in the front yard myself."

"All right!" I shouted. "Give me ten minutes. I'll be down by then."

"Don't forget to shave while you're in there..."

"Jesus, Kat!" I yelled down the stairs at her. Her laughter echoed through the foyer up to me as I stormed down the hallway to my room and its en suite. I slammed the door behind me for effect, letting Kat know that her words had me irritated. Unfortunately for me, her points were valid. I didn't like leaving my room, let alone venturing out. Not after what had happened in the yard that day.

The boys had been good about not pressing the issue because they knew something was still wrong with me— that I wasn't myself. Nobody knew why I was acting the way

I was. About the shame I felt. The thing about Kat was that she didn't care.

In fairness, she really did care. She just wasn't going to let whatever it was that I was such a mess about be a weight that dragged me down. Bowl through everything, that was Kat's motto. Maybe she was right. Maybe that was exactly what I needed to do.

I stood in front of the bathroom mirror, not wanting to undress, but I really did smell funky. It was time to start to coexist with the eternal reminder of my attack. I pulled my shirt up over my head, exposing the marred flesh that lay beneath. My entire abdomen and most of my back were covered in a topographical scar, its pattern full of lines and edges that carved themselves into my healed skin. The pigment of it was different, a shade or two darker than my own, as if it was permanently sunburned, but not severely.

I hated everything about it.

Turning away from the person in the mirror, I jumped into the shower, the water still cold. I just wanted the whole thing to be over with so I could cover myself again. Hide the gift that Kingston had bestowed upon me.

After showering, I got dressed and threw on my boots, racing down the hall to meet my ten-minute E.T.A. Kat stood by the door, a smile on her face.

"You smell better already."

"Let's go," I said, punching the security code into the keypad. Once it beeped and flashed a green light, I swung the massive metal door open and stepped through to the breezeway between the actual exterior door and the one inside. When your existence depends upon you not setting foot out in the sunlight, or someone accidentally allowing it inside, such precautionary measures are necessary.

"Where are we going, anyway?" I asked as I sped toward

her silver Boxster. It was every bit as curvaceous and beautiful as she was. They were a perfect match.

"Nowhere exciting. I didn't think you'd be up for that," she said with a tight smile, looking over the top of the car's roof at me. "Baby steps, kiddo. We're taking baby steps."

"So where is nowhere exciting?"

"The grocery store. I'm tired of you eating that crap you order or have the boys pick up for you. It's disgusting. Your body is a temple, Piper."

"Not anymore," I muttered under my breath.

"What's that?" she asked, seeing the window of opportunity I'd given her.

"I don't really want to talk about it, Kat," I said, folding my arms over my stomach as she pulled out of the driveway.

"I can see that," she replied, clearly refusing to drop the subject. That didn't bode well for me. Kat had a way of bulldozing her way through your defenses one way or another. It's how we became friends in the first place. I could tell by the set of her shoulders as she drove that the grace period was over. She was going to get answers come hell or high water.

Seeing the futility of denying her, I sighed heavily, preparing for the conversation I really didn't want to have.

"I said," putting a little heat behind my words, "that it isn't anymore."

"Isn't what?"

"A temple."

"Oh. Wait, why isn't it a temple?" she asked. There was a brief moment before her body went rigid, her hands white-knuckling the steering wheel. "What exactly happened to you that night?" Her voice was soft and sorrowful when she asked her question, but her tone belied the anger building inside her. Per the king's instructions, I'd kept all details of that night to myself, claiming that I couldn't remember anything other than going for a run and waking up in excruciating pain when the boys found me.

"I was burned," I answered sarcastically.

"Yeah. I got that, Piper."

"I said what I said because I'm not the same anymore," I explained before she could start in on me. "My body was hardly perfect before, but it sure as hell isn't now. That's what I meant by what I said."

"How is it not the same?" she asked, stopping at a red light.

I closed my eyes and slowly drew up the bottom of my shirt just enough for her to see the scars. The sharp inhale of her breath let me know that she'd never expected to see that.

"Now do you see why I'm not really up for going out? Or bathing, for that matter?"

"I'm so sorry I said that to you, Piper."

"Please don't. Don't pity me. That's the last thing I need," I snapped. "You didn't know why I was acting the way I was. You said it because it's your way of caring. I get it. Really, I do. Just drop it, okay?"

"Sure, Piper. Whatever you want."

"And don't you dare tell anyone else about this, Kat. Not even Jensen."

"I won't say a word," she agreed as the light turned green. She pulled away, heading off toward the Brooklyn Bridge.

"Good," I bit out, turning to look out the passenger window. "The last thing I need is for all those models of perfection back at the mansion to catch wind of this. I'm already a leper at the prissy little vampire get-togethers. And

God forbid that the bitch squad hears about it. I'll never be able to survive those parties again."

"They won't," Kat replied. I could hear the honesty in her voice.

"Great, now can we just go get some food and head home? I'm getting antsy just seeing all these people on the street."

"Piper, you're safe. You're with me. And beyond that, the king said the warlocks were on shutdown after their last little performance. You told me so yourself. There's nothing to be worried about. I promise."

If only that had been true.

As we sped onto the bridge, I turned to ask her why it was that we needed to go to Brooklyn to get groceries, but the question never left my mouth. It was cut short the second I saw Monroe, one of Kingston's minions, walking along the pedestrian bridge. He smiled at me as we drove past—an ugly, all-knowing smile that sent a chill up my spine.

Seconds later, Kat's car went careening toward the bridge's guardrail. Then it flew through it, picking up speed as it hurtled over the side. Kat and I were soon plummeting toward the East River.

"Fuck!" she screamed, trying to undo her seat belt. I, however, was paralyzed by fear. I watched silently as the dark water came nearer and nearer, finally crashing against the windshield of the sports car.

I felt Kat reach over to undo my belt, but the water was coming in fast through the open windows. It wouldn't be long before we no longer hovered near the waterline, but were settled on the river's bottom. I fought against the stream of water surging into the car and managed to get myself out, grabbing hold of the roof that had yet to submerge. I wriggled my body out and swam toward the driver's side of the car.

The side that no one had emerged from.

"Kat!" I screamed, panicking as the car started to fall below the waterline. The situation posed a major problem for my werewolf friend; I knew she couldn't swim. As I understood it, none of them could. If I couldn't get her from that car and fast, she was a goner.

And it would all be my fault.

I took a massive breath before diving down, holding onto the edge of her open window. I reached in to find her belt still done up and Kat struggling to unfasten it. She was batting at my hand, her way of telling me to get the hell out of there, but her blows were weak and slowing. She was running out of time.

Once I was able to free her, I grabbed her under the arms and kicked for dear life, trying as hard as I could to drag her out to the surface. My lungs burned, screaming for oxygen while I exerted myself to save her. She was heavy, far heavier than I ever could have imagined, but that only made me better understand why they couldn't swim. Too much body density.

My mind begged for someone to help us. For something to pull me to the surface. I knew I wasn't going to make it without aid.

Then suddenly my adrenaline kicked in, shooting through me like a rocket. I swam like a fish to the surface, gasping in ragged, frantic breaths once I reached the air. I scanned the area, looking for the nearest bank. I didn't know how I got her there; all I did know is, the second I did, I pulled her from the water and started to assess her. She wasn't breathing. Her lips had the faintest hint of blue to them.

I was already too late.

"Somebody help me!" I screamed, hovering over her to start chest compressions. I set my hands on her sternum and felt an intense warmth. There was no way she was dead yet. Werewolves always ran hotter than normal and she was no exception in that moment.

Then I felt a heartbeat. It was subtle and erratic, but it was there.

"Help me!" I yelled again, putting my face down by her mouth to see if I could feel her breathing.

Just as I pulled away from her, having felt nothing, she coughed up an insane amount of water.

"Kat!" I screamed again, rolling her to her side so that she could purge the East River from her body. "Oh my God, you're alive!"

She tried to sit up, but faltered at first. When I moved to help her, she waved me off, giving me an ugly look between coughing fits.

"What...happened?" she asked, her voice hoarse.

"We went off the bridge," I replied, unable to hide the confusion in my voice. Did she not remember?

"We did? How the fuck did that happen?" Before I could reply, her eyes widened, looking over to the river I'd just pulled her out of. Then they turned back to me. "Piper, how did I get out of there?"

"I pulled you out." She stared at me in disbelief. "I know what you're thinking—that I shouldn't have been able to—but I did. I could feel the adrenaline, Kat. Maybe I was like those moms that lift cars off their kids or something..."

"Or something sounds about right." I could feel her assessing me, trying to figure out just how this tiny little nothing had dragged her heavy werewolf ass out from a sinking car. But I had nothing to offer her, and luckily we were interrupted before she could ask any questions.

"Are you two all right?" a police officer called from his boat on the water.

"Yeah. We're okay."

"The ambulance is coming for you. Just hold tight."

"That won't be necessary," Kat said with a smile. "But we sure could use a lift home."

Not long after our ordeal, we pulled up to the mansion in an NYPD cruiser, dressed in New York's Finests' sweats. The kind officers let us out and Kat thanked them, pouring on the charm. They both blushed, got back in their vehicle, and drove off.

"I need to get this stench off of me," Kat groused, walking up to the front steps. "And you're showering too. No arguments."

"No arguments," I agreed, holding the door open for her.

She stopped just in front of me, pinning deadly serious eyes on me.

"I know I didn't just drive off the bridge, Piper. Something happened up there and I want to know what."

"Kat, if I had a damn clue, I'd tell you, but I don't. One second we were headed to Brooklyn, the next we were headed to the bottom of the river."

"To sleep with the fishes..."

"Yep."

She frowned.

"I don't like this. Something about it doesn't sit right."

"I know, Kat, but I don't know what you want me to say," I replied with a shrug. "Can we discuss this once we don't smell like rotten fish and garbage?"

"Yes. We can."

I followed her into the breezeway and waited for her to

enter the code for the security door. Once inside, we parted ways. I made my way to my bedroom, all the while mulling over the implications of the day's events. I had no doubt that Monroe was behind our impromptu dive into the East River, but what I didn't understand was why. If the king really had settled things with Reinhardt, then either the warlock leader had boldfaced lied to him, an act that would bring about his death, or worse yet, Kingston and his boys had gone rogue. The latter seemed far more likely. If I was right, it meant that I would never be safe again.

And judging by what had happened that day, neither would anyone near me.

6

"Tell me again how you two ended up in the East River in the first place," Jensen said, his confusion barely masking his fear-driven anger. He knew how lucky Kat was to be standing in front of him, but that didn't stop him from releasing his frustration with the situation on us both.

"Like I said before," Kat shrugged, "one second we were driving, the next we were plunging into the river."

"And you don't remember anything after that?" he asked, skepticism in his tone.

"I blacked out at some point."

"I remember," I interjected, trying to calm him. "But I don't know that you want to hear about it. It was scary. You shouldn't have those visuals in your mind."

"Do you know why the car went over?"

Sort of...

"No. Not exactly. It felt like the steering yanked us to the side. Maybe there was something wrong with the car?"

"I just had it serviced!" Kat argued, not wanting to blame

her baby, who was currently being fished off the riverbed for a hefty price.

"That doesn't mean it didn't have issues, Kat," I countered. "Sometimes problems occur when cars have been worked on. I've seen shows about it on TV."

"I don't know, Piper," she replied, looking doubtful.

"I'm not saying that's the case. I'm just offering it as an option. The reality is that we won't likely find out why or how we drove off the bridge. I'm just grateful we're both okay."

"So are we," Jase called out from the hallway before entering the room.

"How long have you two assholes been listening in?" Jensen asked, finding a new outlet for his irritation.

"Long enough to hear what happened." Jase turned questioning eyes to me. "I don't know how you two are alive."

"Well, we are, so can we just move on? Please? I don't like reliving this. I almost watched Kat drown. It's not a fond memory."

He frowned.

"You're right. I'm sorry," he said, coming over to hug me.

"I just want to find someone to blame so I can kick their ass," Dean added, coming to stand beside his brother, who refused to let me go.

"You're going to kick the car's ass?" I asked him, feigning amusement, though in actuality, I was freaking out. I needed to divert their attention from retribution. "Besides, you two are on especially short leashes with the king at the moment. Merc too. There's no indication that this was anything other than a mechanical defect in the car. You can't go on a proverbial witch hunt, cracking skulls until you get an answer you like. You know what the king said about the treaty..."

"Fine," he grumbled. "You're right. I'd just feel better if I got to kick somebody's ass."

"Kick Jase's. He could use a good beating," I suggested.

"Hey!" Dean's brother exclaimed, pushing away from me.

"I'm just sayin'."

"Some thanks I get for being concerned."

"Are we done here, Jensen? I'm exhausted. Hauling your mate's heavy ass out of the water has me beat."

He nodded once, his eyes darting over to where Kat stood.

"Thank you, Piper," he said solemnly. "I forgot to thank you in all of this. I don't know what I'd do without her."

"You'd get laid a lot less, I know that," Kat added to lighten the mood. She never was one for being sentimental.

I burst out laughing, as did the others. Leave it to Kat to bring everything back to sex somehow.

"I'll leave you two to that," I said, turning to exit. The brothers fell in behind me, closing the door behind them to the sound of Kat and Jensen crashing into the wall. It appeared that they were going to have quite the evening.

The thought made me blush.

The boys and I parted ways when they headed toward the media room and I made my way to my bedroom to crash. As I walked, I thought about the dream I'd had of Merc and me doing exactly what Kat and Jensen were at that moment. The heat that spread through my body made my cheeks even more flushed and chased away the remnants of fear from my afternoon's excitement. I rounded the corner to the wing of the mansion that held my room, smiling to myself.

Then I walked right into the source of my lustful thoughts.

"Gah!" I squealed, grabbing my chest. "You scared me. You have to stop doing that." He eyed me curiously. I almost thought I saw a hint of a smile cross his face. "Jase and Dean are in the media room, if that's who you're looking for." I started to slip past him, my awkward avoidance of him so obvious it was painful.

"I was looking for you," he replied, which startled me yet again.

"Oh."

"I overheard Kat talking about what happened."

"You were eavesdropping?"

"Strategically listening," he replied unapologetically.

I shrugged, letting out a heavy sigh.

"Yeah. It was a rough day."

"Do you truly believe it was the car that led you over the bridge?"

I tried to suppress my rising panic.

"I really don't know what it was."

"Just as you don't remember how you came to be burned the night we found you in the park?"

"No. I remember going over the bridge very clearly. I don't, however, remember the night I was attacked."

His eyes narrowed as he leaned toward me. I instinctively took a step backward.

"You care deeply for your friends, don't you?"

"Yes."

"You would protect them at all costs?"

"I would," I said softly. "They're my family."

His jaw tensed at my reply, flexing so hard that the tension cut deeper angles into his face.

"Be careful the choices you make, Piper. Your desire to

help them may very well endanger you, as well as those you endeavor to keep safe in the process."

He hovered for a moment, looking as though there was more he wished to say. Then, abruptly, he walked away, disappearing around the corner.

I let out a loud exhale.

I couldn't explain it, but it was as though he knew that I was lying, that I was withholding information. But how could he? He could manipulate the minds of others, but I knew nothing of his ability to read them. Regardless, he'd struck a nerve. He spoke the truth, though I was loath to admit it. I was a danger to myself and others. My track record supported that wholeheartedly.

I schlepped my way down to my room and locked myself in, not wanting to see anyone. Why bother? I already had my guilt to keep me company.

❦

I'D FALLEN ASLEEP EASILY, exhausted by the entire ordeal Kat and I had faced. Soon after, I found myself sitting on the edge of a bed that was not my own, but I recognized it. I'd been pinned down by Merc in it once before. What a sweet dream that had proven to be.

A sound from behind me startled me, and I turned to find Merc leaning against the wall on the far side of the room. Only the bed and an expanse of open floor separated the two of us. He lingered there in silence for a moment before pushing off of it to approach me.

"Wait!" I blurted out, throwing my arm out to ward him off. To my surprise, he stopped. Then a smile spread wide across his face. "What's so funny?"

"You." He continued to stare at me, creating conflict

within me. Part of me wanted to run from him. The other wanted to run into his arms. "You don't fear me when you are awake. Why now do you choose to be afraid?"

"I don't choose to be afraid…" The fall of his expression told me he didn't agree. "Am I dreaming right now?"

"Do you think you're dreaming?"

"I have no idea." Everything there seemed so real—so clear. I just couldn't be sure. "Why are you here?"

His smile returned.

"It's your dream, Piper. I can't answer that for you."

"Fine, then answering something else for me," I countered, hopping off of the bed. "Why are you and your brothers always having silent conversations about me? And why do they selectively tell me what you've said?"

The smile morphed into a smirk.

"You'd have to ask them about that, Piper. I can't speak for them."

"Ugh," I groaned. "Okay, then tell me something else."

"Such as?"

"Tell me why you saved me the night that Kingston attacked us."

His expression sobered.

"Would you have preferred that I didn't?"

"No, but—"

"I saved you for more than one reason that night, Piper." He started toward me again, but this time I did nothing to stop him. "My brothers love you. That point was made very clear to me before we left for the club. Jase was busy with Kingston when we realized what the warlock was doing. Dean was guarding the vortex they'd opened. That left me. And I had no intention of being the reason that they lost you."

"Oh," I replied. The note of disappointment in my tone

was surprising to hear. Perhaps in my dreams, I could not deny the truth like I could when conscious. "And in the park —after Kingston—"

I cut myself off, wrapping my arms around my waist.

He gently took my wrists and lowered my hands from my abdomen to rest at my sides.

"Your suffering was hard to bear," he said softly. "Watching you—the pain you were in—was impossible. I did what I did to take it away."

"Because it hurt you to see someone that hurt?" I asked, thinking that trait was one deeply contradicted by what the boys had told me. That he was essentially a soulless killer. A mercenary. I needed to know if he really was more than that.

"No." My heart sank for a moment, thinking that maybe all I'd experienced him to be wasn't as true as I would have liked. He leaned in closer to me, our bodies touching. My heart perked back up at the contact. "It hurt me to see *you* like that."

"Oh."

"You like that response, don't you?" There was laughter in his voice when he asked. My eyes shot up to his immediately.

"You surprised me, that's all. Sometimes it takes me a minute to wrap my head around things."

"Then allow me to give you something else to wrap your head around," he said, his hands cupping my face to angle it up toward him. "You didn't ask my other reason for saving you the night Kingston attacked us outside the club." My breath caught in my throat as his lips drew nearer to mine. "I may be everything you've been told, Piper. I'm cold. I'm a killer. And yes, at times, unstable. But not with you." I felt the tickle of his breath on my mouth and I leaned toward him, desperate to feel his lips upon mine. "That is something I am not willing to lose. I like how it feels far too much for that."

※

I SHOT UP IN BED, sweaty and panting as Merc's words ran through my mind. I wanted to process them—to make sense of them—but then I remembered that there was no point. It was a dream. A machination of my subconscious, which seemed hellbent on making sense of the mystery named Merc. The mystery I couldn't escape.

With a sigh, I threw back the covers and dragged myself from my bed. It was just about one in the morning—prime vampire time. I really didn't want to see anyone, so I did what I could to sneak around unnoticed, which is no easy feat in a household of super-hearing beings. I made my way down the hall to the butler's staircase and sneaked down into the kitchen. Once there, I went through the cupboards quietly, hoping to pilfer some snacks I could bring back upstairs.

I could hear voices arguing from the ballroom that was just down the hall from where I stood. The high ceilings and sparse furniture in that room allowed for the voices to carry easily. At first, I couldn't make them out well. But as they got louder and louder, they became more clear, as did the subject of their heated discussion.

"If things are as bad as the king said, then there's nothing we can do," Dean argued.

"She's a liability, plain and simple," a male countered. I couldn't quite make out who it was.

"Liability or not, she's our responsibility by order of the king. That hasn't changed."

Holy shit...they're talking about me.

"Maybe you want to take on that responsibility, but I don't," the unidentified male proclaimed. "She's a death trap."

"Maybe you should hone your skills a bit more so you're not so scared to take on whatever chaos she attracts," Jase countered, disgust plain in his tone.

"Do what you want," the mystery male said dismissively, "but I'm telling you right now, you'd better not leave her with me. I won't lift a finger to save her. And don't think I'm the only one that feels that way."

The distinct sound of a fist hitting a face echoed down the hall from the ballroom to the kitchen just before a full-on fight broke out. I didn't want to hang around just in case someone happened upon me listening to the infighting I'd created.

I had to get out.

Before I knew exactly what I was doing, I was sprinting through the woods on the property, the cool wind blowing my hair around me. It looked as I felt: wild and chaotic.

The words of the unidentified vampire ran over and over in my mind. I wanted to dispute them, but history had proven him right. I'd attracted trouble my whole life, and now I'd brought it upon the enforcers.

I would have eventually fallen victim to Kingston and his crew if it hadn't been for the safety the king had offered me. He had done something no one else was willing to: take me in. And all I did to thank him was put him in a politically difficult situation on numerous occasions. Knowing that the treaty could fall at any time, I hated that I could somehow be the straw that broke the camel's back, unraveling the balance that had been struck amongst the races long before I was born.

Nobody needed that outcome.

So many would die if it came to be.

The worst part of all was the knowledge that Jase and Dean would do all they could to protect me when the races began to war with one another, and that made them a target. Kingston would relish the freedom to come at me full force until he got what he wanted, and the brothers would put themselves directly in the crosshairs to keep him from succeeding. I feared that they would eventually fall because of it. Jase and Dean were warriors, but they had a code of conduct—a sense of honor. Warlocks, however, had none. They fought dirty.

My interactions with them were a case in point.

So I ran as the guilt rose within me, crashing through the brush and low-lying branches. I don't know what I was trying to escape, but I knew I had to get away. Away from the mansion, away from the boys—away from anyone that I could ever bring harm to, however indirectly.

I soon found myself standing on a narrow wooden bridge that hovered high above a gorge that sliced its way through the ground. That bridge had seen better days, its planks rotted right through in places, the handrails dubiously attached. Still, I stood there, overlooking the deep crevice the creek had cut through the earth, and I wondered.

I closed my eyes, trying to focus. I was always more able to do that in nature. There, I could think. There, I could find clarity. I inhaled the sweet, clean smell of the running water, letting the cool night air dance around me. It calmed me slightly, but when I opened my eyes to stare down at the black abyss below, my fears snapped back to me.

There would be no escaping them.

Before I fully grasped what I was doing, the rough wood of the handrail bit into the skin of my hands as I pushed myself up to balance upon it. Slowly, carefully, I uncurled

From the Ashes

my body to stand. The wind gusted, causing me to wobble, but I remained on my perch. Looking down, I felt the breeze on my face, blowing my hair behind me.

It calmed me.

It called to me.

"I'm sorry," I whispered to the night, the wind carrying my words deep into the woods. Extending my head back, eyes closed, I reached my arms out to the side and let the now harsh air whip around me.

Then I felt my body lean forward.

I knew the exact moment when there would be no turning back. That millisecond where I fully realized what I was doing—that my impending descent could no longer be stopped. A jolt of fear shot through me instinctively, my survival instincts cutting through the fog of guilt that had settled in my head. But they were too late.

I was going to fall.

I was going to die.

And yet I didn't. With my body at an angle impossible to recover from, I felt a blast of wind crash into me, so strong that it was not only enough to right my position, but also forceful enough to knock me backward. I fell to the safety of the bridge behind me, landing hard on my butt. As I fought to stand again under the siege of the gale force wind, I heard the voices it carried. When the weather calmed itself, I turned to find Jase and Dean approaching me, their massive frames shaking the dilapidated bridge.

"Piper!" Jase cried, scooping me up in his arms. He crushed me against him painfully. I couldn't breathe. "What the fuck are you doing, crazy girl?"

"I—"

"I don't want to hear it," he shouted, interrupting me. "I

know exactly what that was. What I want to know is why you were about to do it?"

"I just—"

"Did you think that one trip into the water this week wasn't enough?" Dean asked, yanking me from his brother's grip to angrily embrace me. "Fuck, Piper. What the fuck were you thinking?"

"I...I don't know," I replied, my voice muffled by his chest.

"You don't know what?" Jase shouted, pulling me away from Dean to face him. "You don't know that you just tried to kill yourself?"

"I wasn't trying to," I whispered, wondering how I could possibly convince them that I wasn't doing what they clearly saw me trying to do. I dropped my gaze to the weathered boards of the bridge underneath my feet. I had failed yet again. "I overheard you guys talking. I was in the kitchen..."

"Aw shit," Dean spat.

"Piper," Jase said more calmly. "Piper, look at me. Please." I did as he asked, lifting sad eyes to meet his. "You need to ignore what you heard, understand?"

"But I can't," I argued, my anxieties rising. "He was right! You'll all get hurt. And if a war comes, the king will need you. Both of you..."

"We won't get hurt," Dean snarled.

"You guys can't keep fighting my battles for me, don't you see that? It can't be this way forever. You can't keep me safe, and I'd never forgive myself if something happened to either of you while trying to do that."

"Never gonna happen," Dean scoffed, garnering my attention. "Where is this all coming from, Piper?"

"I told you I overheard—"

"No, where is it really coming from?" he pressed, leaning

in closer to me. The bridge groaned in protest under his weight.

"We need to get her off of here," Jase ordered, ushering me carefully to the end of the rickety structure.

"Answer my question," Dean continued from behind me. "Do you remember something about the night you were attacked?"

"No," I lied.

Jase eyed me tightly.

"Is there something you're not telling us about the Brooklyn Bridge incident?"

"No! Jesus," I yelled, storming away from them right into Merc. I jumped back from him, startled by his presence. His pale blue eyes practically shone in the moonlight while they pierced mine, looking for the truth behind my words.

"Something's wrong with you, Piper," Jase observed, his tone controlled and kind. He was trying a different approach. "You haven't been yourself since the attack, and while I can see that there is a definite amount of mental and emotional trauma you suffered because of it, I don't understand why you're shutting us out. Why you're suddenly trying to take a dive off a shitty old bridge in the middle of the night. That's not you, Piper. You're too strong for that..."

"Ha," I scoffed, the bitterness in my tone so thick I could practically taste it. "Strong..."

"You think differently?" Merc asked, shocking Jase and Dean. He hadn't spoken to me in their presence since the night I was attacked in the park, and I guess they thought that was a one-time deal. If our little secret was out, Merc didn't seem to care. He continued to speak to me like they weren't present. Like I was all he cared about in that moment.

"I think that whoever was talking in the ballroom was

right. That anyone close to me is likely to meet their end trying to protect me. You said as much to me the other night. That's a lot of burden for me to bear," I explained, doing all I could to fight back the tears that threatened to escape. "I think that strong people aren't victims. I think the night I nearly burned to death etched that reality into my mind and my body. And I think that you all would be far better off without me, especially if the treaty falls. I'm a distraction. A distraction that will get you killed, if you let it."

Merc stared at me, his expression unfaltering.

"I think you're wrong."

That was all he said, those four words his entire argument to the harsh realities I'd just pointed out to him and the others. It seemed a ridiculous rebuttal, and yet somehow, for some reason, those words had a weight to them that I couldn't explain. A persuasive quality that I couldn't deny.

"Wrong about what?" I yelled, frustration overtaking me.

"It takes great strength to protect those around you, especially when the cost is yours alone to bear. It takes great strength to pull an unconscious werewolf from a body of water. And it takes great strength to endure the very incident you just cited as an example of your weakness," he said, taking a step closer. "Kingston did not attack you because you are weak, Piper. He attacked you because you are a force beyond measure. You just haven't realized it yet."

I stared at him as though he were speaking a foreign language, and yet everything he'd said made some measure of sense. Merc didn't think I was prey. He thought I was a badass who had yet to emerge.

"Piper," Jase said, spinning me around to face him, his hands resting firmly on my shoulders. "I don't care if you're weak, strong, or otherwise, you need to know that whatever may come—whatever happens with the treaty—we won't leave your side. Do you understand? You can't make that choice for us."

"Damn right," Dean chimed in, seconding his brother's sentiments. "You're stuck with us whether you like it or not. We ride or die."

"I just wish you didn't have to," I said meekly, my emotions a cross between frustration and adoration. I loved those two more than I could explain, but I hated that that love inherently put them in danger.

"Your powers will come to you one day, Piper," Jase reassured me. "I mean, look what happened with your burns! Kat said they healed up when you went outside— when you laid on the ground in the sun. We know you're a Magical, we just don't know what kind or what powers you can call."

"And nobody has ever helped me explore that," I said curtly. *Except for the one that now wants me dead...*

"Maybe if the treaty falls, one of them will," Dean countered.

"Yeah, that's a big if. And I hardly think we should wish for that to happen on the off chance that some rogue Magical might be interested in mentoring me to get on the good side of the enforcers and the king."

He shrugged in response.

"Would you want to be on our bad side if this all goes to shit?"

I contemplated his words for a second.

"Fair point."

He smiled wide.

"Jase isn't the only one in the family with brains, you know?"

"I see that," I said with a halfhearted laugh.

"I think it's time we take bridge-jumper here back to the

mansion," Jase said, putting his hand on the small of my back.

"And lock her in her room," Dean muttered under his breath.

"That won't be necessary," Merc said, startling me for the second time that night. "This will not be an issue again."

Jase and Dean stared at him with confusion that quickly bled to anger.

"You didn't, did you?" Jase asked. Merc said nothing in response—at least nothing I could hear. But judging by the put-upon exhale from Jase, they were having a silent conversation. "Careful, Merc. That didn't end so well the last time," Jase pointed out, his words a mystery to me. "Remember what Doc said."

Merc said nothing, just looked over at me again, his eyes lingering uncomfortably long before he started back toward the mansion at a fast pace.

"What did he say?" I turned and asked the boys. Neither answered.

I ran after Merc, catching him by the arm to halt him.

"What makes you so sure that I won't...you know," I said, squirming a bit under his heavy gaze.

"Because what was done has been undone." He said those words in a way that made shivers crawl along my spine. There was a subtext in them. One that I couldn't read, but it was clear that he wasn't alluding to my failed attempt at suicide straightening me out. Something else had happened. Something I desperately wanted to understand.

He leaned in close to me, shooting a cautious look at his brothers before he whispered in my ear.

"And it will not be done again."

With that, he turned and continued on toward the mansion. I looked over at the boys and sighed, then headed off after Merc. Jase and Dean were soon at my side. They were understandably concerned for me and unwilling to give me much room. I could hardly blame them for that.

I was still trying to piece everything together myself—especially what had just taken place.

I couldn't understand why my mind had taken such a sharp dive into depression. It was as if, for the first time ever, I'd considered that there was an out—a way to escape my existence of perceived weakness. Though the king's words had been harsh, they were in fact true. The supernatural world wasn't for the faint of heart. The helpless. I did have a choice to make. Maybe the one I'd just made had been ill advised, but I could make a different one now.

It was time I stopped being fodder for others. It was time that I found a way to embrace what I was and inherit the powers that were my birthright.

... As soon as I figured out how.

FOR THE NEXT FEW DAYS, I spent just about every waking moment I could outside, doing all I could to try and re-create the connection I'd had with the source of my power when I'd healed. To put it kindly, I failed miserably. It had been a shot in the dark and I knew it, but I'd still hoped that perhaps something would just happen. That maybe because I was actively seeking it this time, it would let me find it.

But all I got for my efforts was a sunburn.

Frustrated, I took a break, hoping that if I let myself relax, I could approach the whole thing again with a new take on it; let the magic come to me. That seemed to be how it had worked before. Maybe it would again if I just let it in.

It was worth a shot.

My efforts, however, got waylaid when I got the most distressing news. The king had called for a soirée at his home. And there was no declining that kind of event; not if you were me.

Like it or not, I prepared myself for the inevitable.

7

Vampires loved to have parties, or balls, as they insisted upon calling them. They were formal affairs, complete with gowns and tuxes and all the finery one might come to think of when the term "ball" is used. I hated them with a passion, and they couldn't stop finding reasons to have them—even when the treaty was in jeopardy.

When I learned that the vampire king himself was throwing one, I cringed, knowing I couldn't wriggle out of that one. Not showing would be a clear slap in the face, and that was an affront that few, if any, would survive. I most certainly would not, especially after everything that had happened. So I swallowed back my resentment at being made to go and started searching for a dress. I had a closet full of them, but you never wore an outfit twice to an event like that.

It was social suicide.

While I scrolled through sites containing the season's hottest looks, straight off the runways in Paris, someone knocked on my bedroom door.

"Come in!"

"Hey, Piper. It's me," Jase called out as he strolled across the large room. "I just wanted to make sure you got word of the king's shindig this weekend."

"Yep. Shopping for it now."

He looked over my shoulder at the screen, pointing to a stunning black gown. It was form-fitted and sleek, without any embellishments at all, save the cutout in the side that spanned from hip to breast.

"That one has you written all over it," he said with a smile.

I cringed internally, rolling back over onto my stomach.

"I was thinking of something more like this," I replied, pointing to sapphire-blue dress that was equally simple-but-stunning, and was conveniently without gaping holes that would expose my scars. Jase shrugged, disappointed that I didn't jump at the chance to purchase his choice. If he'd known what I'd have shown off if I did, he would have been far more understanding.

"Whichever. Just be sure you let Mia know so she can reach the designer. If we need to send the jet for it, she'll have to make arrangements ASAP."

"Yeah. I'll talk to her about it before I go to bed for the night."

"You're not coming out again?"

"Sorry. I'm still just not up for it."

He forced a smile, trying to wrap his head around something he couldn't possibly.

"Okay, but expect an early morning wake up call, then," he warned, ruffling my hair. "Dean will probably want a drunken cuddle before he heads to bed."

"Deal."

"And don't forget to talk to Mia."
"Going now."
"Good. Talk to you later, Piper."
"Later, Jase."

WALKING into a party full of vampires was like walking backstage at New York Fashion Week. There were perfect faces and bodies as far as the eye could see. I, however, wasn't one of them, a fact that the females in attendance loved to point out every chance they got. It was like a supernatural *Mean Girls*. I usually did my best to find a corner to hole up in and watch the clock as it slowly ticked away. Sometimes Jase and Dean would take turns saving me from the bitchy firing squad, but even they could only handle them for so long.

The king's party was every bit as opulent as all the others I'd been to that year, but as always, his was sprinkled with an extra dose of grandeur. The old ones seemed to like things to smack of an era long gone, a nod to the aristocratic feel that the 1700s had boasted. Personally, I was never impressed by it. It felt like having a party in a museum; everything was old, priceless, and not to be touched.

When we arrived, the butler showed us in. Jase and Dean made their way toward a group of stunning females on the far side of the room, and I quickly found a servant with a tray of champagne flutes and hijacked her, grabbing two drinks and downing the first in two rather unladylike gulps. I placed the empty back down with a sheepish smile. The young vampire had the good form not to comment, though I could see the flash of judgment in her eyes.

With the second glass in hand, I searched the room for a safe place to hang out, making my way to the edge of the crowd so I could navigate around it rather than through. As I did, I caught a glimpse of the king far off on the other side of the vast room. He was talking to Merc. My hand tightened around the stem of my glass instantly. I stood there staring silently, wondering why the two were having what appeared to be a very private conversation while surrounded by the other guests.

I hoped I hadn't gotten him into trouble with the king.

Now watching intently, I tried to read the expression of the vampires' leader. I needed to know his mood. But even I knew that he was a master of emotional control. He was more than capable of explaining in great detail how he was going to kill you, all while smiling politely. I doubted that Merc was much different.

Hoping that I might be able to read his lips, I squinted hard, trying to watch the king's mouth as he spoke. When it stopped moving, I turned to Merc, thinking that surely he wouldn't dare to not respond to the king. That kind of stunt could get him sent away again. Even killed. But as I looked on, practically willing him to say something—anything—I realized that Merc would indeed continue his selective mute behavior. His mouth never moved.

"Son of a bitch," I whispered to myself as I stared, taking a swig of my drink.

"I hardly think the king would agree," a familiar voice said beside me. A rush of cold ran down my spine. The bitch squad had found me early. Or at least its ringleader had. "Shall I tell him your thoughts on his mother? That should make for an interesting start to the evening, don't you agree, Katrina?"

I turned to find myself nose-to-nose with the two people I loathed most. Sylvia and Katrina were daughters of the vampire elite. Blood-sucking socialites. They were also the bane of my existence at these soirées.

"I do, Sylvia. Let's go," she said, taking her friend's pale hand in her own.

"He doesn't like to be interrupted," I warned, trying to maintain some modicum of control over my rising fear.

"You think?" Sylvia countered, quirking a pale blonde eyebrow at me. Her elvish features were lovely, her piercing, nearly-too-big eyes almost impossible to ignore. But no matter how beautiful her exterior, all I saw when I looked at her was the foulness that existed within that exquisite shell. Nothing was uglier to my eyes.

"Listen," I started, doing my best to defuse the situation. "I wasn't talking about the king."

"Were you talking about Merc, then? I highly doubt he'd take your sentiments any better."

I shrugged, then slammed what remained of drink number two. With a quick turn, I started off in search of more alcohol.

"Running away won't save you," Sylvia called after me. "And as memory serves, it didn't do much for you last time." Katrina let out a laugh to punctuate her friend's sentiment. I, however, stopped dead in my tracks. "Did you even run at all?" she asked, her breath suddenly hot on the back of my neck. "From what I was told, you didn't make it more than two steps before the warlocks brought you down." *How could she know,* I thought, my mind reeling so hard that it almost rendered me dizzy. "You don't belong here, you know that?" she continued, her words barely a whisper. "Vampires are predators. And you? You, my dear Piper, are prey. Nothing more." I remained where I stood, breathing deeply, trying to control my rage as I fought back angry tears. "Did you wish for death when they burned you, I wonder? Did you wish to die and rid the planet of your useless life?"

I felt the first tear betray me as it slid down my cheek. Then I looked across the room to see Merc staring at me. His expression was tight. Nostrils flared.

Sylvia followed my gaze across the room and laughed to herself.

"Do you know why the king has thrown this extravagant party, Piper? No, I don't think you do. Allow me to enlighten you. Merc is to pick a mate tonight. The king demands it. And so he is to pick from the eligible females here, the operative word being *eligible*. You hardly qualify, so perhaps you should run along then, hmm? Maybe do what you couldn't when the warlocks attacked you in the park, and run far, far away. And this time, don't stop until the stench of your burning flesh is far downwind of us so I never have to smell that vile combination of fear and surrender again."

I blinked hard, trying to shut out the sound of her voice, but it was no use. Her words echoed in my mind far too loudly. When I opened my eyes, I started to walk away from her, but her torment wasn't over. She had one last bomb to drop.

"Vampires loathe imperfection, Piper. It's in our nature to seek the most perfect specimen to mate with, and you and I both know that you don't qualify. You never really did, but now? Now you are ruined beyond measure."

By this point, we had drawn the attention of the rest of the party attendees. Their perfect eyes were staring at me down their perfect noses. My stomach turned beneath my marred skin. She was right; I would never blend in with their kind. It was utterly impossible. There was no longer a point in trying.

With that revelation fueling my rage, I ripped my dress up over my head as a clap of thunder shook the house. Standing before the gawking crowd in nothing more than my bra and underwear, I flaunted my imperfections for all to see.

"You think I give a shit about being like you?" I shouted, no longer caring about being invisible. That ship had long sailed. "I'd rather have burned to death in that park than be like you. You're an empty, soulless sack of shit, and there's no amount of beauty or perfection that can make up for that." I threw my dress at her, quickly followed by my stiletto heels. "You think you have something over me, something you can leverage against me? Well guess what, bitch? You haven't got shit. Here's your trump," I screamed, pointing to the massive scarring that disfigured my body. "And I just played it for you."

I turned on my bare feet and stormed through the crowd in my skivvies, headed for the grand French doors at the back of the room. I had to get outside. I'd find sanctuary in the surging storm, if I could just get out there.

If I could just escape.

Then I was running. Crashing into everyone in my path, I finally reached the doors, throwing them open to a flash of lightning that nearly blinded me. It was so close that I could feel the prickle of its residual energy. Though the punishing winds pushed me back into the room, I darted out toward the lightning's pulse.

Rain beat against my bare skin, pummeling me. The sting felt good—more than good. It felt right. It was what I deserved. With arms outstretched, I lifted my face to the sky, the movement accentuated by another thunderous boom that shook the very ground I stood on.

I awaited the lightning strike with an open embrace.

But it never came.

Instead, I felt a grip like steel clamp down on my biceps, forcing me to turn around. I found Merc's harsh beauty staring me down in the middle of the thunderstorm. His eyes drifted to my stomach for a moment before returning to my face. There was no pity in his stare.

"I did not come here tonight because it was demanded of me," he shouted over the gusting wind. "...because I am required to choose a mate."

"Then why are you here, Merc? And why are you standing out here in the rain with me? Did you just need to get a closer look? Did you want to see just how ruined I am?" I yelled, my misdirected anger flowing from me in waves.

He paused for a moment.

"I came for you," he said simply. "And I do not need a closer look. I already know what I see. You are not ruined, Piper. These scars," he said, gesturing to my stomach, "they are your story; a map of your existence. And though I loathe how you came to have them, I would not see them erased, because it would mean erasing a part of you that makes you who you are. A part of the one I want." He stared at me with those intense pale eyes, and I soon found myself lost somewhere deep within them. "You are more than the sum total of your parts, Piper. You have a soul so amazing—so powerful—that it inspires everything around you, even nature itself, to celebrate your joys and suffer your pains alongside you, almost as though it were a part of you. Nothing is more beautiful than that to me. Nothing." Again, tears escaped my eyes. "Your mind is such a beautiful puzzle, Piper. I want to spend eternity solving it. What I need to know now is: will you let me?" His grip on my arms softened, his hands sliding down to hold mine. "Come inside. Let me tell the king I have made my choice."

The rain started to slow.

"But I barely know you," I whispered, my kneejerk tendency to push people away rearing its ugly head.

"You know all you need to," he said, his head hanging low, lips brushing mine. "So tell me, Piper. What do you say?"

"Yes." I breathed the answer instinctively.

"Excellent," he said softly. My eyes closed, awaiting his kiss. I'd dreamt of it so many times, my shameful, traitorous body craving that which it should not have. And then suddenly, there stood that desire, wanting me too. I leaned in closer in anticipation. "Not yet, Piper. Not yet."

Instead of a kiss, I got his jacket wrapped around my soaking wet and almost-naked body while he ushered me toward the mansion. With my rage dissipated, the thought of facing everyone that I had just stripped in front of—shown my secret to—scared the shit out of me. My hesitation was plain.

"They will never have what you have, Piper—a pure soul. That is why they resent you. That is what will always set you apart from all of them."

"And that's why you want me," I whispered to myself.

He growled a low, rumbling sound.

"That, and so, so much more."

My whole body tensed at his reply. I felt the tightening all the way to my very core, but it wasn't from fear. It was desire in its most raw form.

Once we re-entered the party, the entire place fell silent. It was eerie—like a horror movie. Robotic heads turned to face us, their expressions a mix of indifference and revulsion. Then my eyes found Jase and Dean. The confusion and concern in their eyes were plain.

As the crowd parted like the sea for Merc, the boys tried to make their way toward me, pushing their way through the masses. I turned to them, giving them my best "everything is okay" look, but I could see that they were unconvinced.

"Piper," Jase called out as he worked his way toward me.

"I know what I'm doing, Jase," I said quietly. *At least I think I do.*

Merc then turned to his brother and gave a single nod. After a moment, Jase mimicked the gesture. Dean too. Merc and I made our way to the king, who stood stoically, his face a study in calm. Stopping only feet away from the vampire leader, I couldn't help but fidget with the edge of Merc's coat, pulling it closed more tightly. The king and I had a secret, one that made me uncomfortable standing before him. Our last conversation still didn't sit well, even if I did understand why we'd had it. It left me unsure of where I stood with him. I also knew that he would not be overly pleased by my antics that evening. In truth, he was well within his rights to punish me because of them. Severely. Whether or not he would exercise that right still remained to be seen. And yet Merc paraded me right in front of him, totally unafraid (or unaware) of the potential consequences.

He was going to declare me his own. He planned to claim me in front of all in attendance.

"Mercenary," the king said in an even tone that belied his irritation. I could see the anger flash momentarily in his gaze. Merc only nodded in response, not addressing the king directly. "Am I to assume that this is your choice?" He nodded again. The king sighed heavily. "I would be lying if I said this pleased me. I'm not certain that Piper is the most...*adequate* candidate. I do not feel that this pairing is beneficial for our kind, especially given the political climate we are in. She brings nothing to this partnership. Nothing but chaos." He then turned dark eyes to me, addressing me specifically. "Have I not been gracious to you, Piper? Have I not provided you with a safe haven? The protection of my most competent enforcers? Retribution for the wrongs done to you, even in the face of a failing treaty?"

"Yes," I replied meekly. "You have."

"Are you not thankful for all these things?"

"Of course I am, sire."

"Then I am at a loss as to why you would endeavor to take even more from me. Why you would be so greedy—so ungrateful—as to demand the hand of one of my most valued soldiers. One who could help turn the tides should war come. One who cannot afford to be distracted by your particular shortcomings." I cowered away from him slightly, the sting of his words cutting deep. "I could have left you on the streets to die as all the others did, and yet, for no benefit of my own, I saved you. And this is how you choose to repay me?" he asked rhetorically, his voice rising with every word. He was far angrier than I could have imagined. I understood that he had done much for me and that he thought I was trying to take something from him, but even with that, his growing rage seemed excessive. It made me wonder if the stress of the treaty had finally gotten to him, and I was a convenient outlet for that tension.

Which didn't bode well for me.

My eyes nervously looked up at Merc, who never broke contact with the king. "Answer me, you ingrate!" the king shouted, startling me so much that I jumped. Merc squeezed my hand tighter. "You will look at me when I speak to you, and you will answer my question. Is this how you choose to repay me?" the king continued, his anger no longer withheld. "By manipulating my most prized enforcer into choosing you over his own kind?"

"No," I whimpered, knowing that the king's outburst was certain to be followed up by one of two things: my exile or my death. I needed to do something to prove I had no foreknowledge of Merc's plan.

And I needed to do it quickly.

But I could find no words that would absolve me from the guilt he saw in me. Nothing I could say to clear my name. Just as I felt my world close in around me, I felt Merc release my hand to step forward, eclipsing the king's view of me.

"This was my doing," he said aloud, drawing a collective gasp from the others in the room. "Not hers. We will be an *excellent* pairing and will serve you well. You will see the advantage to having Piper as one of our own one day." As he spoke, I could feel a shift in the air around us. The king's brow furrowed for a moment, then relaxed. His entire demeanor changed, from his head to his toes. He sidestepped Merc so that his eyes could once again fall upon mine. But this time, they were not full of malice. Instead, they brimmed with acceptance.

"Perhaps you are right, Mercenary. Your persistence in the matter speaks to your commitment to your decision. In light of this, I will grant you your request. Tonight you will be bonded to Piper. All here will bear witness to the ceremony."

For the first time since we'd stood before the king, Merc dared to look down at me. An uncharacteristic and mischievous smile played across his face. Somehow he'd gotten exactly what he wanted that night, and he was clearly pleased. Though my heart still raced with fear from the threat of the king's wrath, I smiled back at Merc, knowing that, finally, the bond I felt between us would be officially consecrated, making us one.

Forever together.

Forever bound.

"Let us begin at once," the king said, raising his arms in a grand gesture to the crowd. He continued speaking, but my attention drifted back to Merc, whose steel blue eyes remained fixed on me. There was something in them, an intensity, a longing, that I'd never seen before. Then, before everyone present, Merc shared the reasons for the look in his eyes. The passion that he felt for me was so plain in his words.

"I choose you, Piper, to be bonded to me for eternity," he started, taking my hand in his to place over his heart. "The curse of the vampire is an emptiness so profound that I cannot begin to explain it to you. But you...you are a light in the darkness I face, both figuratively and literally. Your vibrance is a beacon that leads me from the black abyss that I have fallen into countless times. I see the sunset I can no longer face in your eyes. I smell its radiance in your hair. Feel its warmth in your skin. Make no mistake, Piper, you are a fire that could consume me, and I would gladly let it. Such sweet agony..." He released my hand to cup my face, brushing a tear I didn't know I'd shed from my cheek. "You've cast a spell on me, little one. Such power you possess, and yet you doubt it. I am your mirror now, Piper. The strength you see in me will now be reflected in you. You are every bit my equal. Every bit the being that you see me as. And you—you are my soul. You will forever fill that emptiness in me."

I stood in awe, staring at the being before me, wondering

what in my life had changed so drastically—erased a lifetime of bad luck and unfortunate circumstances—to allow me that moment. All he'd said, everything he felt, spoke to a part of me that I'd never known. Never felt before. Just as I'd awakened something in him, so had he awoken something in me.

Something I would never let go of.

"Piper," the king called, distracting me from my realization. "Do you accept Mercenary as yours?"

"Yes," I breathed, my heart racing wild.

"Do you know what happens now?" he asked, his tone not unkind. I shook my head. "There is an exchange of blood." He looked at me, willing me to see the complication.

"Oh," I said as my eyes widened with surprise. I hadn't known about that little snafu. Perhaps that was one of the reasons the other races didn't mix well with the vampires. Maybe they knew about that little caveat going in.

Merc, seeing my anxiety rise, smiled before unleashing his previously retracted fangs. He lifted his index finger to the tip of one and pricked it just enough to draw a single drop of blood, which he offered to me. I leaned forward, hesitating only for a moment before I took hold of his hand and placed the droplet on my tongue, drinking back the sweet liquid. My eyes rolled back in my head as I swallowed; the heat I felt from that small taste was all-consuming. I practically moaned as it traveled down my throat. Thankfully, I remembered that an entire ballroom full of guests was staring at me, and I managed to stifle that response. But when my eyes shot open, they were all for Merc.

And judging by what I saw in his, he approved.

It looked as though it took a great amount of control on his part to not leap forward and grab me, but he managed, if only barely. Instead, he looked to the king for confirmation, then, once given, he gently reached for my neck and drew me to him, tilting my chin up to him. Still, my heart raced.

"Do not fear me," he whispered, his lips brushing mine. "Never fear me..."

Then he pushed my long black hair off of my neck, exposing the throbbing vein he sought. The source of my life. The life that spoke so deeply to him. With the sweetest of pains, he bit down into it and drank of me, filling himself with the radiance he saw in me. And with every draw, I saw flashes of his memories—memories of me outside the mansion, at the club, and during Kingston's attack. The first time he touched me. My charred body limp in his arms, the ride home from Central Park, my screams from the infirmary. The first time he spoke to me. My leaning form perched on the bridge's railing, the king's ballroom, my fight with Sylvia. The first time he claimed me. So many memories came at me like a freight train, assaulting my mind with the images of me that he held most dear.

When he pulled away from me, that connection broke, but remnants of it lingered. I *felt* him, and he undoubtedly felt me too.

"What has been freely given cannot be revoked," the king boomed, addressing the crowd. He then turned his attention back to us. "You are forever bound."

Forever bound...

I smiled at the thought.

But my excitement was tempered by trepidation. I'd never been in love before. Never known that it could override all logic and rationality. To have known someone for such a short time and already feel the way I secretly did about him made no sense to me at all, but even still, I knew it was right. The second he showed me how he truly felt— the second I experienced that for myself through his eyes—

my heart sang. Its song eclipsed the voices in my head that tried to steer me the way of reason. I didn't want reason; I wanted love. Acceptance. Passion. Safety. And with Merc, I would find all four.

If only for a while.

8

Merc looked down at me with a steely reverence that made my blood rush through my veins. He'd already seen me nearly naked that night; I knew that in my mind. But the heat in his eyes was hard to comprehend. He truly didn't see my scars when he looked at me. He only saw what he wanted—me.

And I wanted him too, there was no denying that. Like the dreams of him I'd had, filled with visions of him on top of me, inside me, consuming every bit of me that he could. That night, with him standing half naked at the foot of his bed, I wanted to be exactly where I was, and it was plain that he could read that in my eyes.

The dream had finally become real.

Like the predator he was, he stalked toward me, climbing onto the bed with the elegance of a lion about to pounce on his prey. But he stopped himself, hovering just above my legs to stare down at my expression more closely. Always watching. Always assessing. Then I saw the doubt flicker through his eyes. He may have viewed me as strong, but even he couldn't deny that a part of me had broken the night I was attacked. He was far too intelligent to think otherwise. He'd studied my every move afterward, undoubtedly analyzing everything I said and did. His quiet contemplation when he was around me made far more sense. He was torn between what he wanted and what he thought I needed. If I did nothing to reassure him, then our wedding night would fizzle out in a hurry.

Time to man up, Piper...

"So...I know it's been a *really* long time since I've done this, so I might be wrong, but I'm pretty sure you need to come a bit closer if you want to have sex with me," I said playfully, trying my best to be funny yet seductive. There was no reason those two things had to be mutually exclusive.

His eyes narrowed, the desire in them pushing through the reservation they had just displayed.

"I didn't want to appear too eager, but I won't lie to you, Piper. I've wanted this since the first time I saw you," he replied. "I have since realized that my intentions may not have been clear to you—that my nature made it difficult for you to see what seemed so obvious to me. But make no mistake, the thought of you has all but consumed my every thought since that night. Especially the thought of you beneath me. " He stared down at me while he knelt between my legs, and I spread them wider, enticing him to lie between them.

He took the bait.

In a flash, his body was pressed tightly against mine, and it became clear just how badly he wanted me. His breathing was ragged and erratic, and his erection pulsed against me. Even with his pants on, I could tell he had a lot to offer a girl, a revelation that both excited and terrified me. It really had been a long time since I'd been with someone—years, to be exact. But what worried me most was the damage I'd sustained in the fire. It wasn't only my abdomen that had been burned beyond recognition. Everything down to my upper thighs had been as well. Though I'd healed, I hadn't exactly explored that part of my body beyond the occasional naked stand before a mirror. And that never ended well. I'd basically blocked my girly bits out of my mind, trying to forget what they looked like after the attack. I certainly hadn't played around with them to see what, if any, feeling still remained.

With my luck, there was probably none.

"I want to see all of you," he whispered into my neck, grinding his body against mine. My breath caught in my throat, which pulled a growl from his. He reached behind me, unclasping my bra, and let his fingers trail along the bottom edge of it, teasing the underside of my breast devilishly as he did. He traced the clear delineation between scarred skin and smooth, kissing a line along my neck to my chest. As his lips made their way down to the top of my breast, a desperate gasp escaped me.

He stilled instantly.

"Nononononono," I protested, locking my hands in his hair. "Don't stop. Please don't stop."

I lowered my gaze to find mischievous eyes staring up at me.

"But you said no," he countered, pulling away from me slightly.

"NO! I meant 'no, don't stop'! Not 'stop'," I argued, my heart racing with anticipation.

A smile spread wide across his face.

"Perhaps you're not ready for that," he said, sliding down past my breasts to my stomach. "Perhaps here would be a better place to start." He dragged a single finger down the line of my once-perfect abs, stopping as he met the top of my underwear. I felt my body clench at the thought of him dipping below that elastic barrier, willing him to do it. Instead he backtracked, trailing his finger back up to where it had started.

"Nonononono!" I protested again, the note of pleading in my voice impossible to ignore.

"No?" he asked with a quirk of his brow. "No what?" He shifted his weight to his elbows, sliding down the length of my body, his pace painfully slow. "No this?" he inquired as he grazed the skin above the line of the thin black fabric. The only thing keeping him from where I wanted him to be. "Is that what you're suggesting, Piper?"

Before I could answer, his hand dove just below my underwear. Again I gasped, arching my back in a futile attempt to force his fingers just an inch or two lower. I needed him inside me.

Just as he started to draw his hand out from underneath the black fabric, I caught his arm, thrusting it back down again. I positioned it right where I wanted it to be—his intended target. This time, it was his turn to gasp. Then he growled, tearing the thin fabric from my body with the flick of his wrist. I could feel his breath fall heavy and erratic on my tender flesh. The tingle of anticipation it caused was unlike anything I'd ever known.

Then his mouth fell upon my core, and my body erupted into a fiery ball of need that bordered on pain. It was hard to process all the feelings at once. I felt like I wanted to pull him closer and shove him away as the pressure built. My body rocked rhythmically against his face as he continued to do things I'd never experienced before. I felt his finger slide inside me, drawing a guttural sound from deep within me. The tension building inside my core couldn't sustain itself much longer, and I begged him to put an end to this sweet, sweet torture. As if he'd been toying with me all along, waiting for me to tap out of our sexual exploration, he reached his finger deeper, expertly finding the exact spot needed to allow my body to let go. With a cry, my body convulsed as I let the wave of energy crash over me—through me—my muscles clenching tightly against the finger that remained behind, caught in the crossfire.

"Oh my God," I repeated over and over again, my head extended so far back that all I could see was the headboard. "Please..."

"Please what?" he asked, his words suddenly tickling my ear. While I fought to put together a coherent sentence, I could hear him unzipping his pants.

"That!" I finally blurted out. "I want that. All of it."

"All of it?" he said incredulously. "Are you sure about that?" He pushed his body away from mine, once again kneeling between my legs, his pants around his hips. With a smooth slide of his hands, his boxer briefs found their way down as well, exposing everything I had just claimed to want. All of it.

I gasped at the sight.

My mind demanded that I withdraw my previous statement, but my body told it to fuck off. Whether it was anatomically possible or not, I wanted him to slide himself deep within me until I begged him to stop or I passed out from pleasure. Whichever came first.

"Yes. I'm sure."

"Then say it," he demanded, collapsing on top of me. The raspy tone of his voice told me his control was waning.

"I want you," I breathed, writhing underneath him.

"To do what?"

"To fuck me," I moaned as I felt the tip of him press against my opening.

"And how do you want me to fuck you?" he asked, pulling away from me. I wriggled down, trying to reconnect us.

"Hard? Now? Whatever, I don't care, I just want you inside me." I was practically begging at that point. I was senseless need and little more. Merc had reduced me to that, and I loved him for it.

Again I felt him pressing against me, splitting me open, but not entering. Always testing. Teasing.

"Whatever am I going to do with you," he asked rhetorically, catching my earlobe in his mouth and biting it lightly. "Have you no manners? Say please."

"Please," I exhaled, arching against him.

"Say it again."

"Please!" I cried out this time, whimpering with desire.

"Now," he said, thrusting himself inside me, "that wasn't so hard, was it?" The shot of pain that jolted through me was as intense as the pleasure that followed in its wake. He worked over every inch of my body with every inch of his, driving me to the brink of insanity. With every thrust of his hips, every hungry kiss, he consumed me until we climaxed in beautiful synchrony. He owned me then, mind, body, and soul. There was nowhere else in the world I could dream of being other than by his side.

9

I woke up early to find my body entwined with Merc's. His eyes were closed, still heavy with sleep, but I knew he was awake. The smile that spread across his face while I stared at him told me as much.

"You're staring," he said, his voice low and raspy.

"How did you—"

"I could feel the weight of your eyes on me."

"That's freaky."

"It's convenient," he countered, finally lifting his lids to expose his piercing gray-blue eyes. My body shuddered when they fell upon me. *And he thought I was staring...* "How are you feeling this morning?"

"Me? I feel fine. Why?" I asked, laying my head back down on his shoulder.

He shrugged it lightly beneath me.

"Much has happened to you in the last few hours. I want to be certain that you have wrapped your head around all of it."

"And that I don't regret anything," I added, seeing where he was going. His silence was all the confirmation I needed.

I propped up on my elbow so that I could look down at him. So that he could see my face clearly, in case my words were not reassuring enough. "I am exactly where I want to be. Last night went from horrible, to desperate, to shocking, then amazing in a flash. I wouldn't change a thing about it." I smiled at him, leaning forward to kiss him lightly on the nose. "Well, that's not entirely true. I could have passed on the king part. That was scary as all hell."

"I would not have let him harm you," he said matter-of-factly.

My eyes widened at his treasonous admission.

"Don't say that," I said, my heart racing with fear. "You cannot stand against him. To do that is to sign your own death warrant. If anyone ever hears you say that..."

"Calm yourself, Piper. Nothing will happen to me."

"You can't guarantee that if you challenge the king."

He smiled widely.

"Do not be so certain of that." He leaned in close to whisper in my ear. "Haven't I already?"

My mind started to race with the implications of his words, but before it could get too far, he shot up and tackled me, pinning me back down to the bed. The weight of his body against mine was more than sufficient to derail my train of thought.

"Do you still wish to discuss my imprudence where the king is involved, or would you prefer to do something else?" he asked, grinding his pelvis against mine. I spread my legs a little wider to accommodate him.

"King who?" I breathed as he bent his head low to kiss along the side of my neck.

"Exactly," he murmured against my skin.

"Venturing out of your love nest to get some food?" Jase called after me as I attempted to sneak into the kitchen for some snacks. Keeping up with Merc was going to require a trip to the grocery store soon. Preferably not one in Brooklyn.

"Something like that," I replied, turning to find him striding down the hall toward me.

"Piper, I need to talk to you."

"If this is going to be some lecture about staying away from Merc, I hate to inform you but I think you've missed the boat on that one." I kept making my way toward the kitchen, not waiting for Jase to catch up, but he inevitably did, grabbing my arm to halt me.

"It's not about that, Piper," he explained, his dark eyes soft and kind. "I want to talk about what happened before that. When you and Sylvia were fighting."

"Oh. That," I said, my arms drifting up to cover my midsection.

"Yeah. That. Why didn't you tell me about your scars? Or Dean?"

My eyes fell away from his gaze to the floor.

"I was embarrassed." My words were a whisper.

"Aw, Piper," he sighed, pulling me into an embrace. "Nothing could ever make either of us feel differently about you. You have to know that by now."

"I'm sorry—"

"You have nothing to be sorry for. We're the ones that are sorry. What I said that night on the bridge—I had no idea that your post-attack trauma was so deeply rooted. That you had a constant reminder of it."

"You didn't know because I didn't want you to, Jase. And there's a reason for that. I knew you'd blame yourself and I couldn't stand the thought of seeing pity in your eyes every time you looked at me. So please don't start now. What's done is done. I've found love and acceptance where I least expected to. Merc doesn't see my scars when he looks at me. He sees something much greater. I can't tell you how amazing that feels."

Jase sighed heavily, a tentative smile tugging at his mouth.

"I don't know how you've managed to bewitch him, Piper, but it is a sight to behold. I guess what I'd thought was fascination with you was something else entirely."

"Seems like it," I replied with a playful wink, hoping to lift his spirits a bit. "But wait a minute, wouldn't bewitching someone require power? Power I likely don't have?"

"I wouldn't be so sure of that," Jase quickly countered. "I've never seen him the way he is with you. About you. There is something magical behind it, make no mistake about that."

"Are you seriously implying that I've put a spell on him?"

"No," he admonished, "nothing like that. Think of me using the world magical as if I were a human. Not *magic* magic—the kind that we know exists—but the kind that results in the mundane world. The kind that explains events that would otherwise be considered inexplicable."

"Oh," I said softly, my cheeks flushed with embarrassment. "It's really that odd, huh?"

"You have no idea."

"What are you two conspiring about?" Dean called from behind his brother as he approached us.

"What do you think, asshat?" Jase replied, smiling wide.

"Merc."

"Bingo!"

"Jase was just informing me that I've somehow done the impossible by taming the beast, so to speak."

"That's an understatement, Piper," Dean said, his expression full of disbelief and reservation. "I'm still unsure about it all. I mean really, how does that even happen?"

"Got me," Jase added.

"Well, I'm going to leave you two alone to contemplate this further. Meanwhile, I'll be in the kitchen pilfering as much food as I can to take upstairs."

"Good idea," Dean laughed. "And remind Merc that he needs to eat too. It's been a few days since he's had a full feeding, and he gets a bit...*grumpy* when he's hungry. Best you not see that side of him just yet, Piper. You might rethink your bonding to him."

That statement stopped me in my tracks.

"You still think he'd harm me?" I asked, turning to face them.

They shook their heads in unison.

"No way," Dean started. "That's virtually impossible."

"Impossible?"

"Think about it, Piper. How many of the vampires in this house that are bonded have you seen fight? Yell? Have anything but sheer and utter bliss in the other's presence?"

I considered his question for a moment before realizing the answer.

"None," I said quietly.

"Exactly," Jase replied. "When we choose a mate, there is a reason for it. They balance us somehow. And there is a power to the bond that only strengthens that."

"Are you saying that they *can't* fight?"

"I'm saying that for as long as I can remember, I've never seen it. It's unprecedented."

"Even in an interracial bonding?" I asked, trying to remember if I'd ever seen Kat and Jensen fight before. My mental search came up empty.

The boys both nodded at me in response to my question.

"Well, if what you say is true, then Merc could be starving and still be sweet as pie to me?"

"Yes," they replied simultaneously.

"Ha!" I laughed. "So you're just trying to get me to save you the wrath of your brother! Some tough guys you are."

"You haven't seen it before," Dean muttered under his breath. "He can be such a dick."

"It's true," Jase agreed. "You'd be doing us a solid, Piper. And let's be honest, I think you kinda owe us one. I mean, we did introduce you to him, right?"

"You two are ridiculous," I said, giggling to myself as I turned back toward the kitchen. Their pleas to make sure my lover ate soon followed me down the hall until they were cut off by the closing kitchen door. "Pussies," I mumbled under my breath, still entertained by the big bad enforcers scared of their hungry brother.

Once I'd grabbed a bag of chips, an orange juice, and an entire bunch of bananas, balancing them precariously in my arms, I stepped back into the empty hallway and made my way back to Merc's room, his bed, and his arms. It was there that I found a comfort once unknown to me. A love that defied all logic.

But it was also where a darkness dwelled. A growing evil that would taint that love until it was no longer recognizable, eating away at the ties that bound us. And time was already running out.

Such a cruel fate would soon befall us.

Such a twisted love ours would prove to be.

10

Merc and I holed up in his room for two days just getting to know each other—that and having copious amounts of sex. Both experiences were amazing. It was crazy to see how his mind worked, hear of his life spent in the service of the king, and learn more about his brothers. Incriminating things. Things I'd be sure to leverage against them later on if I wanted to get out of going to the bar with them. Merc was a veritable wealth of information.

Before I could suggest that we actually leave his suite and join the rest of the crew in the mansion, he received a call from Jase (who'd given up on trying to knock on the door to get our attention a day earlier). It appeared as though trouble was on the rise, and the enforcers were needed to settle things down before they got any more out of hand.

"I must go," he said solemnly, walking over to the bathroom to clean up.

"Did he say what's going on?"

"Yes."

"Is it dangerous?"

"I cannot say, Piper. Enforcer matters are private. You might be bonded to me, but that does not make you privy to that kind of information."

"Oh," I said, deflating slightly against the headboard. "Okay. Well, can you tell me where you're going? Or who it involves?"

"No." He emerged fully dressed, his hair pulled back in a tiny ponytail at the base of his head. "But you must stay in until I return. It isn't safe to go out."

"I was supposed to meet Kat at the club tonight—"

"Then you must call her and cancel. She wouldn't want you in danger either."

I followed him as he walked toward the bedroom door, grabbing yoga pants and a tank top along the way. As I hopped into the pants and pulled the shirt down over my head, we exited into the hallway, me trailing him slightly. He made his way down the grand staircase to the foyer, where a large group of the others was waiting for him, all of them armed to the teeth. Whatever was going on, it wasn't good, that much was clear. I searched for Jase and Dean amongst the crew of enforcers hovering by the security door.

When I found them, they both shot me dubious looks.

"Please tell me what's going on," I pleaded, hoping someone would tell me what they were heading off to face. "You look like you're about to go fight a war."

"I told you that you cannot know," Merc replied, repeating his earlier answer.

"I know, but I've never seen so many of you so heavily armed," I continued, coming down the final step to grab his arm. "I'm worried, Merc. I don't want anyone to get hurt."

"And we won't," he said, though his response was tight and clipped. It wasn't reassuring at all.

"Jase," I started, turning my attention to him.

"I said everything will be fine!" Merc snapped, wheeling around to pin harsh eyes on me. I startled at the anger behind his voice, then realized that maybe he was stressed about what he was about to face. My constant badgering couldn't have been helping that. "I'm sorry," he apologized, both his expression and tone softening. "There is no time for weakness now. The mates of the enforcers must stand strong. We must go now, Piper. Remain here until we return." He came over to me, wrapping his massive arms around my tiny frame and pulling me into him. "And we will return. All of us. I promise."

"Okay," I replied, my words muffled by his chest. When I pulled away, I found him looking down at me as he had that night in the entryway of the store when Kingston had attacked. There was an intensity in his eyes. A commitment. He would be back. Nothing could keep him from me.

He walked past everyone else in the group and punched in the code to the security door leading out to the containment room that separated them from the outside—the failsafe to keep someone from accidentally stumbling out into the daylight hours, and ultimately their demise. The others just stood still, their eyes traveling back and forth between Merc and me. Their behavior was unnerving at best. By the time I mustered up the courage to ask them what their collective problem was, the metal door swung open and Merc stepped through it. The second he did, the others followed.

Everyone but Jase and Dean.

Those two continued to look at me, their expressions a mix of confusion and concern.

"What's wrong?" I asked quietly, stepping closer to the pair.

Neither replied. Instead they turned and looked at each other. I wondered if they too were capable of having telepathic conversations.

"Piper, did you feed Merc recently? Like a true feeding, not just the blood exchanged at your bonding?" Jase finally asked, staring at me as though he could discern the answer without my help.

"Yesterday. Why?"

He hesitated a moment, pondering my reply.

"I don't know if you should do that again," he said, his response surprising. "Nobody knows what you are—what magic runs through your veins. I'm not sure that Merc should take that into his body. Maybe a donor would be best for the time being."

"What am I missing here?" I asked, feeling as though something that was so clear to everyone around me had flown right over my head.

"Merc just seems a bit...on edge," Dean added. I'd never seen him be more delicate about anything in the time I'd known him. "Maybe your blood isn't good for his system."

"You're a variable that's hard to account for sometimes, Piper," Jase added. "Just do me this favor and don't let him feed from you again. Will you? For me?"

"Sure," I said, my voice distant.

A blaring of a car horn carried through the door. The boys were getting restless waiting for Jase and Dean.

"We have to go now, but we can talk more about this when we get back," Jase said, leaning in to kiss my forehead.

"Be careful, you two."

"Always," Dean tossed back at me as he walked through the door. Jase just waved over his shoulder as he followed his brother out.

Suddenly I was alone in the vast foyer of the mansion,

left to wonder what in the hell had just happened and why everyone seemed so freaked out by it. Maybe Merc wasn't the only one on edge. Maybe the whole crew was privy to something I wasn't. Maybe the war had already begun.

That thought made me more afraid for those who'd left that night.

I sat down on the bottom step, propped my elbows on my knees, and rested my chin in my hands, the words "there is no time for weakness now" running through my mind. Kingston had said something like that to me once during my training. I'd been tired and frustrated, and I was looking for some comfort from him, but there was none there to be found. Seeing the similarities between him and Merc in that moment was far from comforting.

Neither were the looks and Jase's and Dean's faces.

I was afraid for my friends and my mate. But why were they so concerned for me? That was the question that I couldn't quite answer. The turn of events that had occurred after Merc's little outburst that night didn't make sense to me. The boys had told me that he would never do anything to hurt me—couldn't do anything to hurt me—but surely he wasn't immune to irritation or disagreement where I was concerned. That was just too farfetched to even fathom.

While I contemplated all the possibilities, I sat and waited anxiously for the enforcers to return home. I needed to find out what was really going on. And if no one would tell me, I needed to find a way to get answers on my own, without their aid. Ill-advised or not, I had a plan to do just that. I was going to test Jase and Dean's little theory and see just how far I could push the boundaries with Merc.

Hours later, they all filed through the security door, unharmed but weary. Whatever they had faced that night had worn them down both mentally and physically. I knew it was bad when Dean couldn't even bring himself to make a smart remark about how cute it was that I'd waited up for them.

My need for answers only heightened as a result.

Merc entered the mansion last, wiping his blades off on the hem of his bloodied t-shirt. When his stormy eyes fell upon mine, he smiled lightly, then continued past me toward the stairs to the basement. He was headed to the infirmary.

I shot up from my perch on the stairs and ran after him, hot on his heels as he sped down the multiple flights leading to Doc's domain.

"Merc, what's wrong? Are you hurt?" I called down after him, winded from trying to keep pace with him.

"It's just a flesh wound," he replied, indifference in his tone.

"Then why do you need Doc?"

"I don't."

"So why is it you're headed to the infirmary then?"

"I need something."

I could see that getting answers from him while descending the stairs was going to prove futile, so I shut my mouth and poured on speed, catching up to him as he reached the final landing. As he reached for the door to the main corridor, I clamped my hand down upon his.

"Merc," I said, still breathing heavily, "please. There's already so much mystery surrounding tonight. All I want to know is what is going on with you. Just you. Please, give me that much."

He stared at me, his masked expression from when I first met him taking over his countenance.

"My wound is of the magical variety. It must be cleansed if it is to heal."

"Was it the warlocks?" I pressed, not liking any of the potential scenarios playing out through my mind. If it was indeed them, then Reinhardt had gone back on his word, and the war had begun.

"I have told you already that I am not at liberty to discuss such matters," he said curtly, turning the knob and opening the door while forcing my hand off of his.

"Fine, but I'm coming with you. I want to make sure you're okay."

"And what will you do for me if I'm not, Piper? Will you heal me? Use your powers to remedy all that ails me?" he queried, a notable heat tainting his words. "I have survived for centuries without your help. I will continue to survive without it."

Unlike earlier that night, I felt the true anger that coursed through him. He was more than on edge. More than irritable. He was pissed off.

And it appeared that he was pissed off at me.

"Wow," I said quietly. "Please, don't hold back. Tell me how you really feel." It seemed that he wasn't the only one who was angry.

My reply did little to improve his mood.

"You mock me?" He was fuming as he stormed toward me. I suddenly realized just how alone and isolated we were. Stories' worth of ground separated us from the rest of the enforcers. And even if Doc had been down there, she was hardly a match for Merc.

"No, I—"

"You will shut your mouth and go upstairs, that is what

you will do. And you will do it now." I stood in place, my body trembling with an undercurrent of fear. This was the man I had been warned against. The man that until now I had not born witness to. When I didn't move, he leaned in close to my face, the fury in his eyes impossible to ignore. "Are you intentionally defying me?"

"No," I whispered, my voice quivering. Before he could say anything else, I turned and ran to the door, flying up the staircase two steps at a time. By the time I reached the main floor of the house, my heart pounded in my chest so loudly that the sound of it was all I could hear. The pulsing in my ears was deafening.

I tried my best to compose myself as I made my way to the grand staircase, and ultimately my old bedroom. I needed space. I needed to think. If Merc's behavior was a result of my blood in his system, then it was certain that he could never feed from me again. That was an easy enough variable to rule in or out. My concern was that it wouldn't work.

And if it didn't, what that meant for me, Merc, and our bond.

HE FOUND ME LATER, sitting in the middle of my king-sized bed, lost deep in thought. He had the good form to look contrite when he entered the room, hovering near the door that he'd delicately closed behind him.

"Piper, I—"

"You can't drink from me again. You need to find someone else to feed from."

Genuine surprise flashed across his face, as though my

outburst was not at all what he'd been expecting when he'd entered my room.

"Why have you come to this conclusion?" he asked, leaning back against the heavy wooden barricade.

"I didn't. Jase did. I'm just agreeing with him."

"And why has he suggested this?"

"Your behavior. It's...*off* somehow. This is not the you that I've known. This is the you I was cautioned against."

He sighed heavily, squeezing his head between his thumb and index finger.

"I'm sorry, Piper. In truth, I haven't felt myself at all today. Perhaps Jase is right. Perhaps there is something about your blood that is negatively affecting me."

When he released his temples, he brought his gaze up to meet mine, the two of us just silently staring at one another for what seemed like an eternity. I longed to understand what was going through his complicated mind. I prayed that it wasn't breaking.

"You scared me," I whispered nervously, uncertain how he'd respond to that admission.

Seeing me physically tense when he stepped toward me, his expression fell to one of sadness.

"I'm so sorry, Piper. I would never hurt you. You must know this. I need you to know this..."

"That's what I've been told—that our bond somehow insulates me from certain emotions and behaviors—but after tonight, I'm just not sure," I admitted a little more freely. "I thought you were going to hit me in the basement.

He visibly flinched at my words.

"I admit that I cannot account for the anger that overtook me downstairs. I think that perhaps you and I should stay in separate spaces until your blood no longer courses through my veins," he said, an uncharacteristic softness to his reply. "I will speak to Jase about this and see what he thinks. His insight into serious matters is usually beyond reproach. I hope it is in this matter as well." He turned to leave, his hand resting on the doorknob for a beat before he twisted it and opened the door. "Please believe me when I tell you that I have never felt about another the way I feel about you, Piper." His sad eyes gazed over his shoulder, reinforcing his sentiment. "I love you."

With that, he exited my room, softly closing the door behind him, leaving me to my chosen isolation. Isolation from him that would last for the next couple days while we allowed his body to burn up the blood I had given him. I nervously awaited the results of our experiment.

"Piper?" Kat called from outside my room, peeking her head in immediately afterward. She never was a big fan of waiting to be let in.

"Yeah, Kat? What's up?"

"How are you doing?"

"Fine, I guess," I shrugged, climbing out of bed.

"We should get you outside today. Want to go for a run?"

"With you?" I asked incredulously. "You know I can't keep up."

"I'll jog. I promise. No speeding."

"The last time you said that, a squirrel ran past us and you took off. You didn't come back for thirty minutes!"

It was her turn to shrug.

"I am what I am, what can I say?"

"Okay, Popeye. I'll get geared up and meet you downstairs."

She started toward my bedroom door, stopping just short of it.

"It's going to be all right, Piper." Her statement caught me completely off guard. It was rare for Kat to show emotions, at least any with depth to them. She was generally more of the sarcastic type with a wicked protective edge to her. Solemn was new for her as far as I was concerned. "Things were a little rocky for Jensen and me in the beginning. I know that it's considered a bit taboo for the races to mix, but I think there's a deeper reason behind it."

"You don't think we blend well."

She gave a wan smile.

"I think that where vampires are concerned, things are inherently more complicated," she explained with a sigh. "Jensen took a while to get used to my blood. To this day he doesn't feed solely on it."

"Oh," I said softly. "So you think Merc will be okay?"

"I hope so."

When her expression started to harden, I quickly read between the lines. She hoped so because the alternative was one that I wouldn't like. Or maybe I wouldn't survive. I never did ask her to expand on her response and she never offered to. Instead, the two of us went for a run in the woods on the property. We strode alongside one another in companionable silence, letting nature be the soundtrack to our jog. Just being in the fresh air helped calm my soul. Set my mind at ease.

By the time we returned to the mansion, the sun was setting, dipping down behind the peaks of the surrounding pine trees.

"I need to go...you know," Kat said with an awkward jerk of her head back toward the trees.

"Haven't gotten furry in a while, eh?" I teased, stretching my legs.

"I've been busy. You good on your own?"

"I'll be fine. Don't worry about me."

She scrutinized me for a moment, then sped off, disappearing into the tree line that encircled the property. I remained outside to watch the sun fully set, absorbing its final glow before it too disappeared. Then I made my way into the mansion to wait out the final hours of Merc's and my separation. Soon we would know if all was well.

Soon we would know if all was doomed.

I WASN'T aware that I'd fallen asleep in the movie room until a large hand on my shoulder gently jostled me awake.

"Should I assume this particular film isn't worth watching?" Merc asked as he sat down on the edge of the couch just in front of my outstretched body.

"Hey," I said, my voice heavy with sleep. Rubbing my eyes to coax them open, I sat up beside him. "Sooooo...how are you feeling?" The trepidation in my tone was apparent, especially when combined with my cautious expression.

An honest-to-God smile spread across his face. I swear I even saw a twinkle in his eye.

"Like myself," he declared, leaning in to kiss me. "Possibly even better."

"So it was my blood?" I pressed, needing to actually hear him say it to know it was true. To know that the whole ordeal was over.

"It was your blood." I sprang to my knees and threw my arms around him, practically choking him (not that he needed to breathe) with my tight grip. He laughed in response, my antics amusing him, as they often seemed to. "From here on out, it should be smooth sailing, as they say."

"I'll take that," I said, my face buried so deep in his neck that my words were nearly unintelligible.

"I'm glad."

I felt his arms wrap around my back, pulling me even closer to him, as if that were physically possible. As it was, I was practically inside him given how I'd pressed myself against him. The relief I felt was indescribable. Things weren't over before they had begun, as I'd feared they would be. He and I could still have a life together.

An eternity as one.

When I finally felt like I no longer had to cling to him for dear life, I relaxed back from him a bit, still sitting in his lap. We'd just overcome a massive hurdle—one that had threatened to undo us—but there was another still present, and this one would not be so easily circumvented.

"So now that we have that cleared up, I'd like to move on to the second order of business," I started, trying to keep my tone light to belie my growing unease regarding the war that appeared to have started.

"And what would that be?" he asked, tucking a stray piece of hair behind my ear. The gentle gesture sent chills down my spine, derailing my train of thought momentarily. I had to literally shake my head to get myself focused.

"Let me preface what I'm about to say with this: I understand that you can't freely discuss matters directly relating to your duties. I get that. You made that point *very* clear the other night." I hadn't meant anything by my last comment, but the flinch of Merc's eyes when I delivered it made me feel awful. "I'm sorry. I didn't mean it like—"

"What I said," he started, exhaling heavily, "it was not entirely true. I should not divulge certain things to you, that much is accurate, but I need not keep you completely in the dark either. Ask me what you want to know. I will answer your questions to the degree that I am allowed."

"Okay," I said with a tight smile. "Has it started? The war? I mean...how bad are things?"

His lips pressed together tightly in response.

"It has not yet begun, but it is no longer a question of if, but when the treaty will fall."

"Shit," I uttered under my breath.

"You need not worry. That war will never reach you," he declared, taking my face gently in his hands. "Harm will not befall you. I swear it."

"And you?" I asked, my throat tightening around my words as I spoke.

"It will not befall me either." I wanted to question him more, ask how he could guarantee such a thing, but the intensity in his cold blue eyes made me think better of it. He meant what he said. He would stop at nothing to survive to ensure that I would too. It was a gesture so pure in a supernatural life that was anything but. I felt overrun by emotion at the thought. "I mean it, Piper," he continued, seeing the tears escape my eyes. He wiped them away before he leaned in close, kissing me softly at first. Then the fear and uncertainty of the past few days drove us to a frantic pace, each clambering up the other to get a better hold. He finally landed on top of me, pressing me deep into the cushions of the couch, his weight drawing a groan from the springs underneath us.

Oddly, it made me laugh.

"I don't think this thing was built to withstand the rigorous workout you're planning on putting it through."

"It's not the sofa that's going to get the workout," he

whispered in my ear, his voice low and gravelly, filled with need.

"Aw, c'mon, you two! You have a room—two of them, in fact," Dean called out from the entrance to the media room. When Merc and I paused to look up at him, he sauntered in to join us, standing at the near end of the couch. "So, looks like Jase's theory panned out."

"I would say so," I agreed as I looked up at his looming presence.

"Well, I hate to break up your little reunion, but the king wants a word with us. I need you down in the meeting hall, Merc. Now."

With a nod, he climbed off of me, then helped me out of the sag he'd created in the sofa.

"I will find you when this is done," he said to me before bending down to kiss me again. It was still full of passion and it made me blush when he pulled away, knowing full well that Dean had been staring at us.

Dean groaned and turned away, headed for the door.

"I think I liked you two more when you were apart," he groused as he exited.

I looked up to find Merc staring down at me, smiling.

"You're enjoying this a bit too much, you know that, right?" I asked him.

He nodded once before taking his leave as well.

Brothers, I thought to myself, then laughed. But that laughter died off quickly when I realized the implications of the conversation they were likely having down in the meeting room. The king demanding an audience rarely, if ever, was good. Merc's words echoed in my mind. *Not if, but when...*

Perhaps 'when' was upon us.

11

"So you're telling me that the king is setting up a meeting with all the leaders of the various supernatural races?" I asked, unable to hide my incredulity. "But why do that if the treaty is going to fall? Isn't that suicide? It will be a melee!"

"And that's why he wants us there," Jase said calmly, stating the obvious. "He's trying for a last-ditch effort to stop the madness before it all begins."

"His version of a Hail Mary," Dean added.

"Aren't things too far gone at this point to even try?"

Jase shrugged.

"He has to. The others have historically followed his lead. If he wishes to meet, they will. If he wishes to keep the peace, perhaps they will try harder to do the same."

Reinhardt sure as hell hasn't...

"It all sounds pretty shaky to me," I mumbled to myself.

"Us too," Dean agreed from his post against the wall on the far side of the media room. "But we have no choice. The king doesn't either. He has to try."

"And he wants *all* of you there, right?" I asked, turning

my gaze to Merc. "I mean, wouldn't your...*gifts* be handy in this situation?"

The question was innocent enough—at least I'd meant it to be—but the response of all three of them was far from what I'd expected.

"They would, but I have been ordered to stay behind." Merc forced the words out as though they pained him greatly.

"Careful, Piper," Jase cautioned. "What Merc can do—it comes at a price. And his gifts are not something that should be advertised. The king has worked very hard to keep Merc's abilities under wraps. You need to do the same."

"I'm sorry," I said, feeling embarrassed. "I didn't know. I just assumed—"

"Assumptions are dangerous," Merc said, pushing off of the chair he was sitting in. Without another word, he walked out of the room, disappearing down the adjacent hall.

Jase and Dean shared a look, then returned their focus to me.

"Tread lightly when it comes to Merc's ability, Piper. I know he's been better since he's no longer feeding from you, but when it comes to his gifts, his stability can be...precarious," Jase said, coming to put his arm around me.

"What he's trying to say is that those gifts can cause a shit ton of damage in their wake, both directly and indirectly," Dean added. "Because of that, he's often left out of scenarios that seem to call for him most of all. The king learned that the hard way once. He can't risk it again."

I thought carefully about what Dean was saying (and not saying, for that matter). There was subtext there that I couldn't quite find. But I would have bet my life on the fact that it was linked to where Merc was before he'd returned and why he was sent there.

"For Merc to influence that many minds at once would come at a price that none of us could possibly fathom. He would likely never be the same again."

"Making him a liability," I added, seeing where the conversation was headed.

"Exactly."

"So he's being left behind? He's staying home while the rest of you go?"

"Yes. And he's not too happy about it," Jase said, looking at the doorway Merc had stormed through.

"Yeah, I gathered that," I replied, following his gaze. "So when is this all taking place?"

"Two days. Something about a solstice or eclipse or some fucked up thing that the witches can't miss," Dean explained, disgust in his voice. He never did much care for the witches once he'd learned they'd turned me away as a child. And once Dean decided he didn't like you, there was no changing that opinion.

"We have a lot to get in order before that time, so..." Jase said, tension overtaking his expression. "We're not going to be around much. I want you to make sure to stick close to Kat when you can, okay?"

"Yeah. Sure," I replied absentmindedly. "Is Merc going to be helping you guys?"

The boys exchanged another look.

"We're not sure yet. Listen, I don't want you to worry about him, but his thoughts...they're escaping his control."

"Meaning?" I asked, stepping in front of Jase.

"It's like he's talking to himself—but we can hear him. Like silent outbursts."

"And what is he saying?" I pressed, my eyes narrowing.

"Nothing in particular. He's just angry and ranting. He'll cool down soon. It took a lot for him to get through the meeting with the king and not flip out. He's just venting in his own way now."

"You're worried about him," I said, my statement sounding more like an accusation.

"Not really. He's been like this before and been fine in the end," he said, exhaling heavily.

"But...?"

"But I don't want to be wrong about that, so I'm asking you to stay next to Kat whenever you can to minimize any potential risk, regardless of how minute it might be or how insane I might sound for thinking there is something to worry about in the first place. I'd rather be safe than sorry."

"He won't hurt me," I said confidently, staring Jase down. Then I turned to give Dean the same look. I wanted them to know that I believed in my mate, even if they didn't.

"I'm sure you're right," he said, softening his expression. "Just humor me, okay? You've done worse than that before." His boyish smile spread wide, eliciting one from me. The charms of Jase and Dean were impossible to ignore.

"Fine. I'll stick with Kat whenever I can," I said, stepping away from them to go and search for something to eat, then my unwitting werewolf bodyguard. "He'll prove you wrong, you two. Mark my words."

I heard Dean mumble something to Jase in response, but I was too far away from them to make out the words. Knowing him, he was grousing already, well aware that I would gloat about being right for a solid two weeks once all the pressing chaos was sorted out. Until then, it was a wait-and-see situation. Not exactly my favorite kind.

Those two days needed for preparations flew by at an impossible speed.

I did as the boys asked and kept Kat at my side whenever possible (short of hopping in bed with her and Jensen), but it all seemed for naught. Merc had managed to balance himself out, his anger very much under control. When others were present, he was silent, which was pretty much the status quo, but he was also thoughtful and sweet. There was no shred of the hostility he had felt toward the king for leaving him out or the other enforcers for getting to attend the meeting without him. All I saw was the man who had stood before me in the rain outside the king's mansion, asking me to be his.

Every time I thought about that moment, it made me smile.

When it was time for the treaty negotiations to take place, a sea of enforcers flooded the front yard, filing into massive black SUVs. I looked over to find Kat kissing Jensen goodbye before getting into her own vehicle. She said she couldn't stand the thought of staying at home to worry, so she'd asked me if it was okay for her to pick up an extra shift at the bar. I didn't care. A little alone time with Merc sounded pretty good as far as I was concerned. We hadn't had much since our initial return home after being bonded.

He probably needed a good distraction himself.

Jase and Dean came over to Merc and me, had a brief silent conversation with him, then gave me a hug before they too departed. I stood beside my mate as the convoy of vehicles drove off. Nervous but hopeful, he and I awaited their return. Whatever happened, we would have news before sunrise.

With a heavy sigh, I turned and made my way back toward the mansion. When I realized I was alone, I looked over my shoulder to find Merc staring off in the direction everyone else had just gone.

"They'll be all right," I said softly, hoping to assuage his concern.

Instead, my words seemed to anger him

"I do not need your reassurance. I am well aware of what they are capable of handling," he said, turning to pin cold, dead blue eyes on me.

"I'm sorry. I was just—"

"Sorry..." he said, the word rolling off his tongue as though it were offensive to him. "You're always sorry. Sorry is for the weak, Piper. Apologizing is for the weak. Weakness is beneath me, as it is you. Perhaps it is time to stop your sniveling and start acting like a woman deserving of your position at my side." He walked toward me slowly, a menacing wall of man. "If this is how you intend to behave in their collective absence, do us both a favor and remain out here until they return."

With that, he strode past me into the house, never once looking back.

Tears welled in my eyes. I hated both them and myself in that moment. I was proving him right. I was weak, and that weakness was repugnant to him. It dawned on me that every time he'd ever snapped at me the way he just had was when I'd acted fearful. Been overly concerned for those that did not need it. It wasn't my blood that was the problem.

It was me.

With that reality pressing down upon me, I wondered just what I'd gotten myself into. I was bonded to a male that loved who I was capable of being at times, but not the person I regressed to in times of stress. When my fear for myself or others consumed me. Unfortunately, it seemed that both behaviors were equally possible when a crisis presented itself.

And that didn't bode well for my future with Merc.

I stared up at the crescent moon above, letting it bathe my face in its silver-blue glow. If I could not find the bravery inside, there would be no fixing Merc and me. It was then that yet another reality settled upon my mind. Jase and Dean were wrong; Merc could most definitely hurt me.

Just not how they'd feared he would.

12

I stayed outside for hours—as long as I could—but the cold was starting to seep into my bones. It drove me to the warmth of the mansion. Once there, I intended to find an innocuous space to hunker down and await the others' return, but it seemed as though Merc had a different plan.

One that I didn't enjoy in the least.

I was in the library, curled up on the floor in front of the wood-burning fireplace, a book in my hands. Just as I turned the page to start the sixth chapter, Merc's voice startled me.

"Have you managed to pull yourself together yet?" he asked, leaning against the door frame. His broad shoulders seemed to fill the only exit in the room. There was an evenness to his tone, but I was not convinced. It belied the rage boiling up within him.

"Yes," I said, forcing a smile. "I thought I'd take my mind off of things with a little fiction. I always loved to escape into stories when I was young."

"Escape, too, is for the weak," he said, the chill of his words cutting through me like the cold night air outside.

"I guess I never looked at it that way," I replied calmly, swallowing hard against my rising fear. One of the reasons I'd survived as long as I had was my ability to defuse a situation—or at least until recently. I hoped to employ every tactic I'd ever used to calm Merc.

Providing that was even possible.

"Of course you didn't," he said, taking a slow, methodical step into the room. "Stand up." His words were not a request.

Obeying him, I shrugged off the blanket encircling me and stood.

"Are we going somewhere?" I asked, feigning casualness. In truth, I felt little other than impending doom as he continued toward me.

"Who are you, Piper?"

"What?"

"Who. Are. You?" he repeated, leaning in close to me as he did.

"You know who I am, Merc. You're not making any sense right now."

"I know what you pretend to be, and you are incredibly good at it. You fooled everyone, including me—a task never before accomplished. You should be proud of your performance. I'm sure he is as well."

"He?" I asked, abandoning my plan to try and wriggle my way out of the situation. Confusion had overtaken me at that point, blurring my judgment. "Who are you talking about?"

He tilted his head to the side in mocking, staring at me as though he were unsure what to do about my perceived insubordination. Then he grabbed me by the arm and dragged me toward him, shoving his face into mine.

"This ends now. Tonight," he proclaimed. His eyes were

wide and wild. It was then that I realized I was in far more trouble than I'd ever bargained for. If I could not appeal to the man behind the insanity, I wouldn't have to worry about being bonded to a vampire who may or may not love me.

I would be dead.

"Something is wrong," I cried, beseeching him to see what was so plainly obvious to me. He had come unhinged again. "I don't know what to do, Merc. What to say. I want to help you, but all I seem to do is enrage you. Maybe somebody can get through to you—stop this from getting worse. But somebody has to do something or—" I cut off the obvious end to my statement, not wanting to anger him further, but it was too late. I'd already said too much. He knew the direction my sentiment was headed in. The writing was on the wall.

"Or what?" he asked calmly, squeezing my arm so hard that I gasped.

"I just want to help you, Merc," I pleaded, tears welling in my eyes for the second time that night. "The boys...Kat...they all say that this isn't normal. That you shouldn't be able to act this way with me. Not to your mate—your chosen one. It's obviously not my blood that's causing it. We need to figure out what's going on here before it's too late."

He cocked his head slowly, scrutinizing me with a piercing glance.

"Too late? Too late for what?"

"For us," I whispered, turning my bleary eyes to him.

"Our bond is forever, Piper, or did you not understand that?"

"I did. I do," I replied, shying away from the weight of his stare.

"No," he countered. "I don't think you do. You see, if you

did, you wouldn't be acting as if there were a door number two. A plan B. Because there isn't, Piper. It is us or it is death. And with knowing what I now know..."

His words trailed off, only further reinforcing my greatest fear.

"We don't need a plan B, Merc. That's what I'm trying to tell you. But there's something wrong, and it's not me. I know you think it is, but it isn't. It's something else entirely. Don't you see that? Don't you feel it? I may not have much experience with love, but I'm positive that you and I shared something close to it when we were bonded. What we have now—this—this isn't it. Living in constant fear of saying or doing or being the wrong thing. Walking on eggshells so as not to upset you, only to find out that my very being does just that. I'm always wondering if I'm going to get Dr. Jekyll or Mr. Hyde, Merc. Where's the being that saved me from the warlocks? The one that kept my pain at bay while I lay wounded—possibly dying—downstairs? The one that stepped up and claimed me as his in the face of both the scrutiny of his own kind and the disapproval of his own king? That is the man I started to fall in love with. That is the man I want to love forever," I said, pleading with him while the tears I had pent up streamed down my face. "Give him back to me. Please...give him back. I know he's in there somewhere. Don't let the darkness take you. Please. For me..."

For a second, the briefest moment, I saw his expression soften. I was getting through to him. I dared to lean closer to him, lifting my hands to his face with great reservation. It was now or never. I had to lay it all out for him.

"Maybe there is someone that can help us," I whispered, my shaking hand just about to cup his cheek. "Maybe if we go to the king, he will know what to—"

"NO!" he roared, swinging his arm wildly. The force that he backhanded me with sent me across the entire living room to crash into the bookcase against the far wall. The sensation I felt in my back as I connected with it shot through me like lightning, down my legs to my feet. I crumpled to the ground, temporarily paralyzed. I could not move my legs. "You will never report back to him, do you hear me?" he shouted, striding across the room like a man possessed. A man bent on silencing me.

With a few more blows like the one he'd just delivered, it wouldn't take long for him to accomplish that.

"Merc!" I cried out, trying to drag my body across the floor and escape, but it was no use. He easily caught me.

"You've been talking with them, haven't you? Conspiring against me?" he spat, accusing me of crimes I neither understood nor had committed. Grabbing me by the collar of my shirt, he hauled me up to my limp feet, my body dangling only inches from his face. "I will not be sent back. Not for you. Not for anyone."

"I don't know what you're talking about!" I screamed in frustration between my sobs. The feeling was slowly coming back to my legs, but the sensation gained was unwelcome to say the least. It felt like fire.

"You're no different than the rest of them," he continued, ignoring me. "I see you for what you are now, Piper. I *see* you..."

"See what? That I wanted to love you? To help you?"

"Ha!" he scoffed. "You even admit it now."

"Admit what? You're not making any sense."

"You speak in past tense. *Wanted to love*," he ranted, shaking me like a rag doll in front of him. "You're a liar. You tried to play me. He sent you to do that, didn't he? DIDN'T HE?"

"I don't understand," I whimpered, wishing that someone would come home to find us soon. Before Merc killed me.

"Well it hardly matters now," he said, his voice suddenly calm and controlled. His ability to switch from rage to impassivity was beyond unnerving. "The why never does. Only the who and the how." He pulled my face so close to his that I could barely make out his features clearly. "And I will find out both of those answers once you're dead."

Again my body went flying across the room, this time crashing through the glass-topped table in the corner. The sharp, shattered pieces bit into my skin as I fell upon them. One must have cut more deeply than the others, for I soon found myself lying in an ever-expanding pool of blood.

There are moments in life when you see things with perfect clarity—moments when you choose to define who and what you are. And then there are those that define things for you. Lying on the floor, bleeding to death, I realized that fate had interceded on my behalf. It was all very simple, really: stay and be the weakling I had always been told I was. Stay and let my life slowly drain from me, never bothering to fight—a natural born victim. Or, in a rare act of defiance and courage, I could force myself to get up and leave. Force myself to quiet the voices in my head telling me it would all be better tomorrow. But I was no fool.

If I stayed, tomorrow would never come.

Tick tock, Piper. Tick tock.

It was then that I could hear the fighting in the distance. The voices. The others had returned home and come to my aid. I could hear the ruckus around me as they tried to restrain him. Now was my moment. This was my chance. With a surge of adrenaline, I pushed myself off the blood-soaked floor and staggered on barely functioning legs toward the doorway that led to the hall. I needed to get to my room. I needed provisions.

I would not be returning to the mansion again. Ever.

His angered roar chased me down the corridor, spurring me on. I did not know how long the others could subdue him. My failing body was sluggish and uncoordinated from blood loss and a concussion, but I managed to get to my bedroom with considerable speed—my will to live was stronger than I'd thought. I threw open the heavy wooden door and made my way inside. I took only seconds to throw what I could find into a duffel bag: clothes, shoes, a jacket. Then I grabbed my purse and fled.

I tripped just as I rounded the top of the staircase and rolled down the first few steps before I managed to stop myself and slide down the rest in a more controlled fashion. I was almost to the security door. Almost to safety.

"Piper!" he screamed after me. I shuddered instinctively. Hazarding a glance over my shoulder as I tried to punch in the code to unlock the front entrance, I found him looming at the top of the staircase. Four enforcers were trying hard to hold him back, but they were losing. Even against their combined power, he pushed forward after me.

There would be no stopping him.

My hands shook and my vision blurred from the blood dripping into my eyes, both interfering with my ability to type in the code. With his heavy footfalls echoing through the grand foyer, I tried repeatedly to press the proper buttons to no avail. My attempt to live was proving futile; he was closing in.

With only seconds to spare, I managed to unlock the main security door. I could hear his straining breaths approaching as I threw it open, turning to slam it closed behind me. Once I was through, I was free, if only for a moment. The sun would soon be rising. Once that happened, he couldn't follow, and he knew it. He'd have to wait for nightfall to come after me.

And by then I'd be long gone.

I leaned back against the solid metal door, my breath coming in ragged gasps. I needed to get outside, out of the tiny room that separated the vampires from the impending light. Outside, I could heal. Once healed, I could leave.

With ever-weakening steps, I schlepped my way to my final obstacle: the front door. Swinging it open with ease, I fell to the concrete and crawled away from the mansion. By that point, I could barely lift myself off the ground. But I needed nature—the elements—if I had any chance at repairing what had been damaged. And so I pressed on until I felt the familiar touch of newly cut grass beneath me. Face down, I collapsed to the lawn, my mind fading as I did.

"Help me," I whispered to the Earth as darkness overtook me.

And help me, it did.

PART II

AFTER

13

Every day started the same for me: a healthy sense of dread eating away somewhere deep inside of me. It had ever since I'd broken through the front door of the enforcers' mansion, bloody and battered, fleeing for my life. I knew Merc was coming for me. I could see the determination in his eyes when the boys had restrained him. It haunted my dreams.

I was his—there would be no turning back.

From the second I'd escaped, I had been on the run. It had taken me nearly two weeks, thousands of miles, a dwindling supply of cash, and one long ferry ride from Seattle to finally arrive in Alaska—my new temporary home. During that time, I'd slept only when I could no longer keep my eyes open. And always during the day: never the nighttime. Night necessitated my every attention.

That was when they would be hunting for me.

Without a passport, I had few places to escape to. Places where someone like me could easily go unnoticed. So I decided one day, as I wound through the back roads of South Dakota in a stolen vehicle, that northern Alaska's short summer nights would be an excellent option. I planned to stay there until I could find someone to make some fake IDs and a passport. The Last Frontier would be where I started over.

After arriving, it had taken another solid day of driving to get to the middle of nowhere, but the sun was still in the sky when I arrived at the mountain cabin. It didn't take long to unpack my dubiously acquired Jeep, and once I'd gotten myself somewhat settled in, I decided to go out and explore my surroundings while there was still sunlight. It was late, but northern Alaska provided me a great advantage in that realm. It stayed light far into the hours that would have been dark in New York. I was banking on this detail to keep me safe until I could get the materials necessary to leave the country. To go on the run on a grander scale.

Though the area I was in was remote, there appeared to be some abandoned logging trails and roads nearby, so I decided to go for a run along them and see where they took me. I needed to have multiple escape routes if necessary. I had to give myself a fighting chance in case Merc ever found me.

The temperature was warmer than I expected, so I donned my running capris and tank top with a lightweight jacket tied around my waist just in case it got cooler in the shaded areas of the trails. The scenery was breathtaking: all towering coniferous trees so wide through the trunks that they had to have been hundreds of years old. It seemed such a shame that someone had slashed through the area to harvest them.

The graveyard of stumps made my heart heavy.

I turned away from it, deciding to go further up through the woods. The pine-laden air smelled glorious, lifting my spirits as I ran uphill, eventually stopping at a ledge overlooking a small waterfall and river. It was stunning.

"Water source, check," I said to myself, remembering that I was about as off the grid as I could be, and that included a lack of running water. The previous well had run dry, so I was stuck schlepping water around or buying it in town when I ventured that way. In actuality, where I had decided to hole up was not well suited for a city girl. I knew nothing about hunting, fishing, or basic survival at all, but that's what made it a genius place to go. Merc would never think to look for me in such a remote location. He'd see my moving there as a death wish.

Maybe it was.

While I stood there reinforcing the wisdom of my decision to move to the woods, a sound from behind me startled me, and I whipped around to find a massive bear lurking near. When I moved to cover my mouth and the scream that threatened to escape it, he stood up on his hind legs and growled, pawing wildly at the air around him. When he landed back on all fours with a thump, shaking the ground I stood upon, I let out a shrill cry of my own in an attempt to frighten him off. It didn't have the desired effect, but it did seem to give him pause. He cocked his head at me strangely.

Then a growl came from somewhere behind him and my heart raced, thinking another bear had heard his buddy's call and would soon be joining our little standoff. Two huge grizzlies versus little old me didn't seem like favorable odds. I would have bet against myself for sure.

But it wasn't a bear at all. Instead, a light gray wolf came leaping from behind the bear, landing on its back, sinking its enormous teeth into the back of the grizzly's neck. The bear shook wildly, trying to force its attacker off, but the wolf didn't budge. Staring at the fight in disbelief, I realized how evenly matched they were when they shouldn't have been. I'd watched enough National Geographic with Dean to know that the size of a wolf paled in comparison to that of a bear, let alone one as big as a grizzly. This wolf, however, was well over half the bear's height and weight. I should have realized then that I wasn't looking at an ordinary wolf, especially given that I knew full well that werewolves existed, but I'd never seen Kat Change before. I had no idea werewolves could be so large. What made me finally understand what was fighting the bear in front of me was the wolf's constant eye contact with me, as though it was trying to tell me something, willing me to act.

Run. It wanted me to run.

And so I obliged it, darting through the woods carelessly, too scared to keep track of direction or landmarks at all. I wanted to flee as quickly as possible for various reasons, not the least of which was that a supernatural creature had found me. Yes, it had helped me, and I was grateful for that, but the supernatural community, though vast, was still pretty tight. If word got out that I had surfaced somewhere, Merc would be on my doorstep after nightfall, and I'd be dead. I needed to pack up my newly-put-away shit and run. Run far away from what I'd thought would be my new temporary home.

Wrong again, Piper. Wrong again.

By some act of God Himself, I found my way back to the cabin, though I was pretty certain it had taken me way longer than it should have. Long enough for someone else to have beaten me there. Someone I was really hoping to avoid.

"You live here?" the shirtless man asked, rapping his knuckles against the log exterior of the cabin before walking toward me. He brushed his shaggy blond hair out of his face, exposing the most beautiful sage-green eyes. Eyes that casually assessed me and my disheveled appearance.

My breath that had been coming hard and ragged stopped entirely. I was pretty certain I was screwed. Really and truly screwed.

"I'm renting it. Temporarily. In fact, I was thinking of leaving today..."

"Looks like you still haven't unpacked everything yet," he noted unhelpfully.

"Well, I'm not really sure I'm cut out for this 'roughing it' kinda life."

He eyed me up and down, then smiled.

"I'm not really sure you are either."

"Guess I should start packing up the car then," I said, forcing a smile. I moved to walk past him, but he caught me gently by the arm, turning me to face him. Those piercing eyes met mine, searching for something in them.

"You know what I am, don't you?" he asked, sniffing the air casually as he did. His tall frame loomed over me, leaving me with little to look at other than the lean muscles of his upper body.

"Yes." My reply was a ghost of a whisper.

"I know you're not human," he said, letting go of my arm. "But I can't seem to nail down just what it is that you are."

I choked on a laugh.

"Join the club," I muttered under my breath, which was a pointless gesture. Werewolves could hear just as well as vampires.

"Well, if you don't possess superhuman strength, might I suggest not picking fights with the local wildlife. They can be a bit testy." He winked at me before turning to walk back into the surrounding woods, the sunlight picking up the lighter blond pieces in his hair. "And I think you should stay for a while. It'll give you a chance to prove my assessment of you wrong," he called out over his shoulder just before he disappeared into the thick brush. "The name's Knox, by the way."

"Pi—" I started before cutting myself off. The last thing I needed to do was tell some werewolf I didn't know my real name. The vamps would have the supernatural equivalent of an APB out on me. I might as well just turn myself over to them if I planned to be that reckless. "*Pepper*. My name's Pepper."

I heard the rustling of leaves stop.

"I'll be back in an hour to pick you up for dinner, *Pepper*. See you then."

THE HOUR he'd promised turned out to be more like thirty minutes; not enough time to make my escape.

A loud knock on the cabin door let me know that Knox had arrived. He really had intended to pick me up. Whether or not that was for dinner remained to be seen.

"Pepper?" he called, pushing his way into the main room of the tiny one-bedroom home. "Ah, good. You're still here." He eyed the few boxes of provisions by the front entrance, not bothering to point out that I'd obviously planned to be gone by the time he came back for me. His expression said it all with his self-satisfied smile. "The boys are looking forward to meeting you. We need to hurry though, or we'll be lucky if there's anything left over by the time we get there."

"You're not alone out here?" I asked, my blood pressure rising rapidly.

"How many werewolves do you know that roam alone?"

He had me on that one.

"So it's you and your pack then?"

"Yep. Just me and my boys."

"No girls?" I inquired, knowing it was a fairly stupid question. Women didn't weather the Change well. The ratio of male to female werewolves was significantly unbalanced. Kat was by far and away the exception to the rule.

He smiled.

"Nope. Just you. But if it makes you feel better, the boys have been warned to be on their best behavior or else."

"Or else what?"

"They die," he replied with a casual shrug.

That seemed simultaneously comforting and not.

"And this is just dinner? Right?" I asked, squirming under his heavy gaze.

His smiled widened.

"We might watch a movie afterward if that's not too scandalous for you."

Point taken.

"Only if it's PG."

He laughed.

"I'll see if Foust still has that animated movie with the lions that he loves so much. Will that work for you?"

"I guess so," I said, fighting back a giggle.

Knox was inherently charming. Almost all shifters were in their own way. They weren't always as good-looking as the vampires, but they had an undeniably sexy way about them: a swagger that couldn't be ignored. In Knox's case, he had that in spades, and it was combined with a clever sense of humor and level ten good looks. Tan, messy blond hair, and a smile that could melt a girl's heart? He was trouble waiting to happen. Lucky for me, I was pretty immune to all those traits.

Baggage can make you immune to almost anything, especially the charms of any man or beast.

"Shall we then?" he asked, making a gallant sweeping gesture with his arm.

I laughed that time. I just couldn't help it.

"Not before I make something perfectly clear to you: I'm not interested. Okay?"

He looked at me strangely

"In dinner? Fine. I'll eat yours. Feel better now?" he asked, walking out the front door. "Though I have to admit, I think a few calories might do those chicken legs of yours some good."

"I do not have chicken legs!" I shouted after him, storming out of the cabin.

He shrugged again.

"That's a matter of opinion."

I watched him saunter down the front steps, never bothering to look back. He knew I was coming, a fact that was most irritating. But that was the confidence of werewolves; they knew when they had you beat.

I stood there with a smile on my face, despite my best efforts to hide it. Against my better judgment, I was warming up to Knox, which was stupid when the possibility of walking into a trap still loomed over my head. There was little to nothing to do about it, other than plead my case to the wolves in the event that they knew who I was and who was hunting me. Maybe they'd be willing to help me escape. Not everyone feared the enforcers. Maybe they fell into that category.

Then again, maybe they didn't.

With growing trepidation, I followed Knox off into the

woods like the proverbial lamb to slaughter. Perhaps that was a bit melodramatic, but it didn't feel like it. I thought about turning and making a break for it, but outrunning a werewolf fell into the highly unlikely to impossible category. Nope, I was going to have to wait out the night and see where it led.

Only time would tell.

We must have hiked through the woods for a mile or so at a pretty brisk pace before we came to a bit of a clearing. There, in the middle, stood what I could only describe as a massive lodge. It must have had dozens of rooms, judging by the footprint of the building. Though it bore no resemblance, the grandiosity reminded me of the mansion.

What a double-edged sword that memory was.

"You coming?" he called to me. I hadn't even realized I'd stopped walking as I stared at it. He jogged back to where I stood, a genuine look of concern on his face. "I promise, it's like I said. They won't do anything to you. Scout's honor." With that he reached his hand out to me, a gesture of good faith, and I took it, wanting to mask my uneasiness with a carefree façade. It made the smile he seemed to love to wear brighten in the dying light of the sun.

He led me to the grand front entrance of the place, where the doors were at least ten feet tall. The building was really more like a small hotel with a residential dwelling feel. Enormous but homey.

"Prepare yourself for the melee," he announced, pushing the doors open wide. "She's here!"

We stepped into something of a grand foyer that was open to a massive living and entertaining room. The kitchen, with its island the length of a bowling alley, was off to the far right. It too was open to everything else. The vaulted ceiling gave the whole place a sense of grandeur and warmth that I enjoyed. The decor was nothing like the mansion's, lacking the sense of opulence that the vampires seemed to enjoy so much. The lodge was far more rustic, with a mix of woods, textiles, and lighting that was much more appealing to me. And antlers. There were copious amounts of antlers everywhere the eye could see.

"I'm guessing venison might be in my near future," I mumbled. That evoked a roar of laughter from the pack that had filed into the living area while I was taking the place in. When Knox spoke of his boys, I didn't realize there would be quite so many of them. Werewolves had large packs; that wasn't overly surprising. What was surprising to me was just how many belonged to this pack, especially one living in relative seclusion. It made me question why they had chosen this pack in particular, and if maybe they were trying to escape something just like I was.

My anxieties dissipated somewhat at the thought.

"Pepper, this is the pack. Pack, this is Pepper." As if rehearsed, they all chimed in, saying "hi Pepper" in perfect unison. It was mildly creepy. So much for my decreased stress level. "Pepper is our new neighbor. Sort of. She's going to be here for...?" he asked leadingly, dropping his gaze to me.

"Oh, um, a while?"

"A while," he repeated, clearly amused by my answer. "You all have already been read the riot act so I won't bother to do it again." Their faces sobered slightly at his mention of the warning they'd been given earlier. "Shall we eat?" He looked down at me again, still smirking.

"Oh, you're asking me?"

"Well I'm not asking them. This isn't a democracy, Pepper. You know how these things work, I imagine."

"So you're just being gracious for my benefit?" I countered.

"Exactly."

I turned to address the congregation of werewolves occupying the house.

"What do you guys think? Should we eat?" Their deafening cheer sufficed as answer enough. "Looks like we should eat," I told Knox, smiling up at his rather shocked expression. Before he could say another word, I bravely made my way into the kitchen and the crowd of hungry werewolves piling food onto plates the size of platters. The bowling-alley-length island (which, upon further inspection, really was made of an old bowling lane) was piled high with various foods from one end to the other.

"I've never seen anything like this," I said to myself as one of the guys placed a plate in my hands.

"Yeah. Sorry about that. We're running a little low on food, but we did what we could. I hope it's still okay for you."

I looked up at the brown-haired, blue-eyed boy like he had three heads. To the takeout queen of NYC, this was a veritable feast for the masses. No apologies necessary.

"Pretty sure it's fine. Thanks."

I wove my way through the wall of bodies, trying to get to something that resembled a salad with little success. There were just so many of them, and they were big. Not enforcer big, but tall and strong, and no matter how big the kitchen was, it wasn't designed for all fifty of them to be in there at once.

"Let me help you," a voice said from behind me as the owner reached a rather muscular arm over my head to shove some bodies out of my way. "Fucking move, assholes. We have a guest." Once there was enough room to turn around and look at him, I found a pair of chocolate brown eyes looking down at me. There was an unmistakable twinkle in them, a boyish mischievousness that contrasted his hard appearance. His scruffy beard and long, messy dreads pulled back from his face made him look more like a delinquent biker than a werewolf. But his inherent charm spoke to the latter. "Name's Foust." He reached out his hand formally to shake mine.

"Pepper."

"So I heard," he replied in a strange tone. "Knox mentioned you earlier."

"Funny. He didn't say a thing about you," I quipped.

That detail seemed to amuse him.

"That is funny. Normally he doesn't shut up about me. But that's because he loves me so much," he replied with a wink. "At any rate, you need some food, girl. Those legs aren't going to get any meatier on their own."

"What is it with you guys and legs?" I blurted out, exasperation in my tone.

"It's a guy thing," he replied with a shrug. "Besides, you're not going to outrun whoever's looking for you on those scrawny things. You wouldn't make it fifty yards before they caught you."

A shattering sound cut through the ruckus in the room, drawing all eyes to me. I'd dropped my plate when Foust said that. *They know,* I thought to myself, trying to back my way out of the crowd strategically. *Oh my God, they know...*

"What the fuck is going on here?" Knox growled from somewhere on the other side of the island. When the sea of men finally parted wide enough for him to see me, I was shaking. "Foust, what just happened?"

"Nothing, dude. I swear. I was trying to get her access to the food and then she just dropped her plate. I never touched her."

"Then why does she look like she's about to have a seizure or something?" Knox growled, jumping up onto the island strategically so as not to land in the food. With an elegant leap, he was at my side. "Pepper! Pepper, look at me. What happened?" My eyes shifted to his, but what he found in them did nothing to improve his mood, which did nothing to lessen my fear. My silence didn't seem to help things either. "Everybody out. Now!" he yelled and the wolves seemed to disappear in a matter of seconds. When the sound of the final door closing rang out through the house, he softened his expression and placed his hands gently on my shoulders.

"I want to go," I said, my voice wavering slightly.

"I can see that. What I want to know is why."

"I shouldn't have come here tonight," I continued as though he hadn't spoken at all. "I should have left when I had the chance."

"Why? Why do you have to run, Pepper?"

"*Piper*," I snapped, finally gaining some measure of control over my body back. "My name is Piper." I watched his eyes for a flash of recognition. I found none there. "Shit," I gasped. "Shit, shit, shit..."

"Please. We can help you, but we can't if you don't tell me what the hell is going on here."

"Nothing. It's nothing. I'm just a little paranoid. Foust said something and I misunderstood him. That's all," I lied, pulling out of Knox's grasp to head toward the door. The darkness of night that I found awaiting me stopped me in my tracks.

"Scared of the dark?" he asked, coming up behind me.

"No," I replied weakly. "I just don't know which way to go."

"Liar," he said casually, as though he hadn't just blatantly accused me of something he couldn't prove. "Tell me what Foust said to you."

"He said I wasn't going to outrun whoever was looking for me on my scrawny legs."

He paused.

"Well, he has a valid point there. If he offended you, then I will drag him down here now and make him apologize. Will that make you feel better?"

"Yeah. Sure," I muttered.

"More lies," he tsked, walking around to stand before me in the open doorway, framed by the pitch black of night behind him. "Let's make a deal, shall we, Piper? You don't lie to me anymore, and I won't take offense at the ones you've already told me. Sound like a plan?"

"I don't want to lie about things, it's just that—" I cut myself off before I dug the hole I was already in any deeper.

"Finally, some honesty. Now we're getting somewhere," he said with a sigh. "Go on."

"I can't."

He cocked his head at me, his expression pensive.

"That's actually the truth. Interesting. Not helpful, but interesting. At least I know you're capable of it now."

Without another word, he slid past me, heading for the kitchen.

"Might as well load your plate while you can, chicken legs. I'm about to release the hounds. They're probably starving by now, so there won't be a morsel left if you don't claim it."

"You're...you're just going to drop it? Just like that?"

He shrugged ambivalently as he scooped a mountain of potatoes onto his plate.

"You've got some heavy baggage of some sort. I get it. Most of us came here to leave something behind. If you want to keep your reasons to yourself, I can respect that. But if trouble is headed my way, I need to know."

I gulped hard.

"Okay. I think I can handle that."

His eyes narrowed.

"See that you can, Piper. This pack is my family and my responsibility. I don't take it lightly." He gestured to the island chock full of food and resumed filling his platter. With a deep breath, I made my way down to join him, bending over to pick up the pieces of the shattered dish. "Leave it. Foust is a big boy. He can clean up the mess he made." He shouted for them to join us and let Foust know he'd be on cleanup duty before he got to eat anything. I was certain he'd be angry with me, but when he stood before me, he looked so contrite it was almost pitiful.

"It's okay, Foust. Really. I just...it's just that...I get a little paranoid sometimes. That was really my fault."

"It was my bad, Pepper—"

"Oh yeah!" Knox shouted, interrupting everyone. "Pepper's name is really Piper. Carry on."

Foust looked at me strangely for a second, then laughed.

"Guess I hit the nail a little too hard on the head, Piper?"

"Something like that," I mumbled, grabbing a few things from the buffet-for-giants and disappearing into the corner of the room. I dragged a seat along with me and sat cross-legged on it, balancing my plate in my lap. With my head down, I ate in relative silence, just listening to the pack. Learning their dynamics. It was important to know who they were and what they were about. I needed to know I could trust them.

Trust hadn't worked so well for me in the past. To say I was gun shy would have been an enormous understatement.

"Hey, Pepper—Piper! I meant Piper!" someone stammered as he pulled up a chair to sit next to me. I looked up to find a smiling freckled face beaming at me. "I'm Jagger. Really sorry about the mishap tonight. Totally didn't mean to stress you or anything."

"Yeah. We're good. No worries."

"Sweet. Glad to hear it. I don't want you scared off the second you show up. It's kinda nice having a chick around for once."

"That's me, the token estrogen, at your service."

His bright hazel eyes went a wee bit too wide as his mind went wild with the subtext of my statement. To his credit, he managed to rein his excitement in quickly. When he realized that I knew what he was thinking, his skin flushed as red as his disheveled hair. It was oddly endearing.

"Jagger, you're not hitting on our guest, are you?" Knox asked as he approached the blushing ginger. "Because I thought I'd made myself pretty clear—"

"We were just chatting about me crashing the bro-party you guys have going on here. I think Jagger likes the change of scenery."

"I bet he does," Knox said, staring at me with a little more heat in his gaze than I'd seen there before. "I wanted to show you around if you've had enough to eat."

"Sounds good," I said, uncrossing my legs to stand.

"I'll put that away for you," Jagger offered, taking my plate.

"Thanks."

"You ready for the dime tour?" Knox asked, ushering me through the kitchen toward a series of hallways. For what seemed like an eon, we wound our way through the massive house, finally stopping at the end of one corridor. "So, this is what I really wanted to show you." His demeanor was off for some reason. He seemed hesitant. Reaching across me, he opened the door to unveil a small, quaint room with a double bed. There was a mirror framed by an intricate pattern of antlers and a bearskin rug in the center of the floor. It looked exactly how I expected a room at a hunting lodge to look.

"It's nice. Very rustic. Very 'hunting chic'," I joked, looking up at him. His brow furrowed slightly.

"You don't like it."

"No, that's not entirely true. I think it's got a certain novelty kind of charm to it. I guess I'm just a bit uncertain why you're showing it to me."

His expression softened slightly but still held a note of seriousness.

"Earlier...when you went to leave," he started, visibly struggling to find the right words, "you stopped when you saw it was dark. I just...you didn't seem to want to leave because of it. Like it was holding you back." When I didn't respond, he rubbed his hand through his hair in frustration. "Listen, I meant it when I said I don't need to know your past. I don't, really. I just thought that maybe you'd feel better crashing here sometimes rather than staying by yourself." Still I remained silent, doing my best to keep my raging emotions in check. He took my hand gently in his and gave it a reassuring squeeze. "You looked so haunted by the darkness, Piper. All I'm trying to say is that you're not alone. That you have options. That's all. Nothing more. I promise."

My gaze drifted back to the guest room he was offering. I told myself that it was because I wanted to look it over again, but it was really to hide the tears welling in my eyes. I begged them not to fall.

"That's really sweet," I managed finally. "Really, it is—"

"But you're good on your own," he interrupted. "Wouldn't want you to have to break our 'no lying' agreement so early on, so I'll give you an out. You can just nod." I did. "So...you want me to take you home?"

No. I didn't.

I was tired of solitude. Tired of the stress living on the run had caused. The thought of relaxing for even a few hours, surrounded by a pack of werewolves with their own tarnished pasts sounded perfect.

It also sounded safe.

"Didn't you mention something about a movie after dinner?" I said, my voice still weak and small from my emotionally tight throat. Knox had the good form not to comment on it. Instead, he laughed.

"I did indeed. Let's go see if the boys are up for a little PG-rated entertainment for the evening."

IN THE WEE hours of the morning, the sun started to peek over the trees on the horizon and through the windows. The boys were strewn all about the living room: on the floor, the couches, and the chairs. I don't think there was a surface in that room not draped with werewolves. I had claimed a recliner (which seemed a bit selfish since most of the boys were nearly twice my size and crammed together wherever they could) and fallen asleep at some point, pure exhaustion taking me over. I'd been running for a couple of weeks, spending only a few hours during the day to rest. I had been long overdue for a stress-free slumber.

But my recurring dream of the boys detaining Merc ruined that in a flash. I'd had it every night since I'd escaped the mansion. Apparently a piece of my mind remained there.

Once I calmed my frantic heart, I pushed the footrest back down into the chair and gazed across the room, trying to map out a path through the sleeping werewolves. It proved a tricky task. Doing my best not to rouse any of them, I tiptoed my way through the living room and into the kitchen where I'd left my keys. Collecting them quietly, I sneaked my way to the front door, sparing a glance back at the sleeping pack. The sight made me smile. Delicately opening the door a bit, I squeezed through it, closing it behind me as quietly as possible.

Then I turned right into Knox and screamed.

"Jesus, Mary, and Joseph! You scared the shit out of me!"

"If you get scared by people standing harmlessly on a porch, I think a lot about your past is coming into focus for me." He was kidding, judging by the gigantic grin on his face. But still, there was an assessment to his gaze. "Sneaking out? You know that's not really necessary, right? The bears won't judge you for your walk of shame..."

"I was awake. I didn't want to disturb anyone, so I thought it best to just see myself out."

"And right into me."

"Apparently."

"Well, since I'm awake too, you might as well let me walk you home."

"Why are you awake, anyway?"

He shrugged.

"I like to watch the sunrise. It's kinda my thing. You?"

"My internal clock has been messed up for the last couple of weeks," I replied, squirming a bit under his heavy gaze.

"I'm not sure moving this far north in the summertime was a good choice if you're looking to get your circadian rhythm back."

"Yeah," I hesitated. "I guess I didn't really think that through."

He opened his mouth as if to say something, then slammed it shut, giving a jerk of his head toward the tree line before heading that direction.

"The bears won't likely be a problem for you between our place and yours, but I'll have the boys mark it up a bit more just to be sure."

"Mark it up?"

"Don't ask."

"I won't."

"I was wondering about something yesterday...after the grizzly incident," he started, fading off a bit as he spoke.

"About what?"

"It's really bugging me that I can't tell what you are."

"Can you always tell what type of supernatural someone is?" I asked casually.

He nodded.

"You're the first one I can't wrap my head around."

"That seems to be a common problem where I'm concerned," I replied dryly. "I don't really know how to answer that question other than to say that I'm a Magical, or so I've discerned over the years, but I don't really have any powers. Not defensive ones, or ones that I have any control over, for that matter. All the other magical groups I know of won't have anything to do with me. And the warlocks—" I cut myself short, realizing that it was far too easy to share things with Knox, and I was doing so far too freely. My loose lips were going to get me in trouble if I kept it up.

His eyes narrowed as he looked at me, halting me so he could see me better.

"The warlocks what?" he asked, his stare boring through me.

"They'd like to see me dead," I replied with a sigh.

He growled.

"Not a lie."

I shook my head. I could practically feel his desire to ask if that's who I was running from, but it seemed his demand for truth had put him in a tricky situation as well. He didn't want to back me into a corner and force me to lie when it was apparent that my past was dire indeed, and I wasn't willing to trust him with it. Not yet. Maybe not ever.

"If they come, we will protect you," he said, harshness in his tone.

Then, without another word, he started back toward the cabin.

"Will you?" I muttered under my breath, still standing where he'd left me. He stopped and turned, his piercing green eyes searching mine.

"Let me make something clear, Piper: I'm no saint. Like I said before, those of us here—in this pack—chose to come and live in the middle of nowhere for a reason. I understand what it's like to have a past that haunts me. So do the others. But I've learned from mine and have changed because of it. Become a better man, so to speak. And I have zero intention of letting anything wander into my territory and threaten anyone residing here. Do you understand?" I nodded frantically. "Good," he said with a touch more heat to his words. "Then let's get you home so that you can start putting the shit you were packing up away. You're not going anywhere,

Piper. Not until I'm confident you can defend yourself, and that's sure as hell not going to happen unless you can figure out what you are and how to use whatever powers you think you have."

Again he turned and headed through the brush toward my cabin, not waiting for my reply. In truth, he didn't need to. I didn't have one for him anyway. Instead I silently trailed him, trying to make sense of all he'd just said (and not said, for that matter). Knox had a past; I got that point loud and clear, but it left me wondering just what had happened. What had molded him into the alpha he was now. I wondered about that for the better part of an hour while we scurried around my cabin, stocking it up with the few provisions I'd gotten on my way through town. Knox had reverted back to his playful, charming self, showing no trace of the intense wolf he'd revealed to me back in the woods.

Then he left.

Not long after, I found myself standing in the tiniest kitchen I'd ever seen, hovering over the sink, trying to make sense out of all that had happened. In my attempt to tuck myself away in the middle of nowhere, far away from the reach of the supernatural world, I had managed to move in next door to a pack of werewolves. A pack of all male wolves, at that.

Well played, Piper. Well played...

I stood there for an eternity, staring out the window. Too many thoughts to count ran through my head. Could I trust these wolves? Would they turn on me as everyone else had? Was it still possible that they already knew who I was and who was after me, and were just biding their time until the enforcers could arrive and they could collect their bounty? There was a reward for my return, of that I had no doubt. Maybe the werewolves were looking to make some easy money by handing me over to the vampires hunting me. Maybe Knox's behavior was all an elaborate act, and a damn good one at that.

Every question that sprang to mind remained unresolved, leaving that annoying sense of dread to rise up within me again.

"What in the world have I gotten myself into?" I whispered aloud, clutching the worn laminate countertop tightly.

That question, too, went unanswered.

14

I spent the morning scrubbing the tiny one-bedroom cabin down from top to bottom; I doubted it had ever been so clean. It was just about noon by the time I finished. I stood in the center of the common area, scanning it to make sure I hadn't missed anything. When it was clear that there wasn't a speck of dirt to be found, I grabbed a beat-up paperback from the mantle and flopped down in the ratty old armchair.

After about ten pages, I threw the book aside.

Jumping out of my seat, I strode over to the front door and made my way out to the porch. The sky was overcast, the sun hidden from sight. The dullness looking down upon me did nothing to inspire my mood.

I picked at the long blades of grass encroaching upon the stairs, weaving them into an intricate braid. It wasn't long before I had made a length of rope out of it, which I wound around the top of my head to make a crown.

Man, was I bored.

"Does that make you Queen of the Forest?" a voice called from the tree line. I turned to find Knox standing there, his arms crossed over his chest and a wide smile on his face.

"I was just—"

"Ready to go batshit crazy without anything to do?"

"Something like that," I replied, pulling the makeshift tiara off my head. "I guess I didn't really plan ahead for this whole seclusion thing very well."

"No. I don't think you did," he agreed, making his way toward me. A slight breeze picked up when he approached, blowing his scent my way. He smelled fresh, like spring. I inhaled deeply, not realizing that I probably looked like a total spaz. His laughter let me know that I did. "I think you should leave this on," he said, taking the bright green crown from my hands and placing it on my head. "It suits you." I smiled awkwardly at him, unsure of what to say. "So listen, there's a reason I stopped by to see you."

"To check up on me?"

"Well, that too, but I wanted to see if you had any pressing plans for the evening." He managed not to laugh when he asked me that, but I could see he was fighting back the urge with great difficulty. I made a grand gesture of looking around and behind me before giving him my best "are you kidding me?" face. That seemed to push him over the edge, his laughter coming out in a sharp exhale. "I didn't want to assume," he said with a shrug, trying to regain his composure. "All joking aside, the boys and I will be heading into Anchorage tonight to blow off a little steam."

"And how do you do that exactly?"

"Ummm...we drive?"

"No, not how do you get there! What do you do once you're there?" I explained, sounding put-upon. His smile widened.

"Dinner. Clubbing. The usual."

"Like dancing?" My heart raced at the thought.

"If you want to. The boys aren't usually into that, but I'm sure we can convince them...for our guest's sake."

I wanted to scream yes, throw my arms around his neck in gratitude, then ask when we were leaving, but a niggling in the back of my brain gave me pause. I'd been played before. Not once, but twice. There were still too many unknowns regarding Knox and his pack. Too many to so easily drive off with them just because he'd asked nicely and smiled at me.

Judging by the downturn of his expression, my thoughts were playing out in my expression.

"You're still unsure about me, aren't you?"

He'd backed me into a corner with that one.

"Yes."

"You don't trust easily, do you?"

"No," I said quietly, turning my gaze to the trees surrounding the cabin.

"What is it that you think I'm going to do, Piper?" His question was much kinder that time, his tone more gentle.

I sighed heavily, knowing that lying would be of no use to me.

"I'm afraid that you have ulterior motives for being nice to me."

"Truth..." I looked back at him to see a sadness in his eyes. One that showed that he understood betrayal. "Piper," he started, taking a cautious step toward me. "I don't know that I can convince you of this, but whatever you think it is I want from you or plan to do with you, it's not the case. Wolves come to me to start over—to escape their previous lives. You may not be a wolf, but you have the same look about you that they all do when they show up on my doorstep. I've never asked anything of them other than loyalty. I don't want anything from you, Piper. I just don't want anything to happen to you." He reached his hand toward me and took mine. The second he did, the gentle breeze that had been dancing around us gusted, knocking me slightly off balance—and into Knox.

"Sorry!" I said, trying to push myself off of him.

"For thinking I have some maniacal plans for you or for falling into me?"

I hesitated slightly.

"Both?"

He looked down at me and smiled.

"You're forgiven. So will you come with us tonight?"

It was my turn to grin.

"I guess I could be persuaded."

"We're getting ready for lunch now if you want to join us. Bring whatever you're going to wear tonight with you. You can get ready at our place, unless running water doesn't appeal to you."

"I'll be right back!" I shouted, running into my cabin to grab my things. Truth was, I didn't have a whole lot of wardrobe options, so I settled on some skinny jeans and a white tank. I grabbed the necklace that Kat had given me for Christmas and my favorite boots—the ones I was wearing the night Merc attacked me. I loved them despite that connection. The dark blemishes in the leather from the bloodstains I couldn't get out reminded me of why I was running.

I snatched a tiny bag containing the few toiletries and makeup items I owned and made my way back outside to find Knox standing there, a look of amusement in his eyes.

"That was fast."

"I'm a low maintenance kinda girl."

"Just the way I like 'em," he replied, turning to lead the way back to the house. "Want me to carry anything?"

Before I could tell him no thank you, he took the boots that were awkwardly balanced on top of my things from me. He spotted the muddy-brown stains in the cognac-colored leather immediately. Not asking for confirmation, he put the toe of one boot to his nose and sniffed it. Then his angry eyes fell on mine.

"That's a lot of blood, Piper."

"I know."

"*Your* blood."

"I know."

"This wouldn't have anything to do with why you're here, would it?"

"Does it make a difference if it does?" I asked earnestly, not really wanting to delve into my sordid history.

"No," he replied, his jaw flexing hard to retain his anger. "I guess it doesn't."

We walked the rest of the way to the lodge in silence, me wondering what he was thinking and him likely questioning the wisdom of harboring someone with a bloodstained past. I was almost certain that it wasn't a love of Alaska's isolation that had brought him here.

It certainly wasn't what had brought me either.

When we got to the lodge, Knox's mood changed, returning to the more fun-loving wolf that I had found him to be. Strict with his pack, but affable. Approachable. Kind.

I ate with the boys, then excused myself to go clean up. The warm water of the shower beat against my skin. It felt amazing. It had been a couple of days since I'd felt that and not been afraid to stay in too long. Knowing that I was surrounded by a pack of werewolves and enough sun in the sky to ensure no surprise vampire visits helped immensely. But then my eyes made their way down my body to take in my scars, and I quickly turned the water off.

The shower didn't seem so enjoyable anymore.

Knox knocked on the door while I was toweling my hair dry, letting me know that we were packing up to leave in about half an hour. I rushed to get ready, then made my way out to the living room where the others were waiting. They all stood when I walked into the room.

"Shall we?" Knox asked, extending his hand toward me.

I took a deep breath.

"Let's go."

***

They had a convoy of Suburban trucks to drive into the city: seven, to be exact. I got into the front seat beside Knox, wondering precisely what it was that I'd gotten myself into. A night on the town would have normally sounded great, but it would have also involved Jase and Dean and a familiar setting. That night, I was without all three.

But I was willing to bet that I was safer making the journey to Anchorage with Knox than in my tiny cabin alone all night, so I took that chance. I'd been wrong about both Kingston and Merc, but something told me that the third time would be the charm. Knox and his pack had done nothing but welcome me with open arms and all but taken me in. Something about being with them reminded me of being with Jase and Dean.

And they'd never betrayed me either.

"Seat belt," Knox said, putting the vehicle into drive. I eyed him strangely. "Safety first. Accidents don't take vacations."

I laughed out loud. How could I not with such a ridiculous sentiment from a virtually immortal werewolf?

"I'll keep that in mind," I replied, buckling up.

"It's about a five-hour trip, so if you're tired, feel free to knock off for a bit. We'll grab dinner when we get there and then hit the club."

"And all the fine pieces of ass we can find there," one of the guys in the back shouted out, earning him a few high fives from the others around him.

"Way to keep it classy, Brunton," Knox sighed, pinching the bridge of his nose.

"Did I miss something?" I asked.

"Kind of," he replied tensely. "There's really no tasteful way to put this, so I'm just going to lay it out there for you with my apologies first. We're going into town so the boys can get laid."

"Oh."

"It's the full moon," he said, as though that were explanation enough. Apparently I didn't know enough werewolves for it to make much sense to me. Kat and Jensen went at it constantly, regardless of which phase the moon was in. When I didn't respond, Knox elaborated. "It sort of brings out our more...*carnal* qualities."

"He means fucking and fighting," Brunton called out from the back.

"Got it."

"The boys get a little antsy. They need one or the other, so we do this little pilgrimage every time the full moon hits so they can—"

"Scratch that particular itch?" I interjected.

"Exactly. Otherwise, I'd probably have a bloodbath on my hands at the lodge."

"You keep saying 'they' as though you're excluded from this dilemma," I noted, keeping my eyes on the road ahead.

"Normally I'd partake in the festivities," he replied tightly.

"And tonight?"

"Tonight I'm going to let them have their fun and keep you company. It'll be entertaining to watch. We can just sit back and let the shenanigans unfold."

"Sounds promising."

He turned a wicked smile to me.

"You have no idea."

THE DRIVE WENT by surprisingly fast. The banter amongst the pack was entertaining. I learned a lot about outings past. Arrests. Fights. Boyfriends showing up at inopportune times. It was all very scandalous and fascinating. I also learned a bit more about the guys in our particular car: where they were from, how they came to be with Knox, and how long they'd been there. Some of the responses were shocking indeed.

"Wait a minute, you're how old?" I asked incredulously, staring over my shoulder at Jagger, who was sitting directly behind me.

"Ninety-seven. Just like I said."

"But you look eighteen!"

He shrugged.

"It's one of the perks. And I was twenty-five when I was Changed, thank you very much. Don't hate on my boyish good looks."

"I wouldn't dare," I gasped in jest. "I guess it never ceases to amaze me that some supernaturals never age."

"Have you not been around many?" Knox asked.

"I...I have." I stopped myself from elaborating, not wanting to get caught in a lie. I also needed to maintain a certain distance from the pack when it came to my past. I couldn't let them know too much. It was better for all of us that way.

"You're getting better at this already," Knox said with a laugh. "Your evasive truths seem to have become second nature overnight."

"You set up the rules. I found a way to follow them."

"Clever girl," he muttered under his breath.

I smiled.

As promised, we went for a quick bite to eat before going to the club that would be the hunting ground, so to speak, for the pack for the evening. And those boys were efficient hunters. We couldn't have been in there for more than ten, maybe twenty minutes before a solid fifteen of them had claimed their bedroom buddy for the evening. A few of those didn't even bother trying to woo their choices; they just walked out of the bar with their prey on their arms, smiling like foxes in the henhouse.

"Where are they going?" I asked Knox as he handed me a gin and tonic.

"The hotel next door," he shouted over the music.

"Convenient."

"Very."

He indicated a booth-like seating area near the back and ushered me through the masses, reaching back to take my hand. He navigated the crowd with ease, and I soon found myself tucked into the corner of the padded bench seat, surrounded by werewolves on the prowl.

The bass was pounding through the speakers at a punishing volume, but it felt good. Familiar. It made me want to go dance like I used to with my boys back in NYC. So, with a few big gulps of my drink, I slammed the glass down on the table and climbed over the guys to head to the dance floor. There was no shortage of entertaining comments along the way, but the sheer volume of the music soon drowned them out. Once I was on the main dance floor, I didn't care anymore. I felt carefree for the first time since I'd run from the mansion.

Since I'd run from Merc.

15

I'd been dancing so hard, I was sweating like a maniac. Unlike every other girl in the club, I wasn't wearing shorts that looked like underwear or a skirt that required one of those TV blackout bars every time the wearer sat down or bent over. Even though it was summer, I wore nothing but jeans. Even with the lightweight tank top I was wearing, I was just too hot. I needed water ASAP.

I fought my way through the dance floor, headed toward the bar. My path was thick with bodies, and I completely lacked Knox's gift for seamlessly navigating them. It helped that he had about a hundred pounds and about ten inches of height on me. I was hardly intimidating. By the time I squeezed my way through, sweat was trickling down the side of my face. I wiped it off with my hand and rubbed it on my jeans while I waited for the bartender to come my way.

I surveyed the club-goers, scanning the room from the raised bar area. I spotted a few of the wolves getting cozy with their soon-to-be conquests, and it oddly made me laugh. Those girls had no idea what they were in for. The boys were going to ruin human sex for them for the rest of their lives.

Once you go supernatural, you never go back, or so I'd heard. I was pretty set on never going back. But when my eyes landed upon a familiar face, I wasn't so certain that would even be an issue.

Being dead seemed much more likely.

I could literally feel the blood drain from my face as I watched one of the warlocks that had decided to use me as a bonfire stroll through the front entrance. His dark eyes narrowed, he searched the club for something, or more likely, someone. Monroe might not have been the head of the rogue warlocks, but he was high up the chain, and I highly doubted it was a coincidence that he was there. I needed to escape, and fast. But my feet wouldn't move.

"No, no, no, no, no," I repeated to myself, watching him stalk closer to me. He had yet to see me, but where I was standing, it wouldn't take long. I had to hide.

I bolted out of the bar area, knocking into everyone I encountered along the way. I knew there was an emergency exit at the back. I'd become an expert at casing a place for all points of egress since I'd fled New York. If I could make it there in time, then I'd have a chance.

With my heart in my stomach, I continued on, hoping that my frantic escape wasn't drawing too much attention. Just as I was about to smash into the push bar on the emergency door, a hand caught my arm.

"Piper?" Foust yelled over the throbbing bass. The sheer panic in my expression told him all he needed to know. "How many?"

"Only one."

"I'm getting Knox."

With my arm still captive, he nearly dragged me back to

the booth we'd been occupying earlier. There sat Knox, all alone.

"We've got a situation," Foust said, his tone all business. Knox followed Foust's gaze as it turned to me, and his features hardened. "She said there's only one."

"One what?"

"Warlock," I said, looking around for Monroe. When I finally found him, he was staring at me from across the dance floor. Instinctively, I tried to wrench my arm out of Foust's grip. I needed to get away from Monroe at all costs, and standing around discussing his impending attack wasn't helping.

Knox didn't reply. Instead, I heard a very distinct growl come from his direction. It was enough to drag my attention away from my would-be attacker. The alpha looked at me with eyes lit with a glowing shade of amber. His wolf was coming out.

"Not here," I said, knowing full well that if an incident were to occur, it would draw the attention of the supernatural community, even as far as NYC. I didn't need a clean-up crew to be sent this way. If anyone that knew me was dispatched here and they caught my scent in the building, I'd be sunk. "I need to get away from here. Far away. Now! Will you help me?"

His answer came in the form of me being thrown over his shoulder and raced out the back door of the club, which set off the emergency alarm. Panic ensued inside, creating what I hoped would be (and Knox had likely planned to be) a diversion that would slow Monroe down, if only a little. Outside, Knox continued to run with me balanced over his shoulder. I looked up to see Foust tight on our heels.

"The plan?" he shouted up to his alpha.

"I'm taking her back tonight. You stay here. Round up

the boys and take care of the problem. And be careful," he warned. "Warlocks can be tricky."

"Got it," Foust replied, pulling his cell from his pocket while running. He started barking orders at whoever was on the line, putting Knox's plan in motion.

In no time at all, we arrived at the cluster of black Suburbans in the parking lot down the block. Knox tossed me into the passenger side and slammed the door, jumping the hood to get to the driver's side. He said something to Foust that I couldn't hear, then they both shot me a wayward glance before Knox jumped in and Foust took off back toward the club.

"Seat belt," Knox said tersely, firing up the vehicle. Before I could comply, he tore out of the parking spot in reverse, then slammed the car into drive and peeled out of the lot, turning into the main road without even pausing. He ran red lights, broke the speed limit by double digits, and muttered under his breath the entire time about fucking warlocks. It seemed that maybe I wasn't the only one who had a severe distaste for them.

Driving in silence, we left the lights of the city behind us, the stars growing in number as we put distance between danger and us. I stared out the passenger window and contemplated the implications of Monroe being at the club that night. None set me at ease.

"Did he see you?" Knox asked, startling me from my ruminations.

"Yes."

"Can he track you?"

"I have no idea," I replied sullenly. "But I don't think it was a coincidence that one of the warlocks who wants me dead just happened to be at a nightclub in Anchorage."

"Yeah. That's seems a bit of a stretch."

Again silence permeated the vehicle, the hum of the car on the road the only sound to be heard. I knew Knox had to be wondering what he'd gotten himself into when he'd befriended me—offered me protection of sorts. He had no idea what kind of trouble I could bring to his doorstep. And now, having had just a glimpse of it, I wondered just how quickly he would rid himself of the problem I proved to be.

"Why don't you get some rest," he said softly. "I'll wake you when we get there."

My eyelids were already heavy, the rush of adrenaline long gone, leaving me with only exhaustion and fear. Exhaustion was winning out, though I tried to resist sleep's call. Finally I gave in, resting my head against the window, the darkness of midnight and me separated only by the thin pane of glass.

But what, I wondered, would separate the creatures of that darkness and me? What, if anything, could keep them away? Those once sworn to protect me had become the very creatures hunting me, and they were not alone in that endeavor--Monroe's presence in the club was proof of that. I could not depend on others to keep me alive. Not anymore. The illusion of safety that had lulled me so sweetly was a dangerous mirage that, if I let it, would lead only to death. I would then bring that death upon the pack trying to protect me from it, and I couldn't accept that fate. I needed to change it.

As my mind drifted off to the sweet place between wakefulness and slumber, it became clear what I needed to do.

※

I SAW MERC THAT NIGHT.

Unlike all the nights previous, this time it was not a

repeat of the attack and my subsequent escape—the brothers holding Merc back like the wild animal he'd become. The crazed killer he was notorious for being. Instead, it had morphed somehow. Jase and Dean were both there restraining him, but he was not at the staircase as expected. This time he was in his bed, the two of them pinning him down as he bucked wildly against them.

"We'll find her," Jase ground out, working hard to subdue him.

Merc shot him a murderous look but said nothing. Nothing I could hear.

"Then I guess we need to get to her first," Dean said as calmly as he could while straining to hold Merc's legs down.

"Don't worry. She'll believe us. She trusts us," Jase added, his tone placating. Merc relaxed back into the bed, if only slightly. "You'll see her again soon."

※

I STARTLED AWAKE, my mind sorting through what I'd just seen and heard. It was a dream, I knew that in my head, but in my heart it felt so real. So true. My paranoia was ramping up with the recent events in Anchorage.

I wondered when it would finally push reason aside and completely take over.

Taking a breath to calm myself, I let my gaze drift over to Knox, who still looked as tense as he had when we'd first sped away from the club. His white-knuckle grip on the wheel hadn't changed.

"We're almost home," he said, staring out at the rising sun. Then he fell silent again.

After a moment or two, I straightened myself up in my seat and smoothed out my clothes.

"I have to thank you for—"

"Don't thank me yet. We're not sure we're in the clear."

I winced at the reality in his words.

"Well, I likely wouldn't be alive at the moment if it weren't for your help, so just in case we aren't in the clear, I want to thank you for getting me this far."

I saw the slightest curl form at the corner of his mouth.

"You really can circumvent the rules, can't you, Piper?"

A small smile tugged at my lips as well.

"When you're not powerful or strong, you learn to adapt other qualities that are useful in our world."

"How do you know you're not powerful?" he asked earnestly.

I deflated back into the car seat.

"Because I wouldn't be running if I was..."

"Maybe you just haven't figured out how to work your magic yet. That happens sometimes, you know? Powers don't always come right away. Sometimes they show up when you need them most."

I thought about how I'd narrowly survived Merc's attack on me at the mansion. How I wouldn't likely have lived if it weren't for reaching the outdoors. I'd definitely needed my magic then, and it had come. Nature and I were connected somehow, as was the case with most magical beings, but for me, it seemed as though she gave to me as she saw fit. That I couldn't call power from her at will. That hardly made me a force to be reckoned with. I sounded like someone who could barely scrape by, magically speaking.

"Oh, they come to me when I need them most," I countered, bitterness in my tone. "And then they bugger off, leaving me to be a defenseless twit. I hate it. I hate being this way."

"Then change," he said. "Learn. Train. Not all supernaturals wake up one day with unlimited powers. Some have to work to achieve what they have; your warlock buddies are no exception to that rule."

"And who will train me, hmm? The fey that laughed in my face when I was a child, their own king and queen casting me out? The witches? No, I don't think so. Those bitches are evil, despite their best efforts to appear good. And I think we've established why I haven't turned to the warlocks for help."

His jaw tensed as he listened to me, my anger fueling his own.

"So you've been on your own since childhood? You've been running that long?" he asked as we pulled into the long, winding driveway of his property.

"No. Not exactly."

"Where were you before you came here?"

"Seattle."

"Half truth," he observed, shooting me a disapproving glance.

"Fine. New York. I originally came from New York City."

"Better." He parked the SUV by the house and I jumped out, wanting to run into the house without further interrogation. Knox, on the other hand, had something else in mind. He caught my arm as I rounded the vehicle, holding me in place. He stared at me for a moment before letting me go. I stormed up the front steps and into the lodge, running to the bathroom to hole up for a while. It was the only place I could be alone other than my cabin.

And I had no plans to head back there right away. I was way too spooked.

Knox was kind enough to leave me alone, but I knew I couldn't stay in there forever. Eventually I emerged from the bathroom to find him in the kitchen, making some very early morning breakfast. I walked past the island toward the living room and the biggest sofa it boasted, inelegantly plopping myself down on it. I propped my elbows on my knees and dropped my head into my hands. I needed to think. I needed a plan.

The unmistakable sound of a chair dragging on hardwood pulled me from my thoughts, and I looked up to see Knox sitting directly in front of me, mimicking my posture. There was a weariness to his expression that looked wrong on him. I didn't like seeing it.

"Piper," he said with an exhausted sigh, "I really think now might be a good time for you to tell me about your past. If not for you, then for my boys. I need to know what we might be up against. A warlock here and there is nothing to stress over, but if it's something else—something bigger than that—I really need to know. The sooner the better." He reached across the narrow divide between us and took my hand in his. "You can trust me. You can trust all of us."

"That word," I muttered to myself. "I can't. I'm so sorry, but I can't."

His eyes saddened.

"Who betrayed you, Piper? Who turned you into this scared shell of a being?"

"No one," I replied, pulling my hand away from him. "This is just me, take it or leave it."

"Lie," he said sharply before softening his tone. Then he took my hand again and wouldn't let it go. "And I'm not leaving it. You need to eat something. The boys should be back soon—once they're done dealing with the warlock. Let's enjoy the quiet while we still have it."

I nodded tightly, wrapping my free arm around my waist. Around my scars. They were my armor—my reminder. I'd dropped my guard over my time with the vampires, taking down the protective walls I'd erected over the years, and it had nearly gotten me killed. I couldn't afford to get too close to Knox and his pack. I wouldn't survive another betrayal.

"I think I'm going to head to the cabin," I said weakly, trying unsuccessfully to free my hand from his hold.

"You do that a lot," he said, eyeing the arm wound around my midsection. "It's like it's your tell."

"I'm just tired. It's been a crazy night."

"You just slept for five hours."

"And yet I'm still tired. Sue me."

His eyes narrowed.

"You're pushing me away," he said shrewdly. "I want to know why." He let go of my hand.

"I'll see you tomorrow," I replied absentmindedly, turning to walk to the front door. I'd almost made it there, but the low growling sound coming from behind me cut me short.

"*Lie*."

Shit.

"You're paranoid, Knox. Go eat. Sleep. It might do you some good."

With a steadying breath, I continued through the foyer to the double entry doors. Knox made no move to stop me. I turned the handle and pulled my way to near freedom.

"They'll find you eventually, Piper. It would be better if you aren't alone when they do," he said, a certain sadness tainting his words.

"You're wrong." I weakly tossed the words over my shoulder. Even I knew they weren't true. But Knox was wrong about one thing; it would be better if I were alone when I was found.

He had no clue what was really hunting me.

16

To my surprise, Knox didn't follow me. I'd expected him to come storming out of the lodge, telling me that I was acting foolish and that I had a death wish. Instead, he let the quiet sounds of nature alone escort me back to my cabin. Unfortunately for me, they were drowned out by the voices in my head telling me that he was right.

I pushed my way through the dense forest that separated our two properties, all the while trying to convince myself that running was best. But with every step I took, I became less certain of that. I *was* weak. I *did* need others to protect me.

And I hated myself for it.

The sun was beaming on the front porch of the cabin, welcoming me home. I perched myself on the second step and stared at the beauty surrounding me, wondering what it would be like to actually get to stay in such a glorious place. A place I felt so grounded by and connected to. The sensation had been missing in New York, with very rare exceptions. The woods around the mansion felt like home, even though they shouldn't have. I was a city girl to the core, or so I thought. But nature was about to teach me otherwise.

I soon realized I was not alone.

Whipping around on the step, I saw a furry face peeking at me from around the corner of the house. A bear. Another fucking bear. It was exactly what I didn't need.

Once I spotted him, he came out from his hiding spot, slowly ambling around the porch toward me. I could feel my anxiety rising, but I didn't move. Not because I was paralyzed by fear, but because I knew him. It was the bear that had startled me by the waterfall. I don't know how I knew it, but I did.

And he seemed to know me too.

He eyed me with acknowledgment, stopping just feet short of me. Then, awkwardly, he sat down, which made him look ridiculous. It was such a human gesture that I actually giggled out loud, my nerves getting the best of me. He snorted loudly then stood up again.

"I'm sorry. I didn't mean to laugh," I said aloud. He cocked his head at a funny angle, as if he were contemplating my apology, then sat down again. My heart skipped a beat. He understood me.

Now, in all my time spent immersed in the supernatural, I'd never once heard of a werebear, so I knew that wasn't the case. No, this was a regular old bear sitting before me, looking like he was trying to have a conversation. It was beyond strange. Thoughts and questions raced through my mind so quickly that I couldn't seem to grab hold of anything concrete. Unable to think clearly, my instincts took over.

Those instincts drove me to my feet and led me over to the bear without caution. By the time my rational thought caught up, I was running my hands through his thick fur.

The rumble of his chest beneath my hand made me jerk away from him, falling backward with a yelp. Within seconds, the grizzly was towering over me.

"Step away, please," I said, mustering every ounce of calm I could.

He backed up enough to let me up.

I scrambled to stand up but never got the chance. The crunching sound of brush breaking behind me drew the bear's attention. I looked back, wondering if Monroe had indeed found me. I wasn't sure that my bear buddy and I were going to be much of a match for him. Luckily, it wasn't the warlock that came crashing through the tree line.

Knox stood there, breathing hard, his naked chest cut and bleeding, though healing right before my eyes. The predatory growl that escaped him shook the ground I was still sprawled out across. Judging by the way my new grizzly friend pawed and stomped at the earth, he wasn't a fan of the werewolf. Grizz quickly moved to hover over me.

To him, Knox was the threat.

"Shit," I muttered as I tried to wiggle out from under the massive bear without getting accidentally stomped in the process. "Knox!" I yelled, the bear's mass muting my voice a little. "Don't charge him. He's not hurting me. He thinks you're the predator here. Just take a step back and chill for a minute."

I couldn't see Knox, but I knew he'd done as I'd asked, because the bear relaxed a bit. I could feel his body ease.

"It's okay, big guy. He's a friend." The bear roared loudly in disagreement. "No, he really is," I argued, finally getting my footing so I could stand beside the massive grizzly. "Watch. I'll show you." I took a few steps toward Knox, only to be cut off by the giant brown ball of fur. His chocolate eyes stared deep into mine as though he were assessing my mental state. "Everything will be fine. I promise," I told him, gently resting my hand on his head. "He won't hurt me." The bear snorted his objection, but backed up a few steps to let me by. I could feel his eyes on my back as I moved toward the werewolf. "Knox," I said softly. "Don't move."

"New friend of yours?" he asked sardonically.

"Apparently."

"You didn't seem too cozy the other day."

"We appear to have worked things out a bit since then."

"So I see..."

When I reached Knox, I stood in front of him, turning my back on him to face the pissed-off grizzly bear. He was anxiously waiting for the wolf to make a wrong move.

"See? He's my friend. No problems with the werewolf. Okay?" The bear sat down on his haunches with a harrumph. "Now, Knox...I think you should apologize to my new friend."

He looked at me like I had three heads.

"Yeah, I think I'll pass on that."

"Alphas don't apologize?" I said, baiting him.

"Not to ordinary bears. Besides, I'd rather figure out what the fuck just happened here. Are you some kind of bear charmer in your free time?"

I laughed.

"Nope. This is my first bear charming to date."

"Interesting," he replied, losing his sarcasm. "Well, if you don't need me, I'll just head back."

He started off into the woods, not giving me a chance to apologize for how I'd left the house.

"Knox! I'm sorry," I yelled after him. The crunching of pine needles and branches stopped. "I don't know how to explain this gracefully, so I'm just going to say it; I'm a danger magnet. Trouble finds me regardless of what I do, and I have no way to combat it. I hate that about myself more than anything. And I don't want to get you or your boys hurt in the crossfire of a battle you don't need to fight."

He emerged from the woods, an intense expression on his face.

"What if I want to fight it? What if I want to be in the crossfire?"

I exhaled heavily.

"You don't know what you're volunteering for."

"Who cares? I like danger, Piper. A lot. Maybe too much."

"But why would you want to throw yourself into a war for me? You barely know me. It makes no sense."

"It doesn't have to," he said coolly. "And you're far from helpless, Piper. You just don't realize it." His expression tightened slightly before continuing. "You have power; I'd venture to say a fair amount of it too. And if today doesn't make you see that, I don't know what will."

I looked back at Grizz, still sitting in my front yard, waiting for me.

"I don't think my Dr. Dolittle routine is going to save my ass, Knox. I'd hardly call that a power. A cool party trick, maybe, but not a power."

"That's part of your problem, Piper. You don't see things for what they are."

"I can't fight warlocks with bears," I pointed out sarcastically.

"I'm not saying you should."

"Then what are you saying, because I'm clearly missing something here..."

"I'm saying that you're deeply connected to the creatures around you. You shouldn't ignore that."

"Creature," I pointed out. "Singular."

He frowned instantly. Taking a step closer to me, he put his hand gently on my face.

"No, Piper. *Creatures*. Plural." That hand lingered on my cheek, sliding down it lightly, circling the angle of my jaw. "I feel it," he said, low and soft. "We all do."

"Oh," I whispered, my heart suddenly racing.

"We'll stand with you, Piper. Come what may, we'll stand with you."

"You wouldn't say that if you knew—" I cut myself off, reminding myself that the less he knew, the better.

"Well, I'm saying it anyway." I could feel the tickle of his breath on my face; my eyes closed instinctively. "Stay," he whispered, his body pressing nearer to mine. "I know you want to run, Piper. But I'm asking you to stay." His hand reached up, grazing my waist, and I jumped away from him, wrapping my hand around my midsection. Grizz was at my side, growling, in a matter of seconds. "I'm sorry, I didn't mean to—"

"It's fine," I interrupted, feeling a mess of emotions all at once. "I need some space. I need to think about this. Whatever I decide, I'll let you know. Okay?" I retreated from him as I spoke, my stomach guarded by my arms the entire time. The bear remained at my side while I walked backward toward the cabin.

Knox opened his mouth to speak, then snapped it shut, giving a half nod before disappearing into the trees again. His expression haunted me. The sadness in his eyes—the empty, dejected stare they'd held—dominated my thoughts. I'd turned on him so quickly and unfairly. He didn't know what he'd done, and that fact clearly pained him. But all I could think about when he'd laid his hand innocently on my body was how wrong things had gone the last two times I'd let my walls down with another being. How quickly things had gone awry. I was starting to really trust Knox, even against my better judgment, but letting him close to me like I had Kingston or Merc was out of the question. I'd narrowly survived both of them. I didn't dare put myself in a position where I'd be forced to survive Knox. If I were to stay and take him up on his offer of refuge, even for a short while, then I would need to maintain an emotional distance from him and the rest of the pack. That was the only way it could work for me. An arm's length friendship was all I could offer.

Hopefully that would suffice.

I was halfway up the porch steps when I heard Knox shouting for me. He barreled into the yard, a look of horror on his face.

"What's wrong?" I asked, hurrying down to meet him.

He never replied.

For the second time in less than twenty-four hours, Knox threw me over his shoulder and took off at a sprint. This time, he was headed for the lodge. As we neared it, I could hear the boys shouting, Foust barking orders at everyone. Something was wrong. I could feel it. Whatever had happened in Anchorage, it wasn't good.

When we arrived at the lodge, I saw firsthand just how bad it was.

I'D NEVER BEEN a part of such chaos before, and I felt utterly useless. The boys were yanking bodies from the line of SUVs parked in front of the lodge and carrying them into the house. And there were a lot of them (bodies, that is).

Knox and Foust were ordering the others around, but their words were choked off by the mounting grief within me. It blocked out virtually everything. I stood in the middle of the melee, staring at them as they scurried around like frantic bees diving in and out of their nest. I didn't hear what had happened to them in Anchorage, didn't hear how they'd escaped. I didn't know if anyone had been left behind. All I heard was the pounding of my heart in my chest echoing up through my ears.

I had no idea how long Knox had been yelling my name until he grabbed my arm and wheeled me around to look at him.

"Piper! We need you!" he said tersely, not awaiting my response. Instead, he started ushering me toward the lodge. At that point all the others were inside doing God only knew what to save God only knew how many. But I would soon learn just how great that number was.

Soon I would witness the carnage I had brought upon them.

The second we broke through the front door into the foyer, it all hit me. The living room looked like a makeshift triage unit, bloodied bodies strewn about on multiple surfaces. Those not injured raced around assessing their fallen brothers to see who was most in need of help. Knox ran in to grab medical supplies and brought them back to me, forcing them into my hands.

"Can you take care of the two in the corner?" he asked, pointing to two of his pack members I didn't really know. "They're not in too bad of shape. They just need to be cleaned out before they can start healing."

Start healing, I thought to myself. And then it dawned on me why this scenario was so outside the realm of possibility for me. They were all werewolves, strong and powerful and capable of healing injuries almost effortlessly. Just earlier I'd seen Knox's cuts all but disappear from his body before my very eyes. Why then was his pack not only wounded, but unable to heal during the long car ride back to the middle of nowhere?

I nodded to Knox that I could do as he asked.

Satisfied with that response, he made his way over to the far side of the room where two of his pack members were laid out on the kitchen island. I hadn't seen them taken out of the SUVs when they'd returned. I knew that for fact because I would have remembered that sight. It would have struck an undeniable chord.

Both men were charred beyond recognition.

Swallowing the rising bile in my throat, I turned away from the macabre view and did as Knox had requested; I went to the boys with minor injuries and helped to clean them up. One had a deep gash in his arm, most likely from a magical blade. The other had a similar injury across his back. Both were starting to heal, evidenced by the tender pink flesh surrounding the wounds. But they both mentioned something about infection—silver—so I did as I was asked and flushed out the open area as best I could with a bottle of some concoction Knox had given me and then bandaged them up. Once I finished with them, I wandered around the room, helping out wherever I could. By then, the unmistakable stench of burnt flesh and hair had coated my nostrils. It was inescapable, as were the memories the familiar scent gave rise to.

I instinctively clutched my stomach, rubbing the scars I bore—the scars given to me by the very same group that had attacked us in Anchorage. That thought made me keenly aware of something that, in all the chaos, I hadn't yet considered. Warlocks were powerful, Monroe especially, but even he alone couldn't have inflicted that much damage to an entire pack of werewolves. My blood ran cold at the thought. He hadn't been a scout. I'd been ambushed by the warlocks yet again.

Only this time it wasn't me who'd paid the price.

I rose slowly from my crouched position next to one of the wounded wolves, scanning the room for Foust. When I found him, he was standing next to the kitchen island, covering one of the bodies with a sheet, head and all.

"How many?" I asked, my voice too quiet for even the werewolves surrounding me to notice amid the ruckus. "Foust!" I shouted, garnering his attention, along with his irritation. It would seem that he too blamed me for what had happened. By the end of the day, I expected that count to rise considerably. "How many were there?"

"Casualties?"

"No. Warlocks."

His brow furrowed at the mention of the enemy. Then his gaze fell to Knox, silently asking permission to discuss the matter with me. One nod from his alpha was all it took.

"At first, there was only the one in the club. By the time I'd gotten back there to inform the others about what was going on, he was already making a break for it down an adjacent alley. While I followed him, I called Jagger and told him to get as many of the pack as he could quickly find and follow my scent—that I was tracking the warlock after Piper. It didn't take long for them to catch up to me, right about the time I had that fucker cornered in a dead end," he explained, his jaw flexing hard as he tried to restrain the anger he felt, recalling the events that had happened. "He should have been shitting bricks, one lowly warlock against a dozen or more wolves. He was a dead man walking. But the way he looked at me—the smug grin that spread to an evil smile—I should have known something was up. That there was more going on than I realized. And that's when everything went to shit."

"There were more of them," I added, knowing how Kingston's crew operated. They weren't known for playing fair. For a clean fight. Those concepts were foreign to them.

Foust nodded sharply, acknowledging my observation.

"A lot more of them. They came out of nowhere behind us. It was an ambush, and we were caught in the crossfire. Literally."

I hadn't realized that I'd been walking toward Foust as he spoke, the fear and desperation I felt carrying me.

"How did you get away?"

"We took out as many of them as we could, then we got the fuck out of there before any more of us got fried or sliced." He looked at me thoughtfully for a moment before continuing. "If that's who you've been running from, Piper, I can understand why. They're no joke."

"I know."

"You should have called me. I would have come," Knox growled, though his anger was not truly at Foust. He was frustrated with himself. Mad that he had failed his pack.

"I gladly would have if one single cell phone had survived the fight, but none did. And I sure as fuck wasn't going to hang out and search the area for one with flying balls of fire whizzing past my head every five seconds."

"The fire," I whispered, staring at Foust. "Was it blue?"

"What?"

"The fire that you were attacked with, was it blue?"

"Yes," Foust growled.

My face went pale.

"Did you see who attacked you with it?"

Another growl, this time from the entire pack.

"Yes," Foust said, stepping closer to me. "A hand-less

cowardly motherfucker that ran away through some kind of black vortex and left his brothers to die."

"Kingston," I exhaled, not realizing his name had passed my lips until I heard it ring through the room that had fallen silent. "I'm so sorry. I'm so sorry this happened. This is my fault. All of it. Your blood is on my hands."

I looked to Knox, not realizing that he was staring at me. His expression was dark and unreadable. Tears stained my cheeks, but I quickly wiped them away. It was not time for my weakness. It was time to prove that their sacrifice meant something. I would not see any others fall because of me.

I turned and went back to the wounded wolves, helping however and wherever I could. It seemed as though very few made it out relatively unscathed. While I worked, I finally came upon Jagger, whose hands were scorched from trying to save one of his packmates. They had already been cleansed since arriving at the house and were healing, but the gaping wound in his leg had not. I tended to the gash in his thigh, keeping my eyes low and focused. I was too ashamed to meet his gaze.

"I know you blame yourself, Piper," he said softly, wincing a bit when I doused his leg with the liquid from the bottle Knox had given me. "But you shouldn't. After the night we met you, Knox explained that he knew something was after you. Hell, Foust pegged you for a runaway after being around you for five minutes." I dared to sneak a look at his face. All I found in his expression was compassion. "Anyway, Knox told us his suspicions and made it clear that he was willing to do anything he could to keep you safe, but allowed the rest of us that choice for ourselves. But don't say anything to him about that. He'd deny it. He's a tough guy, but he's not unreasonable. In some matters, he lets us have a choice."

"And what did you choose?" I asked, my hands lingering on Jagger's thigh, holding a bandage in place to be wrapped.

He shrugged.

"Look around, Piper. Isn't it obvious what we chose?"

"All of you? All of you chose to be part of this fight? A fight that isn't yours? Against unknown enemies?" He nodded. "Why? Why would you ever agree to something so insane?"

"Because it's been a long time since any one of us has had something worth fighting for."

My eyes dropped to the floor.

"If you knew me—really knew me—you wouldn't think that."

"We don't need to think, Piper. Not about this. We work on instinct. That's our gift and our curse. And our collective instincts said that we needed to protect you. At least until you can protect yourself." I tied off the bandage and stood on shaky legs. "That's not really going to be necessary," he said, unwrapping what I'd just tied up. "Now that we're near Knox, we'll heal up in no time."

"What?" I asked absentmindedly, scanning the room to find evidence that supported his words.

"We needed to be cleaned out first, of course. Magical wounds are infections waiting to happen—and don't even get me started on silver wounds—but once they're flushed clean and we have Knox's power to draw on, we're good to go."

I turned to the kitchen again, only to find that the other wolf on the island was now covered with a sheet as well. Two fatalities. Apparently Jagger's little theory was more complicated than he'd let on.

"They don't seem so good to go," I said, staring at the dead.

"Their injuries were far worse than the rest of ours," he said solemnly. "We had limited supplies in the SUVs and we lost too much time on the ride home to save them. If Knox had been there, they would have pulled through. But...he wasn't, so..."

"Now they're dead." I finished his sentence for him.

"It's still not your fault, Piper," he reaffirmed, putting his hand on my shoulder. I shrugged it off and walked away from him. I couldn't bear to see the earnestness in his eyes. He really meant what he'd said, and yet somehow that made his sentiment all the worse.

"The hell it isn't," I muttered under my breath, walking off toward the hallway that led back to the living quarters of the lodge. Before I could escape there, Knox cut me off, stepping directly in my path.

"I need to talk to the pack for a bit, but I don't want you going home. Not until I know more. Why don't you go get that rest you were so desperate for earlier, and I'll come get you when we're done."

Looking over my shoulder to the room full of healing wolves, I sighed and nodded. Unable to meet Knox's eyes, I brushed past him and made my way to the guest room he'd offered me the first night I'd met him. Sad, scared, and full of remorse, I crawled into that bed and buried myself under the covers.

While Knox addressed his wolves, I racked my brain for a way out of this. A way that didn't involve any more of the wolves falling victim to Kingston's inexplicable vendetta against me. Was weakness really reason enough to want to erase me from the face of the Earth? Was it really that great an offense? As I considered those questions, I remembered that he was far from the only one that felt that way. My own mate had tried to kill me for precisely that reason, or at least in part. If Kingston was so hellbent on killing me that he would take on a pack of werewolves, then it was clear that he, like Merc, would not stop until he watched me meet my end.

By the time my mind had exhausted the myriad possibilities of how I could be caught and killed, as well as the numerous attempts at escape I could employ that would inevitably fail, I fell asleep. It was the only peace I would find for a while. The only successful escape from my reality that existed.

17

The sound of arguing awoke me.

I could hear them talking in the living room, the rush of their murmuring voices broken by an occasional outburst that carried all the way to the back of the hall. So much had happened. Too many were lost. I had never wanted things to turn out that way. It was the precise outcome I'd tried to avoid. And yet, they'd died anyway.

Good intentions gone bad; that was my life story.

Werewolves were not easy to sneak up on, but when they were embroiled in a heated discussion, it was possible to fly under their radar, apparently. I tiptoed down the hall, wanting to hear what they were saying more clearly. I also think a small part of me wanted to be punished for my selfishness. I never should have stayed when they'd found me out, but regardless, I had. That part wanted to hear the pain in their voices, the sting of their words as they cursed the day I'd come around. Revoked their bizarre allegiance to me. Maybe they were planning their revenge. A revenge I deserved. Hearing that would certainly spur me to act.

Maybe that would make me leave.

"We'll get answers when she's ready to give them," Knox growled. The others went silent. Just as the room quieted, I stepped on a squeaky floorboard and my attempt at stealth was crushed in an instant. "Piper?" he called, coming around the corner to find me halfway down the hall. "Good. You're up. C'mon, the boys want to see you."

He ushered me into the great room to stare down a sea of mourning werewolves. It was almost more than I could bear. Then I saw Grayson, the youngest in the pack, just beyond them, pale and in pain, breathing hard on the couch. He had been badly burned, though not as badly as the other two that had already died. By the look of him, he wasn't far from meeting that same end.

I felt a tear run down my cheek as I clutched my stomach with my folded arms. My tell, as Knox liked to call it.

"Is he...?"

"He should make it, but he's in rough shape. Even with his burns flushed out and his proximity to me, he's struggling to heal. Whatever magic that warlock wields, it's dark and it's powerful." *Don't I know it,* I thought to myself. "Pain meds don't work so well on us, so all we can do is watch him struggle and suffer. I can't even imagine how bad it is for him right now."

"I can," I said without thinking, my feet carrying me toward the couch. The burns covering Grayson's entire torso practically called to me.

"Really?" one of the guys shouted out, halting my approach. "You look like you got away pretty unscathed."

"Brunton!" Knox barked, silencing the wolf. "Your bullshit isn't going to help anything right now. Got it?"

"No, it's okay, Knox," I said softly, turning to face him. "I deserve that. He's right. I did get away scot free...this time."

"This time?" Knox asked, his stare homing in on me.

I had the attention of the whole pack, all of them staring at me with myriad expressions. Jagger looked sad. Foust looked exhausted, running his hand over his face repeatedly. Knox, however, was all business. He was about to get the answers he'd been waiting for all along, and I could see that he had already decided he wasn't going to be a fan of them.

Smart guy.

With a heavy sigh, I let go of my abdomen and grabbed the hem of my shirt. With one fluid motion, I pulled it up over my head and threw it down. The collective gasp from the pack was more than I could handle. I could no longer meet their eyes.

"This is what happens to those that the warlocks deem as prey," I said, looking to my right out the window. "And that's all I've ever been to them and all the other Magicals, for that matter: prey. So one day they decided that my weakness should no longer be tolerated and had a little bonfire at my expense." When nobody spoke, I forced myself to turn and face them. "They ambushed me when I was out for a run. They held me down with magic and set me ablaze."

"Motherfucker..." Foust exhaled.

"They watched for a while—until they got bored with my screaming—then they left me in the park to burn. They walked away, laughing the entire time. I was always a joke to them. Apparently my death was, too."

"But how...?" Jagger started, unable to finish his thought.

"How am I still alive?" He nodded his head. "It started to rain."

"But their fire was magical," Knox interjected, coming closer to me. I took a step back instinctively. "Normal rain shouldn't have been able to put it out."

"I don't know how or why, but all I know is that it stopped. I was found by some vampires—some of the king's enforcers—and they took me back to their mansion. Their doc did what she could to save me, but none of their medication had any effect on me."

"Oh my God," Knox breathed, staring at the marred expanse of tissue that covered my stomach.

"So," I said, turning my attention toward Brunton, "I really do know how he feels right now, and believe me when I say that I couldn't possibly feel any more guilt about it. Nobody should suffer like that. Nobody."

"How long?" Knox asked, nearly interrupting me. "How long did it take to heal?"

"There was no change in my condition for a couple of weeks—"

"Weeks!" he shouted. "You survived that hell for weeks?"

"I had some help," I said softly. "One of the vampires...he helped me in a way. I guess it was similar to being in a chemically-induced coma. I didn't feel anything. Whenever I would come out of it enough to start screaming again, he would put me back into whatever state it was that made it all bearable."

"Why didn't you tell me?" he asked, his expression bleeding to one of sadness.

"Would you?" I posed the question to him with a little more heat than I'd meant to. "Would you want to run around airing this kind of dirty laundry to people you didn't know?"

"Piper—"

"No, Knox. I mean it. Is this something I should just parade around? You don't know where I've been, what I've had to do to survive without a family—a pack—to lean on. I was on my own for longer than I should have been and shit went wrong because of it. And I'm sorry that my baggage led to what happened today. I would give anything to change that if I could, even if it meant reliving this particular hell," I screamed, gesturing to my stomach. "And believe me, it has been hell in more ways than I can even begin to describe." Tears were flowing freely down my face by this point, my guilt-driven anger releasing all kinds of emotions that I'd neatly tucked away, never to be dealt with.

A sudden, single crack of thunder boomed through the air outside, shaking the house.

"I'm so sorry, Piper," Knox whispered, looking me in the eyes for the first time since I'd removed my shirt.

"They don't conveniently stop at my waistband either, you know?" I spat, self-loathing plain in my tone. "That might make this a little more tolerable, but those boys were sure to do a thorough job and start where it counts." My revelation was met with silence. "So now you know why they're after me. They want to finish the job they started. And I'm sure they'll make me pay for not dying the first time around. Or the second. Or the third for that matter. This particular group of warlocks' arrogance knows no bounds. Their pride was undoubtedly wounded with the knowledge of their failure. Someone will have to suffer for them to feel vindicated. And that someone is me."

"That's not going to happen," Foust growled as I slipped my shirt back on. "Those fuckers won't be getting within a ten-mile radius of you again if I have anything to say about it."

"Don't you see?" I said, choking on a sob. "Maybe it would be better if they did. Maybe I need to draw them away from here and let fate run its course. The supernatural world is really no different than the human one in some ways. Survival of the fittest. The strongest. The most powerful."

"Don't say that," Knox warned, his voice low and husky. I looked over to find golden yellow eyes staring back at me. He was so overrun with anger that he was fighting hard against the Change.

"I'm not trying to be dramatic, Knox. I'm being practical. Those warlocks are only a drop in the bucket. If it isn't them, then it will be someone else. That's how it's always been."

"The vampires didn't hurt you when they found you," Jagger unhelpfully pointed out. I was hoping to skirt that issue without tipping my hand. His observation was going to make that much harder for me.

"No, they didn't."

"Then you have an ally in them as well, don't you?"

"No. Enforcers are neutral. It's their job to be."

Jagger stepped away from his post next to Grayson and made his way toward me.

"But they let you stay with them until you healed? Until you were well?"

"Yes."

"That doesn't sound neutral. It sounds like they cared."

"I guess. Maybe they grew to know and like me, but that doesn't have much bearing on the issue at hand."

"I'm just saying that maybe you could bring them into this. Maybe they could help, too. I have a friend in New York. He's tight with one of the enforcers. I could call him—"

"No!" I screamed. "No. You can't."

"Why not?" Knox asked, the narrowing of his eyes an ominous sight.

I exhaled heavily.

"Because they turned on me, too. I said that it wasn't just

the warlocks after me. The vamps are behind door number two."

"Shit," Foust spat, launching out of his chair. "Those guys don't fuck around, Piper."

"I know that, Foust."

"You're the one, aren't you?" Knox asked mysteriously, coming to stand right before me, cutting everyone else off from view.

"The one what?" Foust called from behind him.

"There was an APB put out about a missing supernatural a couple weeks ago. I never bothered to click on the photo attached to the email...but I don't need to now, do I, Piper?" I bit my cheek to keep the tears at bay. "They're looking for you right now, aren't they?" I nodded. "Those guys won't ever give up, you know that, right? They'll spend eternity hunting you down. There's nowhere you can run that they can't find you eventually." He stormed away from me, punching a hole in the wall along the way. "Jesus! Why couldn't you have just told me this in the beginning? Why couldn't you have just trusted me?"

"Because I trusted them and look how well that turned out for me, Knox!" I screamed, my emotions unraveling my resolve. Again the thunder rolled, the perfect soundtrack to my swell of emotions. "I barely escaped that place with my life! I dragged my battered, bleeding body out the front door of their mansion, got in a car, and took off as fast as I could. I drove for two days straight to put some distance between them and me. I stole cars...took back roads to stay away from anything that might be able to take a traffic photo of me. I couldn't withdraw money, use my credit cards, nothing. I don't have a passport, and I didn't know what else to do, so I made my way to the most remote place I could find that had the fewest hours of dark and didn't require international travel. My plan was to get my shit together, find some sketchy human who could get me some fake IDs, and then go on the run on a grander scale."

"But I didn't let you..." he said with a frown.

"I should have left that night I met you. I should have just grabbed my shit, hopped back in my car, and driven away, but I didn't, and I'm so sorry. I'm so sorry!" I shouted, choking on the sobs I could no longer withhold. My body shook as I released everything—the stress, the fear, the guilt, the sadness—and Knox was suddenly there, holding me against his chest to quiet me. Soothe me. Offer me something I didn't deserve: absolution.

"Shhh," he said, smoothing my hair down to rest his chin atop my head. "If you had, you'd be dead right now, and there isn't a man here that could have lived with that outcome. Especially not me." I pulled away to look at him, his sage-green eyes full of sorrow. "I know you think the boys are angry with you about what happened; it's written all over your face. But they aren't. Not one of them. Not even Brunton. Grayson will say the same once he's in any sort of shape to do so."

My eyes drifted over to the burned pack member, still lying on the couch. And as if I had been struck by lightning, an idea shot through my mind so acutely that I abruptly pushed off of Knox and ran to Grayson's side.

"Can one of you lift him? Carefully?" They all just stared at me, confused by my request. "Can somebody pick him up and take him outside for me. Please?" I asked, the pitch of my voice rising with every word.

I had a plan. Maybe it was a bad one, but I had one nonetheless.

It had been twice now that I had been wounded and lying on the ground when I'd called for help when dying.

Perhaps—just maybe by the longest of shots—the same would happen for Grayson if I were the one to make the request. I had no clue who or what exactly I was asking for help, but I'd received it both times before. I was hoping that somehow, some way, this might work. If not, I'd look mildly crazy. But if it did, I could not only save a pack member from the pain I was all too familiar with, but also redeem myself to all the others. Give something back to them for all they'd sacrificed for me.

It was well worth trying.

"Piper?" Knox asked, approaching me carefully as though my mind had shattered and he was afraid of what I might do next.

"I'll do it," Foust said, coming to squat down beside me.

"You have to be gentle. Very, very gentle," I said, staring deep into his eyes.

"I will," he agreed. Then he assessed Grayson to see where he could place his hands so as not to disturb the burns any more than necessary. Once he settled on a spot between the werewolf's thighs and shoulders, he hoisted him up with care. "What now?"

"Take him outside."

"What are you doing, Piper?" Knox asked, joining me at my side.

"I have a plan," I replied looking up at him. "You told me I'm connected to nature and to your pack. I think it's time I start exploring just how deep those two connections run."

He smiled wide.

"I like your thinking."

With that, he escorted me through the living area to the foyer and out to the front porch. Foust was already there, holding Grayson, who was shaking from the pain, though he remained silent. I remembered that—being beyond the point of crying out.

Knowing the depth of his suffering only strengthened my resolve to help him.

"Lay him down over there," I ordered, pointing to the sunniest part of the front yard. Foust did what I asked without question, doing his best not to jolt Grayson any more than he had to as he placed him on the ground. "Perfect." *I think...*

"Do you need us to go?" Knox asked. I choked back a laugh.

"I have no idea what I need right now, other than a miracle." I knelt down beside Grayson, placing my hand lightly on top of his head. "I don't know if this will work," I whispered to him. "But I'm going to try my hardest to make this all go away." His eyes fluttered open for a moment, searching for my silhouette in the sun. I moved to block it from his face momentarily. He braved a smile for me, then closed his eyes, doing the best he could to relax into the ground beneath him.

Unsure of what to do next, I laid down beside him, moving my hand to hover just above his torso. I didn't want to touch him—touch the raw open wound that was his upper body—but I didn't know if I would need to or not. I thought physical contact might be better than none at all. So with my body grazing the length of his and my hand nestled on top of his chest, I raised my face to the sky, eyes blinded by the pure light, and spoke the words that I had before. The ones that had only by chance led to my salvation.

"Help me," I said softly, pouring every ounce of desperation I felt for Grayson into those words.

Nothing happened.

I lifted my hand away from him and rolled over to face

the ground, just as I had before when it had worked. Then I repeated those words.

Again, nothing happened.

I toyed with the idea of turning Grayson over, but it seemed cruel to do so when the outcome was so uncertain. Instead, I tried something else.

"Help me," I pleaded, the desperation to succeed in my endeavor bleeding into my tone.

Yet again, I was denied.

"I don't understand," I muttered to myself. "I don't know what else to do..."

I could hear Knox and Foust whispering back and forth, the two of them undoubtedly questioning the prudence of dragging their pack brother outside to carry out my hare-brained scheme. While I moved around Grayson, trying different positions, I heard Knox approaching.

"Piper—"

"No. I know I can do this. I *have* done this. Sort of..."

"Maybe we should just—"

"NO!" I screamed, my frustration boiling over.

What seemed like only seconds later, Grizz came thundering through the trees and over to my side. Knox and Foust exchanged a look of surprise.

"It's a long story," Knox offered before Foust could even ask.

"Hey buddy," I said, running my hand through his fur. "Do you know how to help him?"

The bear shook his head, then nudged my shoulder, pushing me toward Grayson.

"I tried that. It's not working. Nothing is..." The bear snorted, shaking his head. Again he pushed me with his nose toward the wounded wolf. "I get it. I'm trying to help him." The grizzly let out what would have most certainly been an exasperated sigh had he been human and sat down right beside Grayson's head. The act brought about a low but thundering growl from Foust. He wasn't a fan of the bear being that close to his wounded friend. The bear, ignoring the werewolf, looked at me with wizened eyes. Once more, he nuzzled me, but this time he gave a long and hard look at the body beside me after. Then he looked at me. Then Grayson. Me. Grayson.

Then I finally understood.

Not wanting to waste time, I laid my hand down on the wolf's burnt abdomen and whispered the words I hoped needed to be spoken.

"Help me help him."

The flash of light that exploded from Grayson's torso literally forced me back, as it did both Grizz and the boys. The heat emanating from where he still lay on the ground was intense, not unlike the fire that had caused his wounds in the first place (and I would know).

"What's happening?" Foust shouted, pulling me back away from Grayson's body.

"I don't know." Before I could even begin to concoct an explanation for him, everything stopped. The light and the heat dissipated, leaving Grayson lying in the grass, his body healed.

"Holy shit," I mumbled, staring at him in utter disbelief. I turned to look at Knox, who was behind me, but when I did, I found the entire pack standing there, and a few extras to boot. Apparently the light show had drawn just about every creature in the surrounding area. Moose. Elk. Deer. Bears. You name it, it was probably there. And I wasn't the only one that noticed.

The pack looked around, their faces slack with shock as they took in all the woodland spectators the healing had drawn. I would have done the same, but I couldn't stop staring at Grayson's flawless body. There wasn't a scar to be seen. Not a single demarcation to denote what had happened to him only hours earlier.

My hand drifted up to my own stomach, tracing the lines of the scars just below the fabric of my shirt. What had I done wrong—done differently—that I had more than my fair share of physical reminders that I had nearly been burned alive?

But then my hand fell, or rather was pulled down lightly. I looked to my left to find Knox staring down at me in total awe.

"You did it, Piper. I don't know how, but you did it."

"And we all felt it," Jagger added.

"Apparently, so did they," Foust joked, pointing to the wall of wildlife surrounding the yard.

"You should all probably thank the bear," I said, jerking my head toward Grizz. "I don't know that I would have put together what now seems rather painfully obvious without him." They all eyed me dubiously. "What? You can't apologize to him *or* thank him? That seems a bit harsh, don't you think?"

"What's she talking about?" Foust asked Knox.

"It's part of that long story that we weren't going to get into."

"He's waking up!" one of the others exclaimed, running over to Grayson's side. In a second, the rest of us were there too.

"How do you feel, Gray?" Knox asked, helping him to sit up.

"What the fuck just happened?" The young wolf looked stunned and groggy, but when his eyes found me, his gaze sharpened into focus. "You...I remember you."

"She's the reason you're not in excruciating pain anymore," Knox informed him.

"The light. Did you see the light?" We all nodded. "I thought I was dying..."

"No such good luck, I'm afraid," I deadpanned. That earned me a chuckle from Grayson before his expression sobered.

"Thanks, Piper. Really."

"You wouldn't have been burned if it weren't for me, so no thanks necessary."

Foust reached a hand out and helped Grayson to his feet, clapping him on the back in that bizarre way that men do.

"I'm fucking starving. Is there anything to eat inside?" the young wolf asked. This time the rest of us had a laugh.

"I'm sure we can whip something up for you, man," Foust said, throwing an arm around his packmate's shoulders. "Let's go see what we've got." I watched as they headed off inside, the rest of the pack falling in behind them as they walked past. Once the wolves were in the lodge, the other animals—the non-magical kind—started to disappear back into the woods, leaving only Knox and me standing in the massive front yard.

"You're so much more than you seem, Piper. I hope you see that now. I hope you finally believe it."

I smiled shyly, turning away from the intensity of his gaze and the weight of his words.

"We should go inside and check on the others," I said softly, still averting my eyes.

"If by check on the others you mean make sure they don't eat everything in the house in a healing-induced food binge, then yes, we should." I looked up to see him smiling mischievously. I returned the gesture.

Wrapping his arm around my shoulders, Knox ushered me back to the lodge and into an entirely different kind of chaos than what we'd endured that morning. It reminded me of the night I'd met the pack. Witnessing their antics only deepened my fondness for them and their way of life. They truly did function as one.

And I was now a part of that.

18

The entertaining breakfast fiasco was followed up by a rather sobering discussion. One that involved a whole lot of warlock talk. It put me on edge. Warlocks were far from my favorite subject.

"The one thing that's plain is that they'll be coming back for her," I heard Foust say. His words jarred me from the mental happy place I'd drifted off to.

"How can you be sure they'll find her?" Jagger asked, sitting up a little straighter on the couch across from me.

"They will," I said plainly. "It might not be today or tomorrow, but they will eventually."

"And we'll need to be ready," Knox added, walking around the back of the sofa I was seated on. Placing his hands on my shoulders, he gave a reassuring squeeze before continuing around the room. "They had the jump on us last time, but they won't here. This is our turf. It protects us. We'll know they're coming before they get here."

"Their turn to be ambushed," Foust interjected.

"Exactly."

"But how do we contend with their magic?" Brunton

asked, never afraid to play devil's advocate. In fairness, it was a valid question, one that I was curious to hear the answer to, providing Knox had one.

"Warlocks are strong in magic, but their combat skills are shit. How did you manage to take out the ones you did, Foust?"

"By tearing them apart with our bare hands," he answered, eyes narrowed with hatred.

"Exactly. We need to get close enough to them to take them out before they have a chance to work their hocus pocus bullshit."

"Fucking pussies," Jagger added, riling the others up. His sentiment drew a roar from the group, myself included.

"I like this plan and all, Knox," Brunton continued, "but saying we need to get close to them and actually doing that are two very different things."

"We need a diversion, Brunton. Something to draw their collective force so we can come in from behind and strike."

"I like it," Foust agreed. "But what will we use to accomplish that?"

"Not a what, Foust. A who," Knox explained, a wicked grin overtaking his expression. The others all looked around at one another, most likely wondering which of them was going to be volunteered for the unenviable task of being warlock bait. The tension in the room was thick while they all awaited Knox's plan. "I'm going to draw them out. Once they figure out that I'm alpha, they'll do all they can to eliminate me, thinking it will serve them in the long run."

"NO!" I yelled, shooting out of my seat. "You can't. I won't let you!"

"Piper, this isn't—"

"I don't give a shit what you think this is or isn't, it's fucking suicide, Knox. You don't know Kingston like I do.

He's insane. He has no honor. He'll find a way to take you out without even trying and then he'll cheat his way through the fight until every single one of you is dead." I was shouting so loud that I could feel the strain in my ears, the uncomfortable pressure building until it popped, shooting sharp pains through my head.

"This isn't your choice to make, Piper," he countered, a flash of darkness disappearing from his eyes.

"I know you've decided to make this fight your own, Knox, and I'm not going to try and stop you, but you have to listen to me about this. If anyone can buy you time to do what you need to do, it's me. Kingston loves nothing more than to grandstand when he thinks he's going to bring me down. His arrogance is his Achilles heel. You can either choose to exploit that, or you can send your pack to slaughter. It's your choice to make, but you need to listen to me if you want to have any chance at beating him." His eyes were glowing slightly, his anger building. But he was letting me speak, so I continued before he changed his mind and decided to shut me up. "You've asked me to trust you, Knox. Now I'm asking you to do the same. I can do this. I *need* to do this."

"I can't let him hurt you," Knox replied, his voice low and wistful.

It was my turn to smile wickedly.

"Then kill that asshole before he gets the chance."

I could see the war waging behind Knox's eyes; fear and reason were battling it out. But the second I saw the corner of his mouth twitch, then curl up into a lopsided smile, I knew which had won the fight.

"With pleasure."

A GUARD ROTATION was put into effect immediately following the pack meeting. Groups of ten would fan out into the forest, fully Changed, to secure the perimeter while others stayed behind to protect the property itself. I did what I could to contribute to that effort as well. Grizz had been dutifully waiting outside for me, and when I came out after the post-breakfast scheming session, I did my best to convey to him the plan. When I got to the part about me being the bait, he snorted and stomped, shaking his head back and forth in a rather grand display of his disapproval.

"I know, buddy. But I need you to trust me, it sounds worse than it will actually be, okay?" His disgruntled exhale in response was not encouraging. "Listen, I need you to do something for me. If you can..." He raised his head higher, his ears perked to attention. "I need you to help the wolves keep watch for the warlocks. I don't know if they can sense werewolves or not, but I'm assuming they can. But they won't think anything of you and your friends. They'll walk right past you like you don't exist." Grizz growled low and deep. "I know, buddy. They're arrogant pricks, but we'll show them. You'll show them, won't you?" He nodded up and down. "Go and get the others. Make them understand what's at stake. Can you do that?"

I watched as the bear stood on his back feet, his massive form blocking out the sun behind him. He slammed back to the ground and took off in a sprint for the woods, stopping just at the tree line to give me a backward glance. Then he disappeared.

"Recruiting the local wildlife, are we?" Knox asked, walking up behind me.

"Can't hurt, right?"

"No. It certainly can't." I felt the heat from his body warm my back. I wanted so much to lean against it and get lost in the feel of his strength. His confidence. It was a powerful force to deny.

"When do you think they'll come?" I asked, choosing to focus on the pressing matter at hand.

"Your guess is as good as mine, but we have a plan now; that makes me feel better about things."

"I think Kingston will have to regroup before he returns, especially if the boys wiped out most of his crew. He can't easily replace his major players. Not without Reinhardt finding out about what he's been up to. And after his last attempt on my life, the king and Reinhardt had an agreement in place regarding the warlocks and me—Kingston in particular. He's on a tight leash—or at least he was. Either way, with everything going on back in New York, he'll have to make his moves carefully from here on out. And if Reinhardt, or the king for that matter, learns about what he's been up to and how his warlocks have fallen, Kingston might just not return at all," I said, realizing for the first time that that was a very plausible outcome. I mean really, how easily could one hide the deaths of several warlocks?

But the reality remained that, if the treaty had fallen, any deals made between the king and Reinhardt would likely be null and void. And that left me back at square one. A place I didn't care to be.

"Well, that would be a step in the right direction, but you've said it yourself; he's not the only one hunting you," Knox said, pulling me from my ruminations.

"About that," I started, turning to face him. "You deserve a better explanation than the one I gave earlier when I had my mini-meltdown."

"Okay," he said softly. "I'm listening." He guided me toward the porch steps and we sat down beside each other, staring off at the wall of coniferous trees in the distance.

"I told you that a group of enforcers found me the night the warlocks tried to burn me alive, right?"

"Yes..."

"What I strategically left out of that admission was that I knew them. I've known them for a long time."

"And that changes things how?"

"They are my friends—were my friends. I lived at the mansion long before that night." I hazarded a sideways glance at him. To his credit, his expression was controlled and steady. If it weren't for the slight amber glow in his eyes, I wouldn't have thought anything was wrong. "Please don't get angry. I just want you to know the truth."

I heard him inhale deeply, then let the breath out through his mouth.

"Go on."

"The king knew of my existence long before he ever came to me. He knew I was an orphan and an outcast. He also knew that I had a massive target on my back where the warlocks were concerned. One day, when I'd narrowly escaped Kingston's grasp, the king happened upon me on the street. He made me an offer I couldn't refuse."

"That sounds ominous."

"And yet it wasn't. Not at all. He said that he would place me in the mansion—where the enforcers all live—and offer me their protection."

"Now it sounds too good to be true," he said dryly. "What's the catch?"

"No catch. That's the thing. When I ran into him that day, there was something in his eyes—something I just couldn't place—but it was as though he understood me. Understood my plight."

"So you just moved in with the most notorious gang of vampires known?"

"Pretty much," I said with a shrug. "They're really not that bad once you get to know them. I mean, some are, but I just avoided them. Jase and Dean were good to me right from the beginning. They took me under their wings and made sure nobody messed with me. Ever."

"And they didn't want anything from you either?" he asked, the undeniable subtext to his question apparent in his tone.

"No. Nothing like that. Jase and Dean have never laid a finger on me. They treat me like a little sister."

"Good. But that doesn't explain why you ran from them, Piper."

I sighed heavily.

"Things got complicated when their brother, Merc, showed up."

Knox went rigid beside me.

"*Merc?* As in Mercenary?"

"That would be the one," I quipped before realization of his reaction set in. "Wait a minute. You've heard of him?"

"You could say that," he said, the tension still rolling off of him in waves. "But I didn't know he was back in the picture."

"Yeah, well, he is," I said with a sigh. "He's also the one who's coming for me."

"Fuck," Knox exhaled, dropping his head into his hands. "What did you do to get on his bad side?"

It was my turn to tense.

"I existed." He lifted his head slowly, turning it to look me in the eyes.

"*Truth...*" His outburst was barely a whisper. "And you still exist. Is that the problem?"

"Something like that, I think," I started, getting up from the steps. Suddenly, being close to Knox was more than I could bear. "To make a long story short, he went completely postal one night when we were home alone together. At first he was talking about my weakness and how it offended him, but then he just snapped and became nonsensical, ranting about me and why I was there. He thought I was spying or something. I don't know. After that, he nearly beat me to death. If the boys hadn't returned home when they did, I'd be dead."

"Why they fuck did they leave you at home alone with him in the first place?" Knox shouted, launching off the front steps toward me. "He's barely stable on a good day!"

"I know that, Knox. So do they, but there was a reason they did. Two reasons, actually," I tried to explain to the heavy-breathing werewolf with the glowing eyes looming above me.

"I can't even begin to imagine what could possibly substantiate leaving you with a monster like that. If I ever meet those incompetent assholes, I'll tear their fucking heads off."

"No. You won't," I said firmly.

"The hell I won't."

"It wasn't their fault, Knox."

"Really? Because it sure—"

"I'm bonded to Merc!" I blurted out with all the tact of a bull in a china shop. "Jase and Dean left me with him because he was my mate. Is my mate..."

Knox looked as though I'd slapped him. The shock and horror in his expression was a sight I wouldn't soon forget. It seemed to take him forever to regain his composure, but when he did, he was all business. A side I had yet to really see of him.

"You're telling me that you're bonded to the craziest,

most deadly vampire enforcer to ever exist?" He did nothing to try and hide his incredulity.

"Yes."

"Then none of this makes sense because vampires...when they're bonded...they can't act how you're saying he acted."

"Yeah, I've heard that before. Unfortunately for me, things didn't really play out how they were supposed to. Believe me, if I'd thought that getting beaten within an inch of my life was on the table, I'd have walked away from the offer he made me. But I didn't. So now I'm here, and now you know why. All my dirty laundry has been aired."

"All of it?" he asked. His dubious expression let me know that my response wasn't fooling him.

"I couldn't possibly sit here and list off every scandalous thing I've done in my time, Knox, nor do I intend to try. You now know my past with the vampires. You already know that the warlocks despise me and want me dead. Beyond that, nothing else is really pertinent at the moment."

In fairness, I didn't think it was. Laying out every poor decision I'd made regarding Kingston seemed pointless. He wanted me dead. The why was immaterial.

He cocked his head to the left, blocking the fading sun from my eyes.

"Truth again. You're on a roll today."

"I figured now wasn't really the time to be cagey with information."

"And I appreciate that."

"So...you starting to rethink that plan of yours to stick with me?"

"Maybe a little," he said, bumping me with his hip. Then the smile he'd put on his face to reassure me fell away fast.

"Did you love him? Merc, I mean. Did you love him when you were bonded?"

My shoulders slumped as I considered his question. I was embarrassed to say that I did—or at least I thought I had. How stupid or blind did I have to be to miss what was headed my way only days after our bonding?

"Do you love him now?" he pressed, filling the silence I'd created.

"Yes. No. I don't really know how to answer that," I replied, my voice quiet and shaky. "My life has been a mess of seclusion and survival, Knox. Maybe I loved him. Maybe I just wanted to love him. Or maybe worst of all, I just wanted him to love me. Whichever way you slice it, it hardly matters much now. Regardless of what feelings I do or don't have for him, I'm dead if he finds me. Those feelings are irrelevant. Love is irrelevant. I can't afford to sit around and ponder such things. That's a luxury I don't have."

"If you still love him at all—even a little bit—that could be dangerous."

"I'm well aware of how dangerous loving Merc proved to be, Knox," I snapped.

"I didn't mean it like that. I'm saying that if you're not crystal clear on how you feel about him when he's standing before you—"

"Him wanting me dead has been super helpful in clarifying where I stand with him and where he stands with me."

Even as I spoke those words, a small part of me buried deep inside cried out against them. I looked to Knox, who eyed me tightly for a moment, assessing what I'd said, and awaited the verdict. Truth or lie.

"Good," he said plainly. "If he comes here, you can't falter when you see him. You can't interfere."

"I've seen him in action, Knox," I whispered, not wanting

to anger the alpha. But he needed to know what he was up against. If Kingston posed a problem for the wolves, Merc would prove an even bigger one.

"So have I," he countered, leaning in close to my ear to speak. "But he doesn't have magic on his side, Piper. Not like the warlocks do. With the vampires, it's all hand-to-hand combat. And that's what I do best." He lingered by my face for a moment after he'd finished, his warm breath tickling my cheek.

"If the warlocks found me, that means that the enforcers will likely do the same, and soon," I explained, my breath catching in my throat.

"Say what you want to say, Piper." His voice was low and husky, and it made every hair on my body stand at attention in the most unexpected way. I tried to ignore the sensation and put together a coherent thought.

"You could avoid a war if you let me go..."

"Maybe I like war. Did you ever think of that? Maybe I like the thought of taking down anyone who has ever tried to hurt you. And maybe I really like the idea of you staying here with us indefinitely."

"Oh."

"Exactly." He pulled away from me just enough so that I could read the conflicted expression on his face. But I couldn't make sense of it. "We should probably go in now. It's getting dark. The boys will be having a shift change soon. Best that you aren't present when they turn back and stagger through the yard naked as the day they were born."

He took my hand in his and guided me back toward the house.

"Maybe I like naked," I teased, giving his hand a little squeeze for emphasis.

He stopped dead in his tracks.

"I'll be sure to keep that in mind, Piper," he said with a smile, then started walking again, laughing to himself as he led me up the porch stairs. The second shift of scouts came out of the lodge just as we reached the door, Brunton and Jagger leading the group. "Be ready for anything at any time," Knox warned them, his tone serious.

"We will," Jagger agreed with a nod.

My heart seized a bit as I watched them make their way toward the tree line, the ten of them fanning out like spokes on a bicycle. They each had their section of perimeter to guard, and I had no doubt that they would. Knox ran a tight ship, but it was plain to see the loyalty his wolves had for him. They trusted him completely.

I said a little prayer for them under my breath, asking the Earth, or whatever source I was connected to, to keep them safe. Then I pulled my hand from Knox and bent down to touch the ground.

"Take care of them," I whispered, running my hand along the blades of grass. A gentle breeze blew my hair into my face, encircling me before it drifted away to die off.

"No powers, my ass," Knox grumbled from behind me.

"I'm just testing out your theory," I said with a shrug. "At any rate, it can't hurt to try. We need all the help we can get."

"I wish that weren't true," he replied tightly, heading up the steps to the house.

I opened my mouth to offer some meaningless placation, but thought better of it and snapped my lips back together. He always knew when I was lying. Why bother trying?

Once inside, we were soon joined by the returning wolves from the first watch. We ate, watched TV, and did everything we possibly could to act as though we weren't waiting for trouble to find us. Nobody spoke of the attack in

Anchorage. Nobody mentioned the warlocks. Everyone, without exception, acted as though nothing had ever happened—that they hadn't buried two of their own earlier that day. I couldn't figure out if they were doing so for my benefit or their own.

Maybe they did it for both.

Knox and Foust sat beside me on the couch, both totally engrossed in the romantic comedy playing on the massive flat screen.

"You guys have the most unusual taste in movies," I said, grabbing a handful of chips from the bag on Foust's lap.

"SHHH! This is the best part," he growled in an effort to shut me up. Unfortunately for him, it had the opposite effect. I don't know if his reaction had really been that funny, but I started giggling at first. Then it grew to a chuckle. Then a full-blown, body-shaking, uncontrollable laugh. One that garnered me the stank eye from Foust.

"I'm sorry," I said, barely able to spit out the words coherently.

Maybe it was the stress of everything finally getting to me. Maybe I was long overdue for a good laugh. But whatever the reason, I literally could not stop.

"Jesus, Piper," Foust groused, pausing the movie to wait out my outburst.

"I'm stopping...I'm stopping," I protested between breaths as I tried to regain my composure. Once I thought I finally had myself under control, I turned to find Foust frowning at me. That was all it took.

My hysterics kicked in yet again.

"I'll go," I squeaked, nearly out of air from laughing so hard. I got up from the couch, clutching my stomach, and made my way toward the guest room. I really did need to get my shit together. I looked like a total nutcase.

Once I escaped the room, I tried my best to control my breathing as I walked toward my room at the end of the hall. By the time I reached it, the laughter had died off, leaving me with a cramped stomach, watery eyes, and cheeks that hurt from smiling so hard. I lay down on the bed, stretching out on my back to try and get my abs to calm down. With arms outstretched above my head, I continued to take deep breaths, holding them until I couldn't any longer, then letting them out in one aggressive exhale.

"Are you getting ready to have a baby?" Knox asked, a curious expression on his face. In fairness, I probably looked ridiculous. I instinctively brought my arms down and pulled the raised hem of my shirt down to cover my scars. He frowned instantly. "I wish you wouldn't do that. You have nothing to be ashamed of."

"Old habits," I said with a shrug. It was the best I could offer him in explanation. "Anyway, can I do something for you?"

His eyes glowed amber for the briefest moment then faded back to green.

"I was just checking in on you," he explained, still hovering in the doorway. "You've been through a lot, Piper. You've been on the run...alone...and then with everything that happened this morning, I just—"

"I'm fine, Knox. Really. I am."

"I know, Piper. I just think that outburst of yours held an edge of instability to it. We all react to things differently—handle stress in our own way. I wanted to make sure that you weren't silently suffering. That's all."

"I'm not. I promise."

His eyes narrowed.

"Half truth..."

"Jesus, Knox. Enough with the lie detector shit. Please. It

gets old sometimes," I groaned, flopping back on the bed to cover my face with a pillow.

"You can't get mad at me for caring," he argued.

"Try me."

"Piper—"

"Knox, I'm not melting down, okay? I'm tired. And yes, a lot has happened to me, but I've dealt with most of it and I'm processing the rest. That's the best I can do," I told him. The muffled sound of my voice was annoying so I pulled the pillow away from my face. I found Knox looming over me. "What? Did I fail the polygraph again?"

"No. You didn't."

"Sweet. Then is the interrogation over?"

"For now," he replied tightly. There was doubt in his eyes. Something deep inside him was unsettled by what I'd said, and regardless of what his instinctual lie detector told him, he didn't seem to quite believe me.

"I'm going to go to bed for the night," I said, scooting across the bed to stand up on the other side. "I'll see you in the morning."

"I'm going to have guards surrounding the lodge tonight," he informed me as he walked toward the bedroom door. "Just to be safe. You'll find a familiar face camping out below your window, so don't be surprised if you look outside."

With that, he left me alone, closing the door behind him. I couldn't quite figure out what was eating at Knox, but there were too many possibilities to really narrow down the list. He had a lot on his plate thanks to me.

I changed out of my clothes, throwing on some sweatpants and a tank top that one of the boys had brought over for me on Knox's orders. After a quick bathroom stop to brush my teeth and pee, I made my way back to my room.

As I walked past the large mirror above the dresser, I stopped and looked at myself. To me, I was plain—nothing special. Perhaps I'd bought into the opinions of others for too long. My whole life I'd been told I was nothing, at least until I'd met Jase and Dean. Could it have all been a lie?

Lifting up the hem of my shirt, I exposed my scars in the scant light of the room. The mottled, mangled skin greeted me, but somehow it looked different. I used to cringe at the sight, but now I willingly explored the way the skin pinched and puckered, tracing the various lines that swirled along my abdomen with my finger. Maybe Merc had been right that night. Maybe my scars were my story. A road map of my life.

And that road had led me to Knox and his pack.

I was wrong to snap at him, and the guilt I felt about it grew as I lay in my bed, waiting for sleep to find me. But it never did. Instead, I tossed and turned, until I finally threw back the covers and walked over to the window. The bright light of the full moon was there to greet me. I stared, marveling at it. And as I did, I saw the similarities between its texture and that of my scars. There truly was beauty to be found in imperfection.

With that realization in mind, I soon found myself standing outside Knox's bedroom.

19

Staring at the thick, unfinished wood of his door, I wondered why exactly I was there. I owed him an apology, that much was clear, but why I felt the need to give it at that hour of the morning escaped me, making me question if there was another reason I'd gone to him. Was it comfort I sought? Forgiveness? Without knowing the answer, I knocked lightly, knowing that I would soon find out.

When it came to Knox, the truth always had a way of coming to light.

I heard the light fall of his footsteps as he approached. My breath caught in my throat and I broke out in a cold sweat. This was a bad idea. My apology really could wait until morning.

"Piper?" he said with surprise in his voice. "What's wrong?"

"Nothing. I'm sorry I woke you. I'll go." I turned to run away, feeling the awkwardness grow inside me. Really, what exactly was I doing?

"Well, I'm awake now, so...what's up? Can't sleep?"

"Not really," I replied, shifting my body to face him. "Are you alone?"

He looked at me like I had lost my mind for a moment, then the corner of his mouth curled up slightly, forming a lopsided grin.

"Well, Foust and I only cuddle every other night, so you're in luck."

"Right," I said with a nervous laugh, shaking my head in self-deprecation.

"C'mon in." He stepped back, opening the door wider for me to enter. Even with the gesture, I had to squeeze past him. I did my best not to brush up against his naked chest, but it was virtually impossible, unless I wanted to paint my body against the opposite wall as though he had some horrid communicable disease that I was hellbent on not contracting. It seemed a bit excessive.

I heard him laugh as I squeaked past him. Apparently my actions betrayed me.

"So, it's three in the morning, Piper. What's got you so on edge that you needed to see me now? Did you think of something pertinent you forgot to tell me earlier?" he asked, his expression becoming more serious.

"No. Nothing like that. I've just...it's just that..." I stammered, trying to put my thoughts together. His half-naked appearance wasn't helping me out at all. "I wanted to apologize to you. For being grumpy about my scars. I'm just not really—"

"Accepting of them?" he interrupted. "I get it, Piper. Really, I do. I just want you to know that you'll find no judgment here. Not from any of us."

"I know that," I said softly. It was one of the greatest traits of the pack. "It's just going to take a while to sink in."

"Understandable." He looked at me expectantly, as

though I still had something to say. Did he know something I didn't? "Is there anything else?"

"No...I think that's it." I turned to leave but his response stopped me short.

"Lie."

Dammit!

"Really. I came here to tell you I was sorry."

"And?"

"...and I am?"

"Yeah. I got that."

"So what else is there to say?"

He sighed heavily, coming to stand right before me.

"Do you feel like there's a shift in the air?" he asked me. It was not at all what I expected him to say. "Like there's something stirring inside you that you can't explain?"

I contemplated his question, digging deep within myself to see if I did. The answer I found there surprised even me.

"I think so. Maybe that's why I couldn't sleep," I replied, my mind turning over the events of the evening. "I've been restless since you left. I thought it was the guilt, but maybe it was something else."

He ushered me over to the bed and sat me down on the edge of it. I propped my feet up on the bed rail; the thin edge of the metal bit into the pads of my feet. The pain helped clear my head. Helped me focus on the subject at hand and not Knox's naked torso.

"Tell me exactly what it feels like," he said, squatting down directly in front of me. "Better yet, how does it make you feel?"

"Antsy. Fidgety. Like I need to do something, but I'm not sure what."

"Like you need an outlet for that energy?"

"Yes. I think so."

"Okay..." he said thoughtfully, rubbing his jaw. "Does this mean we're going for a midnight jog?"

"I tried that already."

"You what?" he exclaimed, shooting up to loom over me.

"I was roaming around a couple of hours ago and found the treadmill in the fitness room," I explained, thinking that was rather obvious. "I didn't go outside, Knox. Jesus. I don't have a complete death wish. If I did, I wouldn't have ever left New York."

"Right. Sorry," he said, exhaling heavily. Then he started to pace the room. "I think it's your magic calling to you. I wish there was someone out there willing to help guide you...teach you about your powers."

"You and me both," I muttered.

"I don't know how to help you, Piper. I can't begin to tell you how much that pains me to admit," he said softly, staring out the window.

"You are helping me, Knox. All you've done from the minute I met you is help me. Even before that, actually."

"Lot of good it's done," he scoffed. "We can only run defense for so long before someone breaches it."

"I know," I whispered, hanging my head in dejection. "That's why we have a plan. It's going to work."

"I've been thinking about that, Piper. About your plan," he said, turning to face me. "I don't think I can go through with it. You may be getting in touch with the magic you possess, but dangling you in front of this Kingston asshole when you don't have a way to defend yourself...it's not sitting well. You can't ask me and the others to sit back and watch him harm you—kill you. You don't know what that would do to us."

"I'm not asking that, remember? You're going to be busy killing him while I distract him."

"And if we fail? If I fail?"

"Well, the good news is that I survived being burned once. Maybe I'll survive it again?" I said in jest, trying to lighten the situation a bit. My efforts were not appreciated, judging by the look on his face. "Knox, there's no other way...unless you're willing to consider another plan altogether. One that involves me packing up my stuff and driving off into the night."

"No!" he shouted, wheeling around to pin glowing yellow eyes on mine. "Don't even joke about that. You're not going it alone again, do you understand me? It's not happening. I'll be cold and dead long before I let that happen, so just drop that shit."

"Your loyalty is commendable, Knox, but when are you going to see me for what I really am? The magical albatross hanging around your neck," I argued, jumping to my feet to meet anger with anger. "You have sacrificed so much already and for what? What have you gained in this, Knox? Dead pack members that weaken you as a whole? A shitstorm of supernaturals sure to show up on your doorstep and rain down an unholy war upon you? Hell, you can't even get your full moon fix because I'm there, cock-blocking you every step of the way. You're going to go postal and kill someone soon if you don't scratch that itch."

"I could have taken care of that last night if I'd wanted to—before all the chaos happened," he said under his breath.

"Exactly my point, Knox, you could have but didn't because you were busy babysitting me. You deserve more than that."

His eyes bled back to their human color, a hint of sadness hidden away in their green depths.

"I know."

The sound of his voice was wistful and distant, and it

reached into my chest and stopped my heart. He knew I was right. He was agreeing with me. Selfish though it was, a part of me had wanted him to continue our argument. The release of energy it provided proved cathartic for me. But more than that, I wanted him to maintain his stance because, deep down inside, a part of me wanted him to want me. And it took having him show me that he didn't to open my eyes to that fact.

I was falling for Knox.

And he wasn't falling at all.

I gulped hard, swallowing back the swell of emotions rising within me. It was so like me to not realize how I felt until everything around me was falling apart. I stood there as stoically as I could and awaited the rest of his response. None ever came. Instead, he continued to stare at me as though he were assessing something, a war waging inside him that I couldn't see.

I couldn't stand to watch it any longer.

"I'll go," I said softly. I hoped the tiny break in my voice didn't give me away. Without hesitation, I turned and made my way toward the door, wanting to escape his room. It hurt too much to stay.

"Piper," he called after me. I didn't slow. "Piper, stop."

I was almost out, turning the knob of the door and opening it a crack. Then it slammed shut, his large palm spread wide across it in front of my face. I turned into his body, his extended arm caging me in. He was breathing hard —too hard—and the faintest amber glow illuminated the darkness between us.

"It's okay, Knox. You can let me go this time," I breathed.

"No," he said firmly. "I can't."

We eyed each other for a moment, letting the tension between us reach an uncomfortable level. Then it broke. His lips crashed down upon mine, pressing me back against the door. I immediately laced my fingers through his hair, pulling him toward me. My efforts earned me a nip of my bottom lip. I gasped, then sighed, letting my body relax against his. He capitalized on my resignation, scooping his hands under my ass and lifting me up, trapping me with the delicious pressure of his hips.

"Knox," I inhaled sharply, pulling away from him long enough to let his name past my lips.

"Piper," he growled, shutting me up. My body rocked against the door, banging a rhythm for anyone nearby to hear.

"Bed," I bit out between breaths that came hard and ragged.

"Right." He carried me over in a flash, throwing me down to land on top of me hard. Our rhythm never suffered at all. As we ground against one another, I realized that if I didn't get my clothes off soon, he would just wear a hole right through them to get what he wanted. In light of this, I wriggled my hands down between us and started to pull my tank top up over my head. "Good thinking," he said between the kisses he trailed down my neck.

"One of us needs to think under pressure," I replied, my words muffled by the cotton fabric being drawn over my head.

"Thinking isn't high on my list of priorities right now," he countered, pushing the waist of my sweatpants down.

"Getting your full moon fix is a bit more important?" I joked while I tried to help him by wiggling out of my pant legs.

His whole body froze.

I hadn't meant anything by my comment. Hadn't meant to insult him. I was nervous and unsure about what exactly was happening between us, and those words escaped before I really thought them through. Judging by his reaction, he felt very, very differently.

"This," he started, his voice sharp and commanding, "has *nothing* to do with the full moon, Piper."

"I was just kidding," I said, staring up at his serious expression.

"I was never babysitting you either. I wanted to be around you. I chose to forgo getting my monthly rocks off because I had something I wanted more."

"Oh?" I replied, barely breathing even though my heart raced uncontrollably.

He stared down at me, breaking his alpha exterior for a moment to let a playful grin emerge.

"Yeah. You, Piper. I wanted you, and I wasn't going to jeopardize that in any way. I was willing to wait as long as I had to."

"You wanted me to come to you," I observed.

"Yes."

"Why?"

"Because you've always had the look of someone who has reason to be wary of others. It was plain the day I met you. You can't push the skittish. They run."

"I'm not running," I said softly, reaching up to capture his face in my hands.

"You'd better not," he growled, yanking my pants off in one fell swoop and collapsing down onto me. "Not unless you want another supernatural tracking you down. If we do this, Piper, there's no turning back. I'm already in too deep for that. Your call is almost impossible to ignore." He leaned in close, his breath tickling my neck as he spoke. "Last chance."

"I'm still here, aren't I?" I whispered, running my hands

down his back to his ass. "Whatever it is you feel, something inside me feels it too. I don't want to run." He pulled away just enough for me to see his pale green eyes searching mine. "I do, however, want these off." I tugged on the waist of his pants, eliciting a laugh from deep within him. Within seconds, he had them off.

With the length of him against my belly, I moaned, arching my hips up toward him.

"I want you for my own, Piper," he bit out, fighting for control. Then he thrust himself inside me, letting out a howl as he did. An echo of responses rang out through the cool night air. And as we found our rhythm again, working our bodies against each other with perfect harmony, I realized that there was a glimmer of hope left for me. That maybe not all was lost.

I started to believe that, together, we would find a way out of the mess I was in. That we would defeat those that came for me. And maybe, with Knox and his pack, I would find a family once again.

20

"Knox!" a harsh voice called from the hallway outside the alpha's door. I had been in such a deep sleep (something I hadn't had for a long time) that I woke up totally disoriented, searching the room to figure out where I was. Then I saw Knox's naked form stride across the wide plank wood floor and it all came back to me in a hurry.

I quickly wrapped the sheet around me and jumped up from the bed, searching for the clothes we'd carelessly discarded only hours earlier.

"What is it?" Knox asked, his voice full of concern. Given the recent string of events, I couldn't blame him. As I scurried around, throwing on my clothes as I located them, I couldn't help but wonder if something had gone wrong in the night. If something or someone had found us.

"We've got a bit of a situation in the living room."

Knox threw open the bedroom door, wearing only his birthday suit, to find Foust on the other side looking flummoxed. The expression was almost comical, especially on the pack's second-in-command.

Almost.

"I'll be right there," Knox replied, closing the door and walking back toward me.

Lord, was that a sight to see in the full light of day.

"Party's over, I guess," I said with a sigh, tying the drawstring on my sweats.

"The party's only begun, Piper," Knox countered with a heated stare. If my clothes could have melted off my body, they would have. "Stay here while I go see what the fuck is going on."

"Let me come with you," I pleaded. "You can't shelter me. It doesn't do any good."

He stopped by the bedroom door for a second, mulling over the validity of my point. Moments later he gave a sharp nod and walked out the door, expecting me to follow. And follow, I did.

"Stay behind me, but close behind me."

"Knox, it can't be that bad or all hell would be breaking out, which clearly isn't the case."

"True, but that doesn't mean it couldn't any second, and if that's the case, I want you nearby. Understood?"

"Got it."

We made our way down the long hallway, my anxiety rising as we approached the end. But that anxiety was for nothing. When we reached the great open area of the lodge, I had to stifle a laugh.

Not waiting for Knox's approval, I stepped around him, heading toward the center of the living room—and the massive grizzly bear that sat in the middle of it.

"For fucking out loud," Knox sighed. "That bear's got a set of balls on him."

"Grizz, what are you doing? Are you trying to get yourself killed?" I asked, rushing to his side as the pack of wolves inched closer to him. I wasn't sure if they were poised to attack him or just unsure of his proximity to me, but they were on edge. Perhaps the bear had been talking smack before I'd arrived.

The grizzly's eyes darted away from the perceived threat for a second to glare at me. It was clear that he thought I was the insane one of the two of us. The condescending exhale he released followed by the weary shake of his head only confirmed that thought.

"Don't give me that look!" I scolded, coming to stand before him. He cocked his head and raised an eyebrow. I didn't even know bears could do that. "Are you judging me? You are, aren't you? I'm being judged by a bear!"

The wolves started snickering, which did little to improve Grizz's mood. He launched up onto his back feet and roared, shaking his head in agitation.

"That's enough!" I shouted at him, and he slammed down to the floor in front of me, the two of us standing nose to nose. "Do you mind telling me why you're so angry?" His eyes darted around the room until they fell upon Knox. Then he let out a low growl, his lips curling to expose his teeth.

I couldn't believe what I was seeing, or what I thought I was seeing, provided my interpretation of his reaction was correct. He knew what had happened between Knox and me that night. I would have bet money on it.

And it was pretty clear that he disapproved.

"Don't be mad, buddy," I said, rubbing my hand along the side of his face. His growling ceased. "Is it that you don't like him?" The bear didn't move. "Did you think he hurt me?" Silence. I decided to try a different approach. "You know I still need you too, right?" The bear's eyes shot to mine, a sadness in them that was so human that it hurt my heart to see it. "You're not being replaced, Grizz. Not even close." He nuzzled the side of my face with his nose, then let his head hang down. "Aw, don't be like that. Please. I love you too. You must know that." Once again, the bear lifted his eyes to mine, pleading for confirmation. I cupped his face in my hands and kissed him on his nose. "You're my secret weapon, buddy. I need you. Please don't be angry with me. And don't be angry with them either. They've done nothing but take care of me from the moment I met them. You know that's true. Knox attacked you that day because he thought you were a threat to me. He would do anything to keep me safe...just like you would."

Before I could say anything else to help repair whatever damage had been done by what had taken place between Knox and me that night, the bear brushed past me, headed toward the alpha. Knox stood his ground, unfazed by the grizzly's approach. Really, though, why would he be? Grizz was just a bear.

That was the most surprising thing about it all. This lowly bear—a virtual nothing to the likes of a werewolf—was willing to waltz into the pack's home and stand his ground against them because he thought they had done something untoward to me. Knox really wasn't kidding. That bear had a huge set of balls.

Grizz came to stand before Knox, rising up on his hind legs again to stare down at the werewolf. With his back to me, I couldn't see his expression, but the gist of what was going on was pretty plain. He was silently reading Knox the riot act.

"I'll protect her with my life," the alpha said, using his serious voice. "Just as I expect you will."

The bear came down with a thump, then nodded once. With that, he turned his back on Knox and walked over to me, nuzzling my shoulder as he passed. I watched as he strode out the open front door as though nothing in that room could hurt him. That bear was no joke.

"Well, now that we have that matter settled," Knox said, shaking his head. "Anything else interesting to report from last night?"

"No," Foust replied. "Everything was clear. No signs of anyone or anything."

"Good. And just to be clear, nobody is to touch the bear. Got it?" The pack nodded in agreement. "Thanks for leaving him alone until this could be sorted out, Foust," Knox said, walking into the kitchen.

"Yeah, well...we knew he kinda had a thing for Piper, so we didn't want to tear him apart and upset her, especially now that you're..." Knox quirked a brow at Foust's insinuation. "Now that you're having midnight meetings?" he said, doing his best to backpedal.

"It was actually three in the morning, Foust, not midnight," I added, trying to help him out. "And we weren't having a meeting." I gave him a wink before I made my way to the fridge. "Who's ready to eat? I know I'm *starving* after last night..."

Knox burst into laughter at my brazen remark. But really, they all knew what had happened. Their chorus of approving howls hours earlier had told me as much.

"What am I going to do with you?" Knox asked, coming up behind me to wrap his arms around my waist.

"Lock me up and throw away the key?"

"Ha! Hardly," he scoffed. "Unless I'm locked in with you. That doesn't sound so terrible."

"Oh God," groaned Brunton from behind us. "Can you two go get a room and let me grab some juice? I'm going to need to spike it with a healthy amount of vodka if this is how the day is going to go. You do remember that we have a pissed-off warlock potentially heading our way, right? That hasn't slipped your mind in your post-coital bliss?"

Knox's expression was murderous when he turned to face Brunton, whom he clearly viewed as out of line.

"He's a bit grumpy," I informed the insubordinate wolf. "You might want to tread lightly around him. In fact, I think I'll just take him back to his room for a bit."

"Good idea," Knox bit out as I pushed him backward toward the hallway.

"You guys get breakfast ready. I think he might be hungry too. Probably best if we feed him soon. I'll keep him occupied in the meantime," I yelled over my shoulder.

"I'm sure you will," Foust shouted back, punctuating his statement with a hearty laugh. In fairness, I had kinda walked right into that one.

I shoved Knox through the door to his room and closed it behind us, immediately locking it.

"I like your style," he said with a quirk of his brow, no hint of his earlier anger evident.

"I'm trying to keep the infighting to a minimum at the moment. You have bigger things to worry about than Brunton being what I can only assume is his surly self."

"Yep. That's a pretty fair assessment of him."

"But he's right, you know? Canoodling in front of them isn't really what they need to see."

"Did you just say 'canoodling'?" he asked, his features scrunched up in a confused expression.

"Yes. I did. Get over it."

"Officially moving on," he said with a smile, coming to wrap his arms around me again. "You truly do have a way with the animals, don't you? Making them bend to your will?"

I choked on a laugh.

"Well, I certainly had my way with you last night."

"Is that what you call that?" he asked, dipping his head low to nip my ear. "As I recall it, I seemed to be having my way with you."

"Only because that's what I wanted."

"Oh really?" he drawled. "Perhaps there's only one way to settle the matter."

"Nope, no time for that, remember?"

"Ugh," he groaned, falling back onto the bed in an exasperated display. It was all for show, of course, but I didn't care either way. I was too busy trying to pull my eyes away from his naked abs. "Fine. You're right."

"We need to tell them about Merc. It's not fair that they don't know who else is hunting me."

"Who's running this pack?" he asked, leaning back onto his elbows.

"You? It was just a suggestion..."

"And it's a good one," he said, pushing off of the bed. "Let's go do that now." He grabbed my hand and led me down the hall to the kitchen, where the boys had started to put together a werewolf-sized buffet. "We need to have a little family meeting. Piper filled me in on some details about her time in NYC. Some of them you need to know about, most specifically that the enforcer coming for her is none other than Mercenary."

I scanned the group when Knox mentioned Merc by his real name. The reactions it brought forth were a mix of confusion, recognition, and everything in between.

"Who the fuck is that?" Brunton asked, looking around at the others.

Knox looked down at me with a wan smile.

"Do you want the honor of telling them about your ex or shall I?"

I considered the question for a moment before deciding that I was bringing them into this mess, so I should be the one briefing them on the enemy. It was apparent that Knox knew enough about Merc to be wary. Maybe even more than he had let on. But what he didn't know—what none of them could know—was the power he possessed and how easily he could turn it on them if he wished to. That was a secret that only a few others and I were privy to, and even though it seemed ridiculous, the thought of disclosing that information felt like a betrayal, not only of Merc, but of Jase and Dean, who'd entrusted it to me in the first place.

I hadn't realized that my arms were wound tight around my abdomen while I considered my options until Knox gently removed them, placing them down at my sides. "Everything okay?"

"Yeah, I'm fine," I replied, taking a deep breath. "I'll do it."

"You're sure?"

"I know things," I said, turning my gaze to the pack. "Things you all need to know..."

To say that they were all surprised by what I had to say was an understatement. I'd dumped a whole lot of holy shit on them at once, and most were reeling from it, especially the part about Merc's gifts. I'd betrayed the enforcers the second I'd shared that information with the werewolves, but I didn't see any other choice in the matter. If he was coming, they needed to know what he was capable of and do whatever possible to prepare for it.

What my little speech didn't prepare them for was the next exciting event that would happen that day. One that occurred shortly after the next changing of the guards. Someone I hadn't foreseen showed up, providing another variable in the chaotic equation that was my existence.

And judging by the welcome she received, the werewolves weren't happy to see her.

21

"Something's wrong." Knox said suddenly, looking off through the wall of windows to his right. Then he tore out of the lodge at an inhuman speed, racing toward the woods.

"Knox!" I screamed, trying to chase after him. By the time I made it to the tree line, I could hear a ruckus headed my way. Instinctively, I stepped backward, wanting to escape whatever was headed my way. But I stopped, steeling myself for the attack. We had planned for this moment. I just prayed that it would play out as we hoped.

"Piper!" a female voice shouted before she cried out in pain.

"Oh my God," I whispered to myself before bolting through the brush into the woods. Kat had found me.

And that was likely to get her killed.

"Don't hurt her!" I shrieked, navigating my way through the overgrown forest, looking for the pack. "She's my friend! Don't hurt her!"

"Piper!" she yelled again. This time her voice held an

edge of concern. I think that she, too, realized she was outnumbered and in major shit.

"Knox!" I called out, finally able to see the horde of werewolves circling something, or someone, as the case most likely was. "Please. Just let me talk to her!"

I crashed into the outer perimeter, shoving bodies aside until I reached the inner ring. That's where I found Kat lying on the ground, bleeding badly, which spoke volumes about the amount of damage they'd inflicted in a short period of time.

"Oh my God, Kat," I said, kneeling down at her side.

"I'm fine," she said, spitting out a mouthful of blood at Brunton's feet. She looked up at him with a menacing glare. Kat had his number for sure. "This one has a bit of an attitude problem that I'd love the chance to discuss with him sometime, but other than that, I'm good."

"I caught her sneaking around Piper's property."

"Yeah," she said in mocking, "because I was trying to find her, Einstein."

"They sent you?" I asked, unable to suppress the sadness in my voice. In retrospect, it made perfect sense. Kat wasn't restricted by the light of day, and she had keen hunting senses. Why wouldn't they send her to track me down?

She nodded tightly, a look of embarrassment in her eyes.

"I'm in a rough position here, Piper. I think you can appreciate that."

"You'll be in a rougher one real soon if you don't start telling me exactly what I want to hear," Knox said, bending down beside Kat. Her eyes shot to him and back to me, quickly putting the pieces of the puzzle together. Kat knew how packs worked. She also knew how possessive they were of what they perceived as theirs.

"Oh, Piper..." she said, the patronizing tone of her voice unmistakable. "Tell me you didn't."

"She doesn't have to tell you anything," Knox said, snatching Kat up off the ground. It was only then that I saw the anatomically impossible angle of her leg. She winced the second she put weight on it, an action that she immediately regretted. To show weakness to your enemy was dangerous in our world and she knew it.

"We have to set that before it starts to heal," I pleaded, reaching for the protruding bone in her lower leg.

"Later," Knox replied. He started hauling her through the trees, almost dragging her at times when her broken limb gave out under her weight.

It pained me to watch her struggle, but I knew that now was not the time to argue. Undermining him would only make him more angry and defiant. It would also make Kat appear weaker. Neither were ideal outcomes. I needed to play this situation just right, or my friend would be dead. It was really just that simple.

Just before we reached the lodge, Knox shoved Kat toward the stairs. She stumbled and fell, catching herself on the bottom step. I raced to her side, lifting her leg to rest it on my lap.

"Oh no," Knox said, grabbing the wounded limb from my hands. "We're not doing this one your way, Piper. If she wants this fixed, she's going to tell me what I want to know. If I'm satisfied, I'll set it for her."

"I'm not telling you shit," Kat snarled. "I'm here for her, and she's the one I'll answer to. Not you."

Knox quirked his brow at her, feigning amusement.

"She's feisty, I'll give her that," he replied, turning his attention to me. "I don't know what it is with your friends and death wishes, but so far, they're two for two."

I smiled tightly, strategically putting myself between Knox and Kat while the rest of the pack looked on, ready to finish what Brunton had started if they weren't pleased with what she had to say.

"How bad is it?" I asked, squatting down beside her. Knox still held her leg, which made me nervous, a fact that I made plain to her in my beseeching expression.

"My leg or the shit in NYC?"

"I can see the former isn't good. How bad is the latter?"

She frowned.

"I'm not sure, Piper. When I left, they seemed to have him subdued somewhat. After that first day, something in him shifted. I don't know how to explain it, but I could see it in his eyes. He was still as mad as a hatter, but it was for a different reason. Like he'd realized what he'd done and needed to find you at any cost."

"Who sent you? Jase? Dean?"

"The king..."

"Fuck."

"I know, Piper. I'm between a rock and a hard place in this. But in a strange way, I'm glad that they sent me. I came up with a plan over the time I was searching for you. I think I know how I can play both sides of this, but you need to listen to me very carefully and do exactly as I say, understand?"

I nodded frantically.

She reached her arm behind her back for something tucked into the back of her pants. Knox, not appreciating the movement, wrenched her leg in warning. She screamed in pain.

"Knox!" I shouted, pushing him away from her.

"I have a passport in my back pocket, Piper. I had it made for you. I know a guy in Idaho that does that kind of stuff. A rogue fey who flies under the radar. He had it ready for me when I went through that way." I reached behind her and pulled it out. "I knew you didn't have one. I also knew you'd be needing one if you had any chance of ever escaping the king's reach."

"So your plan is to let her go?" Knox asked incredulously.

"Well it sure as fuck isn't to send her back to that nutcase. You didn't see what he did to her..." Sad eyes fell upon me as she spoke. "I'm so sorry, Piper. I should have stayed home that night. When the boys told me what had happened to you—it's all my fault."

"It's not your fault, Kat," I said, leaning forward to wrap my arm around her neck in a half hug, doing my best not to jostle her leg in the process.

"At any rate, here's the bottom line: the king sent me to find you. Every night, the boys show up to see if I have any news on your whereabouts—"

"Jase and Dean? They're checking up on you?" Her expression tightened, confirming my worst fears. Perhaps my dream hadn't been just a dream after all. "But they saw what he did to me."

"I know, Piper. But they're in the king's service as much as I am."

I felt sick. Completely and utterly sick. Jase and Dean had been my rocks for longer than I could remember. To know that they would willingly return me to the very place where I had nearly met my end was beyond unthinkable.

Suddenly, the dream I'd had of them and Merc took on a very different connotation. One where they used my feelings for them against me to get what they wanted: me to return to the mansion. And Merc.

I collapsed onto the ground, Kat's leg propped up in my

lap. I couldn't think. I couldn't speak. All I could do was feel the pain of betrayal tighten around my heart, choking it slowly.

"They'll be here at sundown, Piper. If I don't text them to tell them my location, Jensen will be in a world of shit."

"Who's Jensen?" Knox asked, still looming over the two of us.

"My mate."

"He's an enforcer," I added. Knox's expression twisted to one of disgust.

"Fuck him. He can fend for himself."

"There has to be a way out of this that doesn't result in death," I said, my mind still reeling.

"There is," Kat replied, her voice riddled with anger. She clearly didn't care for Knox's plan. "You need to take that passport and get the fuck out of here now. Put some distance between you and this place before sundown. I'll text the boys and tell them to meet me at your cabin. That I just missed you, but that you'd been there recently. It'll be enough to make everyone think we're close, but give you a head start on your international getaway plan."

"She's not leaving," Knox growled.

Kat ignored him entirely.

"I have money. I took all the cash I had—the cash I have stashed at the mansion from tips. My 'just in case' money," she explained, grabbing my hand and squeezing it tightly. "I know what they'll do to me if they find out I lied, but I'm willing to risk it, Piper. You and I will always be outsiders in their world, no matter how ensconced in it we are. I've saved up that money over the past couple of years because I know that the second something happens to Jensen, I'll be out on my ass. There's just under ten grand in my car. Take it. Run. It's your only chance."

"How do I know this isn't some elaborate scheme?" Knox asked. "How do I know that you're not setting her up with an alias that the king already knows about? Money that can be traced?"

It took me a moment to process what was going on, my mind still focused on the betrayal of Jase and Dean. But once his words really registered, I turned to him with a questioning stare. How did the walking polygraph not know if she was lying?

"Knox, why are you—?"

"Because I can't tell if she's lying or not, that's why." He bent down beside me, taking Kat's leg from my hands. "I think it's about time we set this thing, don't you?" he asked, turning her leg back and forth as though he were assessing the best way to do that. "Here's the thing, Kat. Piper is very important to me. Important to all of us, for that matter. And I don't really like the uncertainty surrounding your role in her retrieval. I'm normally an excellent judge of intention. You could say I have a feel for the truth. But with you, I can't seem to get a read on whether or not you mean what you say, and that's just not going to work for me. So from where I stand, nobody is going anywhere. Especially not you."

A horrific crunching sound echoed through the yard, followed closely by a shriek from Kat. He had apparently decided that fixing her leg wasn't in his best interest. Breaking it further seemed more to his liking.

"Knox!" I screamed, shooting to my feet. He slowly uncurled his body to stand in front of me, not a hint of apology in his stare. Cold indifference met my eyes. "She's not lying. Kat and I have been friends for a long time. She wouldn't lie about this. She's trying to help me."

"Just like your boys are? The boys that had your back all

the time?" he countered, silencing me. "If she's in deep with them, then she can't be trusted."

"But she said that they'll be here by nightfall."

"Not if she doesn't message them."

"And how long do you think it will be before they track her phone, Knox? An hour? Maybe two? They'll hunt her down."

"And we'll be waiting for them once they do."

"This is insane!" I exclaimed. "Even if you take them down, more will come. And they'll keep coming until they get what they want. You can't fight them forever. There are more of them than you. This is suicide, Knox." He stared at me, unfazed by my argument. "I know you made me a promise, but knowing what we know now, you can't keep it. I'm asking you not to. For your sake and the sake of the whole pack, back out, Knox. Back out now. Let me run. I'll be okay. I'll get word to you as soon as I'm out of the country. I'll let you know everything is fine."

"No."

"Why won't you see reason in this?"

"Because they will find you and kill you."

"You don't know that," I argued weakly.

"Yes. I do." There was a finality to his words—a certainty behind them that gave me pause. There was something Knox wasn't telling me, of that I was certain. "You're a target they can't lose sight of, Piper. We end this now. My way."

I could see in his eyes that he was unwilling to cave on the issue. Like it or not, the showdown with Merc was going to happen sooner than later. I feared for the fate of us all.

"Then fix her leg," I said, looking down at the hideous angle he'd created with her lower limb. The sight of it made my stomach roll.

"Why?"

"Because we'll need her."

"And if she's a traitor?"

"That's a chance we'll have to take. Besides, how many of your boys did it take to bring her down?"

Knox scanned the pack for an answer. A show of hands said that three of them had captured Kat. She was a wolf in sheep's clothing.

"You're willing to bet your life on her loyalty?" he asked, eyeing me tightly.

"Yes. I am."

His eyes narrowed.

"Truth..."

"You're the one that keeps telling me I call to nature. That I'm connected to it. That's partly why you all took to me so quickly. Why you chose me," I argued. "Why would Kat be any different? She's fought for me before."

"And I'll do it again, Piper," she bit out from her position on the ground. "But I can't condone this plan. It really is suicide."

"We'll see about that," Knox grumbled under his breath, taking Kat's leg in his hands again. With no more care than he'd taken with it before, he snapped it back into an anatomically correct position. Kat screamed, breathing hard as Knox released her appendage, letting it fall limp to the ground. "It should be fine in an hour. Foust, take her to the holding cell. Lock her in there until I say to let her out."

"It'll be okay," I whispered to her. The set of her features told me otherwise, but she didn't bother verbalizing it. She'd already made her stance clear.

"Take her phone too," Knox yelled at Foust. "We're going to need it later."

"What are you going to do?" I asked, fear rising within me.

"Precisely what she'd planned to, only we're going to do it just a wee bit earlier."

Oh my God...

"They'll burn," I said, breathing the words as though saying them too loudly would make that reality worse somehow.

"They'll get what they deserve, Piper. They betrayed you. They don't get mercy."

"But—"

"No buts on this one. I don't mean to be an asshole about this, but I have to plan an ambush. I'm going to need you to hang out in your room for a while."

Before I could argue, he walked inside, presumably to make sure Foust had Kat locked away. The others followed him in, leaving me in the front yard to ponder what in the hell had just happened. My best friend was taken prisoner. My boys had betrayed me, which, if Knox had his way, was going to cost them the ultimate price. And I was likely to face the male who had nearly taken my life. Maybe both of them, for that matter. It was all a lot to absorb.

But worse than that, there was something niggling at the back of my mind. Something that didn't quite add up. I needed answers, and there was only one place I was going to find them.

I walked inside to find the pack embroiled in a discussion regarding strategy, so I took that opportunity to head off toward my room. At the last second possible, I diverted down a different hall. The one that led to the holding cell.

Kat and I had a few things to discuss.

SHE WAS LOCKED up tight when I found her, so there was no

need for anyone to stand guard. If I was going to get the answers I wanted, it was now or never.

"Kat," I whispered as quietly as possible. "Are you okay?"

"My leg feels like it had a date with a wood chipper, but other than that, I'm stellar. You?" she replied, smiling.

"Things are a bit tense at the moment..."

"Interesting friends you have here. Figures that you of all individuals would try to go underground, only to move in next door to an entire pack of werewolves."

"Who'd have thunk it, right?"

"If I'd have known they were here, it might have been the first place I looked, knowing your luck." Her jovial expression fell to one of sadness. "Listen, Piper. You have to believe that this isn't what I want."

"I know that, Kat. I understand the position you're in," I said, trying to put her at ease. "What I don't understand is why you said the king sent you?"

She paused for a moment.

"Because he did?" she replied, confusion in her tone. "Piper, you know as well as I do that when the king asks you specifically to do something, you don't argue."

"Right. I know that, but what I don't get is why he wants me found so badly. I knew Merc would be after me. Maybe even the boys because they were worried, but not the king."

She looked at me strangely.

"He's worried about you being on your own."

"What?" I asked, not hiding the incredulity from my tone. "Is that what you think or what he said?"

"Not that he stopped to explain himself," she said dryly, "but yes. He did say that he was concerned for your well-being, knowing your history, and asked that I bring you home safely."

"He wants to bring me back to the mansion? To Merc?" I

nearly shouted before lowering my voice. "He tried to kill me, Kat. Why in God's name would he send me back there? Just because we're bonded?"

Realization dawned on Kat's face.

"Piper, are you working under the presumption that the king knows about the attack? About what Merc did?"

"Um, yeah. Why wouldn't I be?"

Kat leaned against the cell's bars and closed her eyes, exhaling heavily.

"We didn't tell him."

Holy. Shit.

"What do you mean you 'didn't tell him'?" I repeated, throwing in some air quotes for effect.

"I mean that once you left and the boys got Merc under some semblance of control, they had a little meeting about how to handle things."

"Who's they?"

"Jase, Dean, Jensen, and Kendrick. They were the first to arrive home from the king's. They're the ones that found you and stopped him from..."

"Smashing me to bits?" I asked sardonically.

She sighed again.

"By the time I got home, Merc was relatively stable. According to Jensen, he sounded nothing like he had when they'd arrived on the scene and found him with you."

"But why the need for secrecy? Why not report him?"

She looked away from me for a moment before turning her wide eyes back to mine.

"Do you remember what he said that night?"

"Um, he said a whole lot of crazy shit that night, Kat."

"Jensen said he was enraged, spouting off about the king and you conspiring against him—trying to get him sent away again."

"And they believed him?"

She shrugged.

"Listen, Merc was sent away before I ever came on the scene, but from what I now gather, he might have been put away for...unfounded reasons. At least that's what Jase and Dean alluded to."

"So they're willing to risk my life because they *think* he was treated unfairly a bazillion years ago?"

"I don't know what they're thinking, Piper. I already told you that they're all over my ass every night, checking up on my progress. But they're acting weird. Weirder than normal. I don't know what to make of the whole thing," she said, pushing away from the bars to limp around the cell. "Do I think they're up to something? Maybe. Maybe not. There are too many unknowns in this for me to even begin to sort through, let alone come to a conclusion. All I know is that I jumped at the chance to be the one to look for you because I knew my own intentions, and they're to get you the fuck away from all this as fast as I can." She turned dead-serious eyes to me. Eyes that glowed a light shade of gold. Wolf eyes that I had never seen before. "But now I can't even do that because Romeo out there has a hard-on for revenge."

"He's trying to protect me—"

"He's going to get you and everyone else in a five-mile vicinity killed!" she snarled a little too loudly. Footsteps echoed down the hall. Someone was coming.

"What do we do, Kat?" I whispered, panic rising in me as I looked over my shoulder to see who was coming.

"I don't know, Piper. I wish I fucking did."

"You two having a nice chat? Getting caught up on old times?" Brunton asked as he approached. Of course he'd be the one to see what was going on.

From the Ashes

"I just wanted to make sure she's okay," I said, trying to calm my shaking hands.

"She looks great," he replied, taking me by my arm to lead me away. "I think Knox asked you to stay in your room until he came for you. In case you've forgotten, that's this way." He walked me down the hall to where it met another, then turned and escorted me directly to my door. I turned the knob and stepped in, but Brunton's grip on my arm tightened, stopping me. "Piper, I'm not trying to be a dick to you or your friend, but I need you to entertain the idea that nothing is as it seems with your former life, okay? That's all. We all have a lot at stake here, and we can't afford for you to be sentimental and have that cloud your judgment." His normally harsh expression softened slightly before he continued. "Take it from me. I know a thing or two about that."

Just as his words registered in my mind, he walked away to rejoin the pack. His sentiment left me with unanswered questions, not the least of which was what exactly had led him and the others to Knox and the middle of nowhere in Alaska. I knew they each had a story to tell; I'd heard most of them on the way to Anchorage. All except Jagger's and Brunton's. But if Brunton could sympathize with me, then things had been bad for him once, that much was clear. Maybe all the wolves had a little more skin in the game than I'd initially thought.

Maybe this war wasn't just about me.

I MUST HAVE SPENT at least a couple of hours in my room just running through various scenarios in my mind. By the time I was done, I was more confused than ever. I walked over to the window to survey the yard, wondering where the boys keeping watch were, and whether or not Grizz and his friends were still patrolling as well.

"Piper?" Foust called, poking his head into my room without knocking. "Hey, Knox needs you. A text just came in on her phone. He wants you to check it."

My heart dropped into my stomach.

"Okay," I replied, making my way over to him, fidgeting with the hem of my t-shirt as I walked.

"You need to play this cool, Piper. I think you can appreciate just how precarious this situation is."

"I know."

He nodded tightly, his mouth pressed into a thin straight line.

We made our way to the common area in silence, both of us too caught up in the unknowns raging in our minds to bother making chit-chat. By the time we reached the living room, everyone was standing around staring at Knox, who held Kat's phone in his hand, staring at the screen.

"Who's it from?" I asked, approaching him.

"Jase."

"Let me see it, please." He offered it to me without question. *What have you found,* it said. "What do we tell him?" I asked.

"That you think you've found her. Be vague, and answer how you think Kat would to avoid suspicion. We don't know everything he knows. We can't afford to fuck this up."

"They'll come either way," I said absentmindedly. "If they think something's happened to her, they'll show as soon as they think it's safe."

I typed in what Knox requested, then stared at the home screen awaiting a response. You could practically feel the tension in the room as if it were an actual being, hovering over my shoulders. The weight of it was hard to bear.

Within minutes, Kat's phone chimed, indicating a text message had been received.

I opened it immediately.

Where are you? Are you still in Alaska?

I typed in my response.

Yes. In the middle of fucking nowhere.

Knox looked it over, then gave the okay for me to send it.

A minute later: *We'll trace your phone once you have her.*

I swallowed hard.

I'll let you know the second she's been secured.

Barely seconds after I sent it, Jase's reply came through.

Do that.

There was no "let us know if she's okay," no "tell her we're coming to help." Jase's replies were strictly business, as if I were a commodity that he was waiting to have delivered. Maybe I was. I couldn't silence the voice in the back of my mind telling me that, if their goal was to try and keep Merc from being sent back to wherever he'd been, I was little more than a loose end. The piece of the puzzle that could put everything into perspective should the wrong individuals (like the king) find out about what had happened. But without me to confirm that those events had even taken place (because I was conveniently dead), that wouldn't really be an issue. Jase and Dean cared about me, I knew that to be true.

The question that remained was: did they love their brother more?

TIME SEEMED to crawl yet speed simultaneously, moments of

the night drawing on forever, like every time a text from Jensen came in to check in on Kat. Then the rest just flew by. Everything that happened was a blur.

I mainly stood and stared out the westward-facing windows, watching the sun sink lower and lower in the sky while the chaos of planning continued on behind me. I didn't need to be a part of it. I wasn't bait this time around. Actually I was, in a sense. I was the reason they were coming.

I would be the reason why they died.

Knox had it all planned out so beautifully. It was foolproof, really. He could tell by the tone of Jase's texts that they wouldn't waste any time in arriving once Kat gave the go-ahead. I tried to get out of telling him how long it would take them to travel once dematerialized (because I really didn't know exactly), but after a long enough interrogation, he was able to narrow it down to a satisfactory margin based on the truths that I knew.

His lie detector abilities would be the final nail in Jase's and Dean's coffins.

So I waited and prayed and did everything I could think of to try and keep the sun from setting. I'm sure the boys, who could clearly hear me, found me highly entertaining. Or they thought I was crazy. Or worse yet, they thought I was a turncoat. But none of them said a word. They just carried on with the night as though dinner and a movie were the order of the evening.

And the sun just kept falling, despite my efforts to stop it.

When all that was left was an orange glow in the distance, Knox came over to me and handed me Kat's phone.

"It's time, Piper." He had the decency to look sympathetic toward me, but it didn't help. I took the cell from him while a tear rolled down my cheek. Then another. Then another. I stared down at the innocuous piece of technology as though it were a bomb about to go off.

"Remember what I told you," Brunton called to me from the far side of the room.

I nodded once, mustering every bit of bravery I had to do what I needed to do.

"I can't...I can't do this in here," I said, suddenly feeling lightheaded. "I need to go outside."

I started heading for the front door with Knox at my heels. He never tried to stop me. Never told me no. He knew that I'd find strength in the outdoors, so he let me go.

Smart guy.

I pulled up Jase's previous text message and started to reply. Before I knew what had happened, I had already hit send. I had signed their death warrants.

All I could do was wait for them to appear before my eyes and pray that I had stalled just enough to buy them the time they needed. Regardless of whether or not they'd betrayed me or planned to in the future, I couldn't watch them die that way. That just isn't who I am.

With the pack spread out across the yard, scanning it methodically, we awaited the enforcers' arrival. With every second we waited, the sun grew fainter and fainter. And just when I thought it had died, stepping aside to let the moon prevail in the darkness, I saw two foggy patches appear near the trees. Smoky silhouettes that, in a matter of seconds, would become Jase and Dean.

"Oh my God," I whispered to myself as I moved toward the ever-thickening clouds. "NO!"

22

I was in a full sprint the second their forms solidified. By the time I reached them, they were fully ablaze.

"Piper!" Knox screamed, grabbing me around the waist before I could grab one of them and burn myself in the process.

"Help them!" I screamed at him, kicking violently in an attempt to free myself. But it didn't work. Nor did it matter.

For a moment, I couldn't see anything at all, my eyes having great difficulty adapting to the sudden darkness that surrounded me. Both the fire and the sun were gone.

"Jase!" I called out, squinting hard to try and make out his body.

"Piper?" he replied. The confusion in his voice nearly undid me.

"Let me go!" My voice thundered through the open area like a storm itself. Much to my surprise, Knox did as I demanded. The second my feet hit the ground, I sped toward Jase, the bright light of the moon now illuminating my path.

"Are you okay?" I asked, crashing beside the boys, both

of whom were curled up on the ground, their burns healing quickly. But the sun did more to a vampire than just torch him. It drained him almost entirely of energy. The two of them were beyond vulnerable lying there before the pack of wolves. I was all that stood between them and another painful means of death.

"I've been better," Dean replied through gritted teeth. His deep, dark eyes turned to me, and the second I saw them, I knew: he meant me no harm. He never had.

"Where's Kat?" Jase asked, turning his attention to the wall of supernaturals staring him down. "I guess we found the welcoming committee..."

"She's indisposed at the moment, I'm afraid," Knox said tersely. He started to walk toward the enforcers, who were pushing themselves up to stand but still weak. Lambs for the slaughter.

"I need to talk to them, Knox," I said, standing my ground.

"Funny. So do I."

"Not funny at all. I mean it. If you kill them now then I'll never know what really happened back in New York. Something isn't right about all of this. I want to know what. If I think they betrayed me, then I'll be the first to step aside and let you tear them to bits. But if they didn't, then you need to leave them alone." The glow of his eyes let me know just how happy he was with my idea. He took a step closer. "Don't let them near," I whispered, closing my eyes. Right on cue, a violent wind picked up from the north, blowing around Jase, Dean, and me before slamming into the pack. They weren't bowled over by it, but they sure as hell couldn't advance into it.

The look in Knox's eyes was murderous.

"Your new friend doesn't seem too keen on us," Jase shouted over the cacophony blowing around us.

"He's a bit overprotective," I shouted back. "Listen, I meant what I said to him. You boys and I need to set some things straight and I mean right now." The two of them wavered on their feet, their skin healed but their energy still perilously low. They needed blood and rest, and they weren't going to be getting either anytime soon. I wondered if I could heal them myself if need be, but I decided to deal with the matter at hand first. "Tell me why you didn't tell the king about Merc."

"What?" Dean asked, seemingly thrown by the question I'd posed.

"I want to know why you didn't involve the king in this. And I want to know why Kat seems to think that you two are in a hurry to bring me back to Merc? Do you want me dead that badly? Just to save his ass?"

The two of them shared one of their glances, then turned their eyes back to me.

"Piper," Jase started, the hurt plain in his voice. "How could you possibly think we would want to hurt you?"

"Kat thinks that because that's what we want her to think," Dean added. "New York is a shitshow right now. You have no idea what happened after you left."

"To put it simply, we don't know who to trust right now, so we're playing the part of impartial enforcers to the letter."

"You couldn't trust Kat?"

"No, Piper. We couldn't be sure since she was—" Dean started before cutting himself off.

"Since she was what?"

"The king sent her, right?" he asked, willing me to put the pieces together.

"That's what she said, but—"

"We don't know who we can trust right now, Piper," Jase said, looking over to the pack. "And that includes the king."

My eyes widened with the realization of what he was saying. Things were beyond bad if the king's motives were in question.

"That still doesn't explain why you want to bring me back there," I argued, the dream I had in the car playing repeatedly through my mind. *She'll believe us...she trusts us.*

"We don't have to, Piper. We just wanted to find you and make sure you were safe—" Jase started before Dean cut him off.

"And we wanted to let you know what happened with Merc once you left. You need to know the truth."

"I'd love to hear that story," Knox interjected, shouting through the wall of wind. Somehow the sarcasm in his tone came across loud and clear. "I'd love to know why you think she should give a fuck about what happened to him after what he did."

"She shouldn't," Jase bit out, doing his best to stand tall and strong.

"Then why bother?" the alpha pressed.

"Because the disparity in his behavior from that night and now is remarkable. Something else is going on. Something outside of his control..."

"Says you!" Knox shouted, lunging toward us.

"It's okay," I said, throwing my arm out to defend Jase. As I did, the wind died down, then disappeared altogether. "I want to hear this. I need to know."

"I don't think you do," Knox countered.

"We know Piper," Dean said. His passive-aggressive slight was not lost on Knox, judging by the werewolf's harsh expression. "We think she does want to hear this."

"Kat told me that he went off the deep end in a different way," I said, returning my attention to the brothers.

"Yeah, that's what she would say since she's been gone almost as long as you have. She didn't see what happened after that—what happened once he got hold of himself." Dean stepped toward me, reaching for my hands. Knox's growl cut him short. "Not long after Kat was sent to find you, Merc settled down. It took a fuckload of work on our parts to make that happen, but it did. And the second he realized what had gone on that night, he started rambling—out loud —about not knowing why he did it. That it was like it hadn't been him."

"And you believe that?" Knox asked sardonically.

"Yes. I do," Dean snarled. "He's my brother. I know him."

"I know him, too," Knox countered. "He doesn't seem like the contrite sort."

"When it comes to Piper, all bets are off where Merc is concerned," Jase added. "You'd be wise to remember that."

"And you'd be wise to remember where you are and who you're in the presence of," Knox said, golden eyes blazing in the dark of night.

"Please," I said curtly. "Let them finish."

"Piper, I don't know how to say this so that it makes sense, but I don't think Merc was in his right mind that night. Not in the way you've heard about before. This was something different. Something unnatural."

"It also makes sense of his behaviors that we'd attributed to the drinking of your blood. The signs were all there. We just didn't see them for what they were at the time."

"So you kept this from the king because you want a chance to get to the bottom of this?" I asked, trying to keep up. "You think something was done to him?"

"We don't know, Piper. But we failed him last time. We don't want to do it again."

"How did you convince the others to keep quiet about it?"

"Jensen and Kendrick owe Merc their lives. Getting them to sit on this information was easy."

"And Kat?"

They shared another look before answering.

"Her loyalties lie with Jensen, but deliberately defying the king ends only one way. We couldn't be certain that she would do right by you. That was why we acted the way we did."

"She tried to help me run when she got here," I said in her defense.

"Good," Jase replied. "Then she's an ally after all."

"As are we," Knox growled from directly behind me.

"We have to tell them about the warlocks," I said, looking up over my shoulder at the alpha. The set of his jaw told me that he wanted to argue that point, if for no other reason than to piss off the vampires, but he knew I was right. They needed to know.

"Not here," he said, scanning the trees. "Inside." He called forth a few of the werewolves, including Jagger and Foust, and told them to escort the vampires inside. If Jase and Dean could have dematerialized, they would have just to show Knox that he wasn't in charge, but neither had the resources for that at the moment, so they begrudgingly followed the pack into the lodge. Knox, however, held me behind for a private sidebar. "I don't like this, Piper. I'm not convinced that they're on your side."

"You don't know them like I do, Knox. I need you to trust me on this. Can you do that?" His jaw once again worked furiously as he mulled over my question. Could he trust my judgment when it potentially put his pack in danger?

"I can, but the second I think something is off, it's kill first, ask questions later. Agreed?" I swallowed hard, knowing that it wouldn't take much for him to implement that plan. The brothers needed to be on their most diplomatic behavior. Jase could do it; I'd seen him pull it off in the past. Dean, however, was a walking loose cannon. If anyone could push Knox's buttons, it was him.

I nodded in agreement, and the two of us made our way inside to where the others were waiting. Foust had brought Kat out as well. She looked as though she were back to normal, if not a little thin. Werewolves burned through calories like a blast furnace burned through coal. She'd need to eat soon if she hoped to regain her strength. Hopefully after food and a good night's rest, she'd be back to herself again.

Initially, I didn't notice that she was eyeing the brothers, a wariness in her expression that on second glance was impossible to deny.

"It's cool, Kat. They're good. They weren't sure if you could be trusted so they put on an act to maintain neutrality."

"They thought they couldn't trust me? I'm not the one keeping secrets."

"But you are the one in the direct service of the king at the moment," Dean snapped.

"So?"

"We're not getting into this right now," Jase yelled at both of them. "Know that all we've cared about this whole time is keeping Piper safe and telling her the whole story about Merc. The story you don't know because you've been gone."

Kat seemed unimpressed with Jase's argument.

"He tried to kill her. He should die. That's how I see it. If you don't agree, then we're not on the same side."

After a long silent standoff, Knox interrupted, getting the group debriefing back on track.

"Here's the deal, kids. The warlocks seem to have tracked Piper down, too. My boys took a few of them out, but the main one got away."

"Kingston," Jase spat as if the name were rancid on his tongue.

"Yeah. That guy. We expect he'll be coming here for her," he explained, shooting a sideways glance to me.

"I knew I sensed them in Anchorage," Kat muttered under her breath.

"You were there that night?" I asked.

She shook her head.

"No. It was early morning when I arrived, but the residue of magic was all around the downtown area. I knew something had gone down. I was freaking out at first, but then I found your trail leading to a car—away from where the battle was waged. I was confident that you had gotten away."

"I did, thanks to Knox and the others."

Jase and Dean turned to face the alpha, a look of respect in their eyes.

"You fought for her?" Dean asked, taking a step toward Knox. He nodded once. Dean raised an outstretched hand toward the werewolf, who accepted it from him. "We are in your debt." The way he said those words—the weight they carried—told me that his sentiment was more than just lip service. He meant what he was saying.

Jase mimicked his brother's gesture, offering his gratitude to the alpha.

"So now what?" Dean asked, losing every bit of the

formal tone he'd just possessed. "If you think the warlocks are coming for her eventually, then we need to get her out of here. He'll think she's still on the run. The last place he'll look is NYC."

"She's not leaving," Knox declared. "She was entrusted to you once and you failed her. We will not do the same."

"Seems like it should really be Piper's choice, boys," Kat observed, coming to stand on my right. "What do you want to do, Piper? Run? Go home? Stay here?"

I hesitated for a moment, realizing that no matter what decision I made, someone would be hurt by it.

"I can't go back, guys," I said, my eyes imploring Jase and Dean to see the truth in that statement. "Merc made sure of that." I then turned to Kat. "But I can't run either. Where can I go that I won't eventually be found? That's no way to live—always looking over my shoulder. I did that my whole life before I met you guys. I don't want to do it again." I lowered my head, unable to face any of them when I delivered my final line. "I'd rather be dead."

"That's not going to happen," the four of them said in unison.

I couldn't help but let a nervous laugh escape.

"Glad we've got that all cleared up," I joked.

"If you're staying, I'm staying, too," Kat announced, flopping down into a recliner. "Until the threat is eliminated, of course. Living in the sticks isn't really my thing. No offense." She gave Knox a half-heartedly apologetic look.

"I'd argue with you, but we could use your help. We lost a couple of fighters against Kingston."

"We will do what we can as well," Jase added.

"But how? You can't stay here," I argued. "And I doubt we'll have time to call you if and when they show up another day, which we're still not certain will happen at all."

"Why do you think that?" Dean asked, looking at me strangely.

"After the stunt he pulled in Anchorage? Reinhardt has to have noticed that a handful of his own are dead, or at least missing. He's no fool. He'll eventually get to the bottom of it."

"Piper," Jase started, using the voice he did when he thought I wouldn't be able to handle the news he was about to deliver. "Reinhardt has other things to worry about at the moment. Dead warlocks wouldn't be surprising to him at all right now."

"Oh," I exhaled. There went the shred of hope that a war with my nemesis could be avoided.

"Would it be possible to...*eat* before we continue this conversation?" Jase asked delicately, knowing that his request would surely be met with resistance. The wolves wouldn't enjoy the idea of being at the fangs of a vampire enforcer.

"You can use me," I volunteered, hoping to avoid an argument. Apparently my suggestion did the opposite.

"Over my dead body," Knox growled, pulling me behind him.

"Oh for fuck's sake," Kat sighed, pushing the footrest of the chair in so she could stand. "You can eat me."

"But you're still weak," I protested.

"Weak?" She turned to wink at me. "Maybe I just want everyone to think that." Without further ado, she headed toward the hallway, waving at the brothers to follow. "I'd like a little privacy, I'm sure you all understand," she drawled, sauntering around the corner. Jase and Dean weren't far behind.

"If they leave here, Piper, we run the risk of them returning with more. They might take you by force."

"They won't. I'm telling you, it's not going to be like that."

Knox started to argue, but a flash of blue light crashing through the window cut him off. The wolves scattered, managing to dodge the fireball that landed in the middle of the room. Eerie blue flames roared to life on contact, engulfing anything in the vicinity. I looked at Knox across the growing inferno, the fear in my eyes telling him everything he needed to know.

Kingston had arrived.

PART III

THE SHOWDOWN

23

Jase and Dean came running only seconds after the window in the living room shattered under Kingston's attack. Blood trickled down their chins. They looked significantly better than they had, even with little time to feed, but I knew they weren't quite back to themselves. And Kat was nowhere to be seen.

"Oh Piperrrrrrrrr," a familiar voice called from somewhere out in the yard. "Let's not make this any harder than it needs to be, shall we? I know you're in there. I know your babysitters are, too. If you'd all be so kind as to make your way outside, it will really just speed things along. And you know how I love efficiency."

I looked to the brothers and saw that they were thinking the same thing I was.

Kingston appeared unable to sense the presence of the wolves.

"Knox," I called as quietly as I could. "You guys need to slip out the back somehow and circle around. I'll buy you time, but Kingston can be unpredictable. It's hard to know when he'll tire of making a show."

"No!" Knox growled.

"You have to. You agreed to this plan and you're going to keep your word."

"We'll be with her," Jase added. "We've kept her safe before. We'll do it again tonight."

Knox appeared to want to argue, but Foust intervened, helping him see reason.

"It's now or never, man. We need to do as she says."

"Fine," Knox bit out before coming over to me. He grabbed the back of my head and pressed my lips to his, kissing me hard. "Do whatever you have to to keep him distracted. Understand?" I nodded. "That goes for you two as well."

With a jerk of his head, he and the pack made their way toward the halls of bedrooms and disappeared down them. The possibility that the warlocks had the place surrounded was there, but not necessarily likely. They generally kept their ranks together. They were far stronger as a whole. Even if they'd had the forethought to secure the perimeter of the lodge, those relegated to that particular duty would be relatively easy to pick off without the benefit of the coven at their sides.

Or so I hoped.

"So you like efficiency?" I yelled from the living room. "Too bad you suck at it. I'd be dead right now if you didn't."

My blow was met with silence. It appeared that his failure to kill me last time was a bit of a sore spot with him. And I'd just picked at the open wound.

"I'll admit I was surprised when I learned of your resilience in that matter," he said, the control of his voice belying the rage that grew within him. "But I promise you this time, Piper, I'll finish the job with little effort at all."

Jase and Dean flanked me as we made our way out to the

front porch. There to greet us was a veritable army of warlocks. Far more than I'd ever seen in one place before. Far more than Kingston had ever commanded.

"Motherfucker," Dean muttered to himself.

"No need to be shy," Kingston said, waving for us to come forward. "I can assure you that you're no safer there than if you come closer."

I tried to pull myself from the throes of panic threatening to take over. Instead, I refocused on the tactical plan that we'd put in place. I surveyed the crowd, doing a headcount. I also did what I could to see just how widespread Kingston's forces were. I hadn't heard any screams from dying wolves, so I figured that was a plus. Maybe Kingston's arrogance really would work to our advantage.

"I must say, Piper, you look far better than the last time I saw you." The evil grin that spread across his face made me sick. He'd truly enjoyed watching me burn.

I had no doubt that he'd enjoy it just as much a second time.

"You look about the same," I replied, doing all I could to keep my legs from quaking.

"And how is that?" he asked, cocking his head at me.

"Thin. Hand-less. Just as arrogant." He laughed at my reply, but there was no joy in it. It was a harsh, cruel, all-knowing laugh that let me know that it was the pain he was about to bring down on me that he found enjoyment in. Not my candid insults. "How'd you find me?" I asked. He shot me a look of disappointment in my question.

"I followed a little kitty kat until I was close enough to use a locator spell. It's all really quite boring and over your head. I'd much rather talk about the here and now," he said, the evil twinkle in his eyes flaring in the light of the moon. "I must say that your babysitters aren't looking that well today." He turned his attention to the brothers at my sides. With steady steps, he approached us, stopping only a few yards away. His minions mirrored him pace for pace. "Did you have an unfortunate arrival?" he asked, feigning concern. "There was a faint smell of burnt flesh when we showed up."

"We're up for whatever you have planned, Kingston," Jase said calmly, dropping his eyes to the warlock's missing hands. "And I'll be happy to take a few more souvenirs this time too."

"Don't be so greedy, Jase. I think it's my turn to lop something off of him," Dean said, chiming in.

"What did you have in mind?" Jase asked, turning to look over me to his brother.

"I'm up for whatever. An ear...an arm. Maybe something a little more important than that."

"I hardly think you two are in any position to make threats," Kingston countered, his calm expression faltering slightly. The faint blue glow at the ends of his arms gave him away.

We were running out of time.

Where is Knox...?

"Because this night is all about you, Piper, I'm going to let you choose," he continued, folding his arms behind his back.

"Choose what?"

His wicked smile reappeared.

"Which of them you'd like to die first."

While I fought to breathe, the wall of warlocks backing Kingston started to chant. As they did, the familiar blue flame that he normally brandished grew behind him until it was twice the size of his form. With his arms still behind him, the orb of swirling inferno remained there, but I knew that the second he moved, that mass of eerie blue fire was coming with him, destined for one of the boys.

I felt Jase's hand on my back in a weak effort to calm me, but it did nothing to help. One of the brothers was about to die.

"I can't make that decision," I said, my voice cracking as I spoke.

"No?" Kingston replied, amusement in his tone. "Shall I choose for you then?"

"Fuck you," Dean snarled, stepping forward a pace. "You're a pussy. You've always been a pussy. And I'm not going to die at the hands of a pussy, so do your worst. We'll see how you fare once you fail at killing me, but succeed at pissing me the fuck off."

He looked over his shoulder at me, an apologetic and resigned expression on his face.

"Love you, P," he said, just as the streak of blue flame throttled toward him.

"NO!" I screamed, lunging forward with my hands up as though they could somehow deflect the incoming fireball. Dean disappeared from sight just as the strike headed for him veered slightly off target, hitting the support post of the deck behind us. With little time to react, Jase snatched me around my waist and ran for the house at an inhuman speed. The door that slammed closed behind us flew off the hinges seconds later, narrowly missing us.

"Kat!" Jase shouted. "Time to make a break for it."

We rounded the hallway to find Dean there, helping Kat toward us. She was weak and pale. There was no way she could fight.

Not giving it a second thought, I ran over to her and put my hand on her head.

"Help me help her," I whispered, closing my eyes. I

could feel the heat from the healing light blaze through my hand to her. Seconds later, it disappeared, leaving Kat standing there awestruck. But we had no time to admire my work.

The lodge was under siege.

"Where the fuck are your boys?" Dean growled, dodging a flaming log that flew past his head. Surrounded by flying pieces of splintered wood was not a vampire's idea of a good time. "I'm spent from my disappearing act. I don't have another of those left in me."

"Here!" Kat said, shoving her wrist in his face. "And make it quick."

Dean didn't hesitate, taking her offering like a starving animal.

"Something must have happened to the pack!" I shouted over the ruckus around us. "We have to try and find them."

"Hardly the time for a supernatural scavenger hunt, Piper," Kat scolded, pulling her arm away from Dean. "That's enough, you greedy shit."

"Well, we have to do something. We're screwed if we stay here," I pointed out.

"We need to get on the roof to assess the situation better. We can't see shit from in here."

"I'll go now," Dean said, once again disappearing from sight.

"Can you get her up there?" Jase asked Kat, the weight in his stare implying the ramifications for failing at the task should she accept it.

"Yeah. Go find your brother," she said, waving him off.

"I'll see you in a minute," he said, kissing my forehead.

"Men," Kat scoffed, rolling her eyes. "They always leave..." As she laughed at her own joke, she dragged me down the hall to a staircase at the very end leading up to the second floor. Somewhere I hadn't yet been. "There has to be an attic or something. I can punch a hole in the roof if we can get to it."

"You mean before the place burns down?"

"Something like that."

We searched the second floor for an attic access with no success. After what seemed like an eternity, I located a panel inside one of the closets.

"Kat! I found it."

Without skipping a beat, she had it open and was thrusting me up through it, following right behind me. Soon we were standing on beams that spanned the length of the building, the open framework of the pitched roof in plain view.

"Jase!" I shouted. "Where are you? We're in the attic!"

A sharp cracking noise echoed through the vast space and the silvery light of the moon shined through the escape hole that Jase had just made for us. He popped his head in to greet us, though the news he had to share wasn't so welcoming.

"We have a problem, ladies," he said, grabbing my hands to pull me up. Once I was through, he handed me over to Dean, who immediately forced me down flat on my stomach. Kat was at my side a moment later, the four of us lying on the roof, surveying the situation.

And it was grim.

From our bird's eye view, we could see exactly what had happened to the pack. The tree line that encircled the property was peppered with werewolves—some in human form, some not—all of whom were trying desperately to get past some barrier that we couldn't see. Kingston, coward that he was, had eradicated that threat in the easiest way he could. He didn't have to fight them—he had seen how well that had ended for his crew last time. Instead, he'd decided to just remove them from the variables in play. He'd known they were there all along, and we'd played right into his hands. Knox and his boys were no longer a threat because they couldn't get to Kingston.

And if they couldn't get to him, they sure as hell couldn't get to us.

"Shit! What do we do now?" I looked frantically from face to face, hoping that one of them would hold a shred of hope in their expression, but none did.

"They're going to burn us out," Jase said calmly. "He won't risk coming close enough to Dean or me to get hurt. They'll burn down the building right out from under us, or they'll smoke us out. Either way, he'll be ready for us."

"Well, I'm not going to sit up here and burn," Kat spat, pushing to her feet. "If I'm going down, it'll be fighting, not lying here waiting to die."

Jase and Dean smiled, both of them standing as well.

"Jensen always could pick 'em," Dean said.

"He sure could," Jase added.

I scrambled to my feet, the cool night air harsh against my skin, a stark contrast to the heat of the roof. If we planned to get off of the building before flames erupted around us, we didn't have much time. It was time to act.

"Piper," a voice taunted from below. "I'm afraid your hiding place is about to expire. I'd really love to finish our chat before you die. Be a dear and come down to join us. Your friends can come, too. I have plans for all of you." We walked over to the edge of the roof to find Kingston staring up at me, his army of warlocks flanking him tightly. A silvery blue glow peeked out from under his leather jacket, one that matched the color of the fire he'd created.

When I looked to the boys for ideas on what to do next, I found the two of them silently staring at one another.

"I don't see any other way," Jase said to Dean, looking pained by whatever conclusion he'd come to.

"The way I see it, we only have two options. Bring down Kingston and his mob, or bring down the magical wall keeping the wolves out. And since I don't know how to do the latter, we need to figure out how to do the former," Dean replied.

"I won't be long," Jase said, now turning his attention to Kat and me.

"Where are you going?" I asked, the desperation in my voice plain. "You can't leave!"

"I have to, Piper. I think it's the only way to defeat him. I need to speak to someone, though I realize now doesn't seem like an opportune time."

"He's right, P," Dean said with a sad look. "If we're going to take on this army, Jase needs to confirm something first."

"Confirm what?" I pleaded, feeling abandoned.

"My suspicion," Jase said as he stared down at Kingston. "No time to explain. Know that I will be back as quickly as I possibly can." He crushed me to his chest, hugging me as though it might be his last opportunity. "I love you, Piper." Pushing me away from him enough to pin serious eyes on me, he continued. "Buy me some time. Do whatever you have to to keep him talking. Exploit his arrogance."

With that, Jase disappeared into the night.

"Piperrrrr," Kingston taunted from below, impatience tainting his tone.

"Looks like it's now or never," I breathed, glancing over to Kat. "Showtime."

Kat took my hand and gave it a squeeze. I gave her a look of understanding, then she scooped me up in her arms and jumped off the roof. Dean's swearing was quickly muffled by the wind in my ear. Before I knew it, Kat and I hit the ground, rolling wildly across the yard.

Trying to push myself up, I fell back down again, my arm screaming in protestation. It was broken for sure. But not for long.

"Help me," I whispered.

I felt the warm rush of energy course through me, healing me almost instantly. Now able to move, I looked over at Kat, who seemed no worse for the wear. She'd clearly transferred her momentum from the fall better than I.

Dean appeared out of nowhere, helping me to my feet as Kingston approached us, his confident swagger fully intact. Kat came to flank my other side, the three of us united against the army before us. A magical David versus Goliath.

Once again, Kingston smiled at me, amused by our bravado. He knew that he had the upper hand. I could only hope that his sense of security would make him careless. The second Dean saw an opportunity, he would undoubtedly take it. But he only had one shot at the warlock. He had to make sure it was the right moment.

The warlock's gaze fell upon Kat. He flicked his arm toward her, launching her far back into the wall that divided the pack from us. But instead of crashing against it as the others had on the other side, she flew right through it into Jagger, knocking him over. When she regained her footing, she too was locked out with the rest of the pack.

"And then there were two," Kingston mocked, staring Dean and me down. "What to do with the big bad enforcer..." He tapped his chin as if in deep contemplation. "I'd hate to have to kill him so early on and have him miss the big finale. Perhaps I can find a way to keep him out of the mix for the duration."

As if on cue, a wall of twisted blue flame shot up from the earth, encircling Dean. The cylinder of fire was narrow, and I feared that there was no way that Dean wasn't being burned alive (so to speak).

"Dean!" I screamed, lunging toward the flames.

"I'm all right, Piper," he replied through the roaring fire. "Remember what Jase said!"

As I swallowed back my fear and anger, Kingston came closer, leaning into me in a conspiratorial fashion.

"I think that's a better place for your little friend, don't you?" he asked, his breath on my ear. He was far closer to me than I was comfortable with. "Don't worry. I'm not done with him just yet." He leaned toward me, lifting his hand to shelter his mouth from the others as though he were about to tell me a secret. "Would you like to see my big surprise?"

He pulled away so that the light of the moon could illuminate the insanity in his eyes. He was drunk with power in a way I'd never seen before. He was going to succeed with whatever maniacal machination he'd concocted.

And it most certainly involved my death.

While I contemplated that, a swirling vortex of black opened up behind him. A portal to somewhere or something. I had zero desire to see what he was inviting to join our showdown, though I doubted it could make things any worse than they already were. But once I sensed who was about to step through the magical door, our connection as strong as it had been the night we'd exchanged blood oaths, I realized I was wrong.

"Why is he here?" I whispered, staring at Merc as he came to stand next to Kingston. His empty blue eyes eventually found mine, but they gave nothing away. It was like I was seeing him for the first time, like that night outside the mansion. Almost as if he didn't know who I was.

But once his hatred of me boiled to the surface, I knew he really did.

"Him?" Kingston asked, as if he hadn't just brought the enforcer through the portal. "He's here for the main event." At that moment, Kingston extinguished the cage of fire entrapping Dean, who rushed to my side, pushing me behind him. "Ready for your part in this?" Kingston asked him. "I was rather excited when I saw that you and your Neanderthal brother had found Piper. That you'd be here to witness her death, but then something dawned on me." He lifted one of his arms up before his face, turning it back and forth as if he were inspecting his hand—the hand that Jase had cut off. "It's unfortunate that Jase isn't here for this, given that it was he that did this to me, but you'll suffice."

"You'll be missing more than that when I'm done with you," Dean shouted before charging the warlock. In the blink of an eye, Dean was on his back with Merc lying on top of him. The two were struggling with one another, an evenly matched pair. Or so it seemed.

Dean seemed as though he were fighting to get free. Merc, however, was trying to kill his brother. I screamed at the sight.

"Stop! Merc! You'll kill him!"

My words didn't faze him at all.

"This is going to be so good," Kingston said in my ear. "I'll try to drag it out a bit, but I can't make any promises. That mate of yours has crazy on his side, and there's just no accounting for crazy in a fight." I lunged toward the pair still wrestling for control on the ground, but Kingston's iron grip pulled me back against him. No matter how hard I struggled, I could not escape him. "It won't be long," he whispered, licking the lobe of my ear.

I was crying now, desperate to do something—anything

—to stop the madness playing out before me. Merc had never shown violence toward his siblings. Why was he now? What had gone so wrong between them that he would attack Dean without provocation? And most baffling still: why wasn't he trying to kill Kingston? Or me?

My window of opportunity to stall was now clear.

"How are you doing this?" I growled at him, still wiggling violently to escape his grasp.

"I thought you'd never ask," he said, tightening his grip on me. "There's a funny story behind that, if you're interested in hearing it."

"I'm listening."

"A long time ago I heard a rumor about your boy there—a story about his instability and his gifts—and why he was put away." I listened to him as I watched Merc pummel Dean until he was nearing unconsciousness. His body lay on the ground, barely moving. With every blow Merc delivered, I knew Dean was closer and closer to fading. Once Merc deemed it time, Dean would have no means to defend himself against a stake to the heart. "I tucked that information away at the time, hoping that one day I'd be able to discern whether or not it was true."

"Your point?"

"Now, now. No need to rush," he chastised. "When Merc returned, that little rumor came back to me and I wondered..." His grip loosened on me slightly, allowing him to spin me around in his arms to face him. "I wondered if the reason you and your friends succeeded in the alley that night had less to do with their prowess and more to do with his rumored ability, because I know that I wanted you dead one minute, and the next, the spell I'd sent after you had disappeared and I stood still while Jase took my hands." My heart stopped for a beat while my mind processed what he was saying. Merc had made him stop his attack on us that night, but only once he'd thought I would perish because of it. Once he'd thought he would lose me. "And then, of course, I learned of your bonding—the interesting change of heart the king had that evening—and everything became clear to me."

"Who told you about that?" I asked, unable to hide the contempt in my voice.

"A little birdie," he replied with a smile. "But that's hardly important. What's important is what I did with that information."

"What did you do, Kingston?" I breathed, fearing what he was going to say.

His smile widened.

"Merc!" he shouted. "Enough."

I wrenched my head to an uncomfortable angle, turning to see Merc stand like a puppet on a string, leaving Dean limp on the ground at his feet.

Oh my God...

"You see, Piper," he continued, grabbing me by the chin to force my head back around to face him. "Nature—magic—it works within a system of checks and balances. For each and every force, there is an equal and opposing force. It made me wonder if the gifts that made him powerful enough to influence the minds of all the supernaturals around him would in turn make him susceptible to the same, providing one was capable of such magic."

"But you're not strong enough for that," I argued weakly. The fight I'd just witnessed between Dean and Merc said otherwise.

"Fair point, Piper. The truth is that I wasn't in the beginning. The spell I'd cast was enough to create feelings of resentment toward you in your mate, but not enough to make him do what he did in the end."

"What did you do, Kingston?" I repeated, fear building within me as everything Kat and the boys had told me started to fall into place. Things were definitely far worse in New York than I ever could have imagined.

He sighed heavily, feigning exhaustion.

"Reinhardt has grown soft in his old age. He has no vision. No sense of self-preservation for our kind. He valued the treaty amongst the supernaturals far more than he should have," he explained, his eyes narrowing as he spoke. "So I stole from him what he no longer deserved." The light that I had seen emanating from under his jacket flared, forcing me to close my eyes. "I now control the warlocks, Piper. They answer to me. And the first order of business is to see you dead."

"The king will know you did this. He'll never stand for it!"

"The king..." Kingston sighed, looking put-upon. "There's so much you don't understand, Piper, and I haven't the time nor the inclination to explain it all to you."

"Like what, Kingston? What don't I understand?"

"More than you could ever imagine," he replied, his maniacal smile spreading wide. "I know things...things about you. About your parents. Things that nobody else knows. But they don't matter, none of it does, because you'll never know the truth. The only truth you need to know is that you're weak—an abomination that should never have been suffered to live—and I am going to right that wrong. I am going to restore the magical balance."

He shoved me away from him, putting distance between us.

"But first, I think I should finish what has been started

here tonight," he said, stepping back toward his minions. He shrugged off his jacket as he did, exposing an ancient medallion—an amulet of sorts—that hung around his neck. The closer Kingston got to his army, the brighter it glowed. "Kill him!"

I turned, panicking, to see Merc pull a stake out from the back of his pants.

"No!" I screamed, darting toward him. I jumped on his back, trying to pull the weapon from his hands. "Don't do this. This isn't you. I knew it wasn't you before. Now I know why. Please. Stop. He's your brother!"

My pleas fell upon deaf ears.

"Piper!" I heard Jase call from behind me. "It's the amulet!"

At that moment, Merc flung me off of him, tossing me back toward Kingston like a rag doll. A fiery blue ball whizzed over me. I thought I'd narrowly missed the warlock's attack until I heard Jase cry out.

I'd never been the intended target.

I rolled on the ground and looked up to find my friend, once again, burning.

Fire was everywhere around us. The house. Jase. Even the magical barrier to the wolves was now a wall of fire.

So much burning.

It roared like my growing anger. Jase. Dean. How many would fall that night? How much collateral damage was I willing to accept?

"Make it stop!" I shrieked, turning my rage to Kingston.

The second the words left my mouth, thunder rolled and the skies poured down upon us, extinguishing everything. Then, as quickly as it had come, it disappeared. Kingston stood still, his expression faltering for a moment.

And that moment was all I had.

"Help Jase and Dean!" I commanded, praying that somehow those words would be enough to save Dean from Merc.

The wet ground began to rumble, shaking everyone standing upon it. I turned to see Merc stumble back away from his brother, the stake falling from his grip.

"It cannot be," Kingston exhaled, a look of disbelief flashing through his eyes. Then they turned murderous, his longtime hatred of me coming to the surface. "It matters not. This ends tonight."

A growing fireball—one larger than he'd thrown at Jase—developed in front of him. I knew in a matter of seconds it would be headed for me. I closed my eyes, focusing on everything around me, steadying myself for the attack. When I opened them, the fiery mass flew toward me.

I threw my arms up to deflect it, but I failed. Instead, it hovered right in front of me like a dog awaiting a command. I reached out, mesmerized by the ball of energy. The second I touched it, it faded into nothing.

"Fire Bender!" Kingston yelled, frustration overtaking his calm. He stormed toward me, resorting to a hands-on approach to killing me, which would undoubtedly succeed. I was no match for him in combat.

As he closed the distance between us, a familiar growl erupted from my right. In a flash of fur, Grizz appeared, unhindered by the magical barrier, and barreled into the unsuspecting warlock. While Kingston threw a ball of fire at the bear from his position on the ground, I sprang forward, landing on top of him. I snatched the amulet from around his neck and attempted to run, but he caught my foot, bringing me crashing to the ground.

I used the momentum generated by the fall to smash the amulet against a nearby rock. The glowing stone at the center of it shattered. The second that happened, all hell broke loose.

The invisible wall that had served to keep the werewolves out failed, unleashing the extremely pissed-off pack on the warlocks. Without the source of their collective magic, and unable to repair or replace it, they were left to fight with only their individual powers. And they were not holding up well in such close proximity to the wolves.

It was a melee.

I ran to Jase's side, hoping that he had not fallen to Kingston's attack. He was hurt badly, burned from head to toe, but he was moving. I got up, wanting to find Dean, only to see Merc carrying him toward me. A look of guilt, the depths of which I cannot begin to explain, pained his expression.

"You bitch!" Kingston snarled from behind me, his ball of fire already primed and ready to be thrown. I didn't have time to react. Just before it crashed into my body, the body of another passed in front of me, absorbing the deadly blow on my behalf.

Knox lay on the ground at my feet, unmoving.

The fury that swelled in me came flying out. And the power it unleashed was something none of us could have expected.

"Nooooo!" I screamed, slamming to the ground beside the alpha. But my eyes were all for Kingston. The ground that had quaked earlier shook with the force of a ten on the Richter scale. Cracks shot through the earth, extending out in all directions from me, creating vast crevices.

Crevices that started to swallow the warlocks whole.

"What are you?" Kingston asked, the shock in both his expression and words unmistakable.

"I am a Storm Caller. An Earth Shaker. A Wind Walker,"

I said, stalking toward him like my body was possessed by a foreign power, my voice no longer my own. "And, as you said, a Fire Bender. But I'm so much more than that." With a flick of my wrist, a gust of wind lifted him far off the ground, suspending him there. "I'm the one that will put an end to you once and for all."

I felt the flow of foreign energy coursing through me as the growing crevice below Kingston spread wide across the yard. His minions were gone, already taken by my wrath. He, too, would soon feel its sting.

"You cannot defeat me!" he shouted, though it lacked conviction.

"I just did," I whispered, dropping my arm to my side. As if I'd cut his invisible strings, Kingston plummeted into the gap in the earth, careening toward its core, where he would be forever entombed in a molten inferno. It seemed befitting, given his love of fire.

I watched as the ground molded itself back together, leaving no trace of the disturbance that had just occurred. But there were still signs of the battle just waged upon it. Too many to count.

Knox, my mind shouted, bringing me back to myself. My attention fell to the wounded werewolf. I'd half expected to see him sitting up, grinning at me in the most mischievous way, a reminder that he was tougher than I gave him credit for.

But that was not the case.

Instead, I found him lying motionless, just as he had been when he'd taken the magical blow meant for me. I ran to him, skidding to my knees at his side. I lifted his head into my lap and cradled it, tears stinging the backs of my eyes.

"Help me help him," I begged whatever power I was connected to. Whatever power had been there for me that night. But she never came. Panicked, I surveyed my surroundings, looking for anyone who could help me. All I found were bodies strewn about the ground—fallen wolves equally wounded—Kat staggering toward me, and the brothers, Merc still holding Dean in his arms and Jase, now sitting up, but terribly burned. "I don't know what to do," I whimpered, rocking Knox in my lap. I felt a weak nudge from a muzzle on my shoulder. Grizz flopped to the ground beside me. He too was wounded, but not mortally so.

I tried again, asking for the help I had received countless times that night. This time I felt the now-familiar warmth flow through me into Knox, but it dissipated long before he ever roused. I didn't know what I was doing wrong.

"He sustains his pack," a voice called from behind me. Kat crouched down at my side, resting her hand gently on my arm. "It takes all he has to not lose many of his wolves right now, Piper. He and they both are in a precarious situation. If he dies because their demand on him is too great, they all do." She squeezed my arm lightly. "Keep trying. You're his only hope." I nodded tightly, dragging my sleeve across my face to dry my tear-stained cheeks. "I'm going to help them," she said, getting up to make her way toward the boys. I prayed she had enough in her to bring them back. Vampires were hard to kill, but the strength of Kingston's magic that night combined with the sheer amount of it left room for doubt in my mind.

"Help me help him. Please," I whispered. This time, the heat that coursed through me was uncomfortable. I felt like I was burning from the inside out. I pushed through the pain, remaining focused on what mattered most in that moment: keeping Knox alive. My limbs shook, and I could smell the burning of flesh—my flesh—as I soldiered on, maintaining my hold on the wolf's arm, unwilling to break contact with him.

"Piper," a male called to me. "Piper, you have to let go now." Freezing cold hands pried mine away from Knox easily. I opened my eyes to find Merc kneeling beside me, the same look of sadness in his gray-blue eyes. "It will kill you if you don't control it," he said softly, a hint of understanding in his voice. I stared at him, not knowing what to do or say. Thankfully, a pained cry from Knox distracted us both.

"Knox! Knox, can you hear me? Squeeze my hand if you can hear me." I took hold of his hand, hoping that he would do as I'd asked. All I received in return was more of the same horrific cries.

"He is suffering for his pack—taking their pain away," Merc observed.

"I can't help him enough. I don't know what else to do," I said, beseeching the vampire beside me. "Will you help him...like you helped me? Will you ease his suffering?"

He stared at me, giving nothing away in his gaze.

"You love him," he said, his voice calm and controlled.

I said nothing.

"You are falling in love with him."

I bit my lip, nodding once.

He assessed me for a moment before leaning close, tucking a stray piece of hair behind my ear.

"For you, I will do this."

Without further ado, he leaned down to Knox and murmured something unintelligible until the werewolf calmed, his body relaxing into the ground beneath him. Once he did, Merc stood, giving me a long, wistful look, before turning to walk back toward his brothers, who were now standing, albeit with Kat's help, off in the distance. She had fed them, judging by the pallor of her skin and the fact that they were upright at all. Her loyalty to the enforcers had been proven tenfold that night. Jensen would be proud.

My heart tightened as he continued past them, heading off into the darkness. I wanted to say something to him—anything—but couldn't find the right words. We had so many unresolved issues looming over us. So much damage had been done that I questioned if it could ever be repaired—or if I wanted it repaired at all. Losing Merc to the madness had been like a death to me. I'd grieved his loss and moved on. I'd found someone else. Or had I?

Watching him walk away, I wasn't so sure.

Fear had kept my emotions at bay for the past few weeks, allowing me to move past how I felt about Merc. But that night, seeing him again with the veil of twisted magic lifted, feelings rushed back in, clouding my decisions and leaving me confused. I felt slightly traitorous—like an adulteress. He'd helped Knox for me—to help me. His guilt had been palpable as he'd stared at me before he walked away. He hated himself for what he'd done, and it hurt to see it.

He loved me so much that he was willing to walk away.

My heart ached at that realization.

"You need to keep working on him," Kat called to me as she approached, pulling me from my downward spiral. I looked up to find her bearing the weight of a brother on each shoulder—a wobbly threesome. "If you keep healing him, you'll heal the others. Look around. They're getting better."

I did as she said and once again scanned the carnage of the battle. Some of the wounded wolves were now sitting up; a few of them were standing. Feeling restored and refocused, I channeled the energy back into Knox at a more even and controlled pace. What seemed like an eternity later, I felt him move under my hands.

"Knox?" I called, hopeful for a response. When his green eyes fluttered open, I screeched with delight.

"Anyone see that freight train that mowed me over?" he asked, rolling over onto his side.

"You're okay!" I shouted, throwing my arms around his neck, knocking him back to the ground. I fell awkwardly on top of him, burying my face in his neck.

"I'd be better if you stopped choking me," he replied with a laugh.

"Oh. Sorry," I apologized, scrambling off of him.

"I didn't say run away!" He pulled me back down on top of him, resting me comfortably on his chest. "Much better."

"I need to go check on the others," I said, kissing him lightly.

"No you don't," he argued, squeezing me against him. "I can feel them when they're near. They're all alive and accounted for, thanks to you." His earnest expression made me flush with embarrassment. I was the reason they'd nearly been killed in the first place. Praise seemed unnecessary.

Kat hovered beside us, then dropped the boys rather inelegantly to the ground beside Knox.

"You two are going on a diet when we get home," she groused, plopping down between them, breathing hard.

"We're a sad-looking lot," Knox joked, though there was far more truth to his observation than he wanted to admit. "Anyone able to tell me what the fuck happened? All I know is, the second we entered the woods, that fucking force field or whatever the hell it was went up and we were shut down...stuck watching the shitshow." The pain and anger in his voice let me know that it would take him awhile to get over what he'd witnessed that night.

He'd thought he was going to watch me die.

"Everything happened so fast," I said, trying to remember how everything had played out.

"Where did you ghost off to?" Knox interrupted, looking at Jase like he'd deserted us to save himself.

"The amulet," Jase started, shifting to make himself more comfortable. His burns were markedly improved, but not yet fully healed. "I saw it poking out from under Kingston's jacket. It looked familiar, but I could not be certain. I thought it was the one Reinhardt had always worn —the one that he did not have on the night that Merc..." His voice drifted off, realizing that he was navigating a delicate topic. "Anyway, I needed confirmation that I was indeed seeing that. I knew just the person to go to to find out."

"Who?" I asked, thinking that if Reinhardt had been overthrown, he wasn't likely to be in a position to tell Jase, and if the king didn't know what was going on in the first place, Jase certainly wasn't going to turn to him for answers.

"Sylvia," he replied with an evil grin. "That bitch has been screwing Kingston off and on for decades. I knew for fact that she went to him the night of your bonding to Merc. She was so angry."

"Hell hath no fury," Dean added, collapsing onto his back, exhausted.

"At any rate, she sang like a canary when I had her by the throat. Kingston had bragged of his plan to take over the warlocks, and in his arrogance told her all about the prized amulet. How it worked. The power it held. How delicate it was..."

"I'm going to strangle that little shit when I get home," Kat snarled.

"I think I'd like to see that," Jase replied with his trademark smile.

The two of them shared a look and then laughed—hard—both of them falling back to the ground to join Dean, clutching their bellies.

"Knox," Foust called, walking toward us. Jagger and Brunton flanked him as they crossed the lawn to reach us. "We're all clear."

"That we are," Knox replied, standing slowly. "Thanks to Piper."

"That was some serious shit, Piper!" Jagger blurted out, scooping me into a hug. "You blew the fucking ground open! Who does that? Seriously bad ass, girl."

Knox shot me a curious glance, and I smiled at him. He could get the low down on that later.

"I do what I can," I said with a shrug.

"Yeah ya do. Talk about cleaning up."

"Speaking of cleaning up," Foust said, looking at what remained of the lodge. "Do you think you can heal that?"

We all turned our attention to the home, or what was left of it. Fire had destroyed the first floor, leaving parts of the second story sagging down into it. The roof was all but gone.

"I'm so sorry, Knox," I said softly, taking his hand in mine. "Your home...your things...they're all gone."

"But we're all here," he countered, stepping in front of me to eclipse my view of the house. "That's what matters. We can build another place."

"Piper," Dean called from behind us. "The sun is going to be rising on the east coast soon. We have to go." He looked at me with pleading eyes that begged for me to understand the implications of what he'd said. Even with

Kat's help, they were in no shape to dematerialize and needed my blood to help them.

"Here," I said, rushing over to them, wrists extended. They both latched on and drank greedily, forcing themselves to let go before they took too much. When they stood, they looked as they always did, but even more lively. Invigorated.

"That's some serious juice you're packin' in those veins of yours, P!" Dean shouted before realizing the volume he'd used.

"Indeed," Jase agreed, a look of awe in his eyes.

"What about Merc?" I asked, knowing that he'd arrived via a portal that I couldn't recreate.

"He's already gone."

"What? How?" My heart raced at the thought of him being gone.

The brothers shared one of their annoying moments before answering me.

"He can dematerialize, too. Family trait, I guess," Dean explained with a shrug.

"We'll see you at home? Soon?" Jase asked, pulling me into an embrace that Dean quickly joined.

"I...I don't..."

"She's staying with us," Knox answered for me.

Unfortunately, I wasn't so sure he was right.

"Knox..."

"Don't say it, Piper," he interrupted. I pushed away from the boys to face him. "You can't forget what they did to you, not to mention what's going on down there. They told you that it's a shitshow. You can't go back to that."

"I don't know that I can stay here either, Knox. You're the one always telling me not to run. Well, I have a ton of stuff I ran from back in NYC, and I think it's time that I go back and deal with it all," I told him. "Besides, if there really is a war going on, they might need me, especially if I can figure out these powers of mine."

"Looked like you had pretty good control over them to me," Kat added sarcastically.

"I couldn't recreate that if I tried, Kat. I'm not even sure who that was. That's the whole problem. I need to practice. You said so yourself, Knox. What better place than in the middle of chaos? It seemed to work out pretty well here. Maybe I need that kind of pressure."

"That's insane, Piper. I know you've been in the mix of supernatural bullshit before, but not a war. It's nothing like what you've endured. It's insidious and convert. You won't see it coming."

"There are other things I need to go back for." I said, hesitating. I didn't know how to explain to Knox that I needed to resolve things with Merc. To him, he was an abusive, nearly murderous, ex of mine. I didn't want to be that girl—the one who couldn't walk away—but in light of what I'd learned that night, my resolution seemed to be wavering. Merc was not the monster I had made him into in my mind. He was a puppet, one manipulated by an evil warlock. To hold that against him seemed cruel.

If nothing else, I owed it to him to hear him out—absolve him of his guilt that was so plain. One way or another, we needed closure.

"You're right," he said softly. "You should go." Once again, my heart sank at hearing him so easily cave, not that I wanted him to argue with me. I just wanted him to understand, not give up. I looked up at him to find a dark expression flash through his eyes. It held a realization—one that he did not seem to like. "We're coming with you, Piper. Where you go, we go. We're a family—a pack.

There's no escaping that fact. War or not, you're stuck with us."

"You can't, Knox! You all nearly died tonight, and all because of me. You can't walk into New York, knowing what awaits you."

"I can't?" he asked, quirking his brow. "I thought I told you, I like danger."

"You're insane."

"And you love it."

He smiled wide, enjoying how flustered I was.

"You're serious, aren't you? You're really going to pack up the boys and come to New York?" I asked with utter disbelief.

"I think I can handle city life for a while," he replied with a shrug.

I threw my arms around his neck, squeezing him tight.

"And you think Grizz is the one with balls..."

"You can stay with us," Jase said. "We owe you a debt of gratitude not easily repaid." Knox nodded in an official manner to the enforcer, accepting his offer. "Now I'm afraid we really must go. See you soon, Piper."

I watched as Jase and Dean disappeared into thin air, satisfied with the knowledge that I would indeed see them soon.

"I'll call Jensen and get him to make arrangements to get us all back to the city," Kat said, taking out her cell phone and walking around the house.

A muzzle jammed into the small of my back, alerting me to the fact that Grizz was still there. I couldn't believe I'd forgotten about the big ball of fur lying nearby.

"Buddy! I'm so sorry. Are you okay?" He grumbled at me but shook his head yes. "You did great tonight." He exhaled heavily and stomped, chasing after Kat for a bit, then turning back to look at me.

"Kat? What about her?"

He lumbered back toward the pack and then wedged himself between Foust and Jagger, staring at me indignantly.

"Of course you're part of the pack, Grizz."

"Piper," Knox said cautiously. "I don't think that's what he's getting at."

"What do you mean?" I asked before realization set in. He was indeed part of my pack.

And he wanted to go wherever I went.

"Kat!" I shouted into the night air. "Make sure Jensen makes arrangements to bring a grizzly bear with us."

I heard a muffled string of swears erupt on the other side of the house, but I knew she'd do as I asked. The boys, however, burst out laughing as they all congregated around the bear who'd helped save the day. Grizz looked leery of them, but it seemed that he and Knox had an understanding where I was concerned. They would both protect me at all costs.

I just hoped they wouldn't have to once we arrived in New York.

"We've salvaged what we could from the bedrooms," Foust reported as he walked into the charred remains of the living room. "There's barely anything left." Knox's expression tightened, his mouth pressing into a thin line.

"Throw what you found into the SUVs, and let's get out of here. Kat said they've got everything ready for us once we get to Anchorage."

"About that," Jagger interjected, lurking by the front

door. The rest of the pack had already filed into the caravan of vehicles in the front yard, which had managed to escape damage. Only one was lost, but even that made for tight quarters in the remaining SUVs. "I—I can't go."

The three of us looked at the ginger-haired werewolf with a mix of expressions. I was confused, Foust was irritated, and Knox understood.

"It'll be okay, Jags. We'll sort things out while we're—"

"You don't get it. I can't go back there. The second someone finds out I'm in town, I'm dead."

"The enforcers won't let that happen any more than your pack will, Jagger," I said in an effort to calm him. He was fidgeting wildly, practically jumping from one foot to the other while he thought about whatever demons he'd escaped when he'd come to Alaska and Knox.

"I don't know that that's enough, Piper. Your boys said it's chaos there. That doesn't bode well for me."

"I'm not leaving you here," Knox said firmly, but not unkindly. "A lone wolf won't do well up here."

"I'll be fine. I'll hole up in Piper's place until you guys come back."

A look passed over Knox's face. One that both Jagger and I caught. One that told us we weren't coming back.

Ever.

"I'm not leaving you, Jagger. And I swear on all that is holy and right, we will sort out whatever shit is waiting for you in New York. Okay?"

Jagger looked unconvinced.

"Would it help if I told you that I won't let anything happen to you either?" I asked, grasping at straws to calm the wolf.

Oddly enough, it seemed to work.

He looked at me earnestly, making him look younger than he already did.

"All right. I'll go," he said, turning away to the vehicles awaiting us all. As soon as he walked out the door, Knox started to laugh.

"Like I said, Piper, you really do have a way with animals."

EPILOGUE

Everything seemed to come together so easily.

The wolves had been given sanctuary by both Jase and the king. Nobody had been lost in the battle with the warlocks. And their threat had been all but eliminated. So why did I feel such unease at the thought of returning to New York?

I looked out the window of the private jet sent for us by the king himself and wondered. I wondered what would happen when I saw Merc again—what would become of our bond Then I wondered what would become of my budding relationship with Knox? How could the two of them possibly coexist under one roof? What had appeared to be the solution to the wolves' housing dilemma quickly turned into a conundrum I couldn't solve. One that left me questioning my sanity when I'd agreed to the offer made by Jase.

But it didn't matter now. All that mattered was restoring the balance within the supernatural community. Without it, lives would be lost. It might not be tomorrow, or the day after, but eventually those I knew and loved would start to fall victim to the anarchy. And that was a fate unacceptable to me.

Then there was Jagger, whose past was about to revisit him the second he set foot in New York. A past that had sent him running all the way to Alaska to escape it. Whatever he had done—whoever was after him—had to be addressed. I had made a promise to him that I would keep him safe, and I intended to keep it. But to ensure that, I needed to get control of whatever magic coursed through my veins. Whatever earthly power I had access to.

And when it came to those powers, it seemed like all bets were off.

Historically speaking, nobody had ever wanted to mentor me—teach me about my magical abilities. But now I couldn't help but wonder if that would still be the case. There was one out there, providing he was still alive, that might be tempted to join forces with an outcast like me. One that could potentially teach me the ways of the magic I held.

I reached into my pocket and pulled out the amulet that I had broken during the battle, turning the heavy gold pendant over in my hand. The first thing I planned to do upon our arrival in New York was not to deal with the fallout of my relationships or the insidious warring of the supernaturals. Instead, I would endeavor to make a new ally.

The warlocks had always been strong in both power and magic.

And with Reinhardt's help, I would soon be too.

Next in Series

ACKNOWLEDGMENTS

Books don't write themselves. Sometimes it takes a team to do it.

On that note, I'd like to say thank you to my beta readers: Shannon Morton, Simone Nicole, Jena Gregoire, Courtney DeLollis, Kristy Bronner, Janet Wallace, Becky Mutter, Bree Wilder, Jessica Watterson, and Virginia Nicholas. You guys really helped me hone this novel into something I love and am immensely proud of. To my stellar husband, Bryan, thank you for your patience, your tech skills, and your willingness to believe me when I tell you that I'm just going to the bathroom, even though I have my laptop in hand. I know the jig is up, but you pretend not to notice, and I love you for that. And to my amazing cover designer, Regina Wamba, you're never allowed to break up with me.

ABOUT THE AUTHOR

Amber Lynn Natusch is the author of the bestselling *Caged*. She was born and raised in Winnipeg, and speaks sarcasm fluently because of her Canadian roots. She loves to dance and sing in her kitchen—much to the detriment of those near her—but spends most of her time running a practice with her husband, raising two small children, and attempting to write when she can lock herself in the bathroom for ten minutes of peace and quiet. She has many hidden talents, most of which should not be mentioned but include putting her foot in her mouth, acting inappropriately when nervous, swearing like a sailor when provoked, and not listening when she should. She's obsessed with home renovation shows, should never be caffeinated, and loves snow. Amber has a deep-seated fear of clowns and deep water...especially clowns swimming in deep water.

Made in the USA
Monee, IL
28 January 2026

42751865R00204